code Red

code Red

a novel by **Jennie Hansen**

Covenant Communications, Inc.

Covenant

Published by Covenant Communications, Inc.
American Fork, Utah

Printed in the United States
First Printing: October

10 09 08 07 06 05 04   10 9 8 7 6 5 4 3 2 1

ISBN 1-59156-629-0

This book is dedicated to the men and women serving in the United States Armed Forces and to all those people everywhere battling terrorism. A special thanks to the many soldiers who have trained at the army's beautiful Fort Lewis in Washington, and particularly to Rich and Jo. I couldn't have written this book without you.

Prologue

A drop of deep red rolled slowly down the front of her shirt. Nicole touched it regretfully with one finger and noticed it matched the stains on her hands and the streaks spreading almost to her elbows. Mixing with dirt and scratches, it meant she was in big trouble. She didn't doubt there were stains on her face as well, especially around her mouth. She glanced hopefully toward the sky, hoping the faint mist might turn to rain.

Mom and Marcie could pick blackberries without getting more than a speck or two of juice on their hands. Nicole sighed. She'd meant to surprise Mom with enough berries to make a pie, but her mother wouldn't even notice the almost full bucket of fruit. She'd only see the dirt and stains and be angry because Nicole had sneaked away from Marcie and strayed into the woods alone—again.

Other children seemed content to play on the numerous playgrounds scattered across the sprawling army base, but Nicole couldn't resist the pull of the thick tangle of trees and shrubs that covered this base on the edge of the Pacific Northwest's fabled rain forest. She knew all the places within walking distance of home where the soldiers trained, and she avoided those, but there were miles of trails and little-used roads that wound through the forest, and she never tired of exploring them. She'd been warned about bears, but while she occasionally saw a deer or a raccoon, she'd never seen a bear—though secretly she hoped she would someday. That would be a grand adventure! She mostly saw soldiers jogging or riding bikes along the trails she explored.

This was the best place they'd ever lived, and her family had lived a lot of places. Fort Lewis had everything she wanted. Even the rain she'd wished for began to fall. She breathed deeply the rich scent of pine and ocean, and she wished she could stay there forever.

A sound caught her attention, and she crouched deeper into the thicket of thorny bushes. She didn't really think Marcie had come looking for her; her sister was a scaredy-cat. One long, auburn braid caught on a bramble, and her heart beat faster. Her mother had warned her again just last week that a bear had been seen on the hillside close to the houses where military families lived. At eleven, she was old enough to know that even though there were enough berries to fatten every bear within a hundred miles and still make a million pies, she couldn't count on a bear's willingness to share, especially if it were a mama bear with cubs. Cautiously, she freed her braid, but she couldn't resist moving closer to check out the sound.

As it came closer, she recognized the growl, not of bears, but of angry men. Noticing an indentation almost like a path cut by heavy runoff that delved beneath the tangle of berry bushes she crouched behind, she decided to sneak closer to the arguing men. Pretending to be a soldier sneaking up on enemy lines was a game she played frequently. Anyway, she wasn't hiding exactly; Mom had warned her that meeting strangers while wandering through the forest could be as dangerous as any wildlife she might encounter. Besides, something about the approaching voices raised an alarm telling her it wouldn't be wise to show herself.

Adults always seemed to get angrier when they discovered a child had overheard their quarrel, and these men were already angry enough. She huddled deeper into the thick brush where she had been picking berries, ignoring the addition of more scratches. The falling rain obscured any faint sound she might have made.

The voices stopped almost in front of her. Whether it was distance, the rain, or something odd in the way they spoke, she couldn't understand what the men were saying. She knew, however, that they were extremely angry. She could see three men, though one was doing most of the talking. A second man occasionally shouted what sounded like a curse or an insult. The third man finally spoke, and Nicole strained for a closer look. His voice sounded familiar, almost like her father's. He wasn't shouting like the other two men, and she couldn't see his face, so she couldn't be sure. If he was Dad, he'd soon stop the other men from fighting. Her father was a master sergeant, and he didn't put up with anyone yelling or being rude.

Curiosity got the better of her, and she dropped to her stomach to wiggle a little farther along the trail, which was almost a shallow ditch. This allowed her to inch forward under the long, sheltering bramble branches until she could better see the dirt road where three men stood in the shelter of a large fir tree. One man, dressed in an army field uniform, had his back to her, while the other two faces were clearly visible. The man facing away from her looked like Daddy. She didn't recognize either of the men facing her. One was dressed in BDUs like the first man, with his hair buzzed almost into nonexistence, the military style that made all men look nearly the same. Both he and the man she thought might be her father were deeply tanned. The other man wore slacks and a blue polo shirt. His dark hair was longer, but not by much, and his skin was also the deep tan she was familiar with from being around soldiers who trained in the deserts of the Southwest. Except for his thin, foxlike face, Nicole thought he might even be Hispanic.

She examined more thoroughly what she could see of the man who stood with his back to her. Though she couldn't see his face, she could tell he was a little taller than either of the other two men. He had wide shoulders like her father, and the way he stood was the posture she knew so well. Dad wasn't due back until tonight, but he might have come early, she thought with a thrill of excitement. She could call to him and race him down the hill, but something held her back, urging caution. It was more than a fear of getting in trouble for escaping her older sister, who was supposed to be watching her.

The soldier facing her said something, and the soldier with his back to her, the one she was becoming convinced was her father, lunged toward him. That was when she noticed his hands were tied behind his back. The man wearing civilian clothes intercepted him, holding something in his hand Nicole couldn't see clearly, but she heard a small pop and watched the soldier who might be her father crumple to the ground.

Being an army brat, she knew at once that the sound wasn't like the gunshots she was familiar with, but something told her the man had been shot just the same. She wanted to go to him, offer him aid, and make certain he wasn't her father. It couldn't be Daddy; Daddy wouldn't let something so terrible happen. She ached to run for help but was unable to move. Shock held her motionless and locked her throat so she couldn't even scream.

She stared in horrified fascination as the other two men spoke together in hushed tones for a few minutes before the one in uniform crouched beside the fallen soldier. He said something to the man who had fired the shot, who then leaned forward to assist him in raising the body until it hung limply between them. The victim's head sagged downward, and she still couldn't be sure of his identity. The other two men took a moment to scuff with their boots the place where the fallen man had lain, then they hurried down the path carrying the unconscious man between them. She couldn't bring herself to consider that he might be dead.

Nicole stayed hidden until she was certain the men were gone. While waiting, she debated what she should do. She wanted to tell someone what she had seen, but she suspected no one would believe her. Mom would yell at her for going into the forest and say she'd made up the story. She would punish her for disobeying Marcie. Besides, the men were probably taking the fallen man to the hospital—and he couldn't be her dad anyway. Dad wasn't expected back from the training ground at Yakima until tonight.

Eventually she crept out of the bushes and stared for a long time at the ground. There was no sign that the three men had been there. The mistlike rain grew heavier, and tiny rivulets of water smeared the scrape marks left by the men. She could almost believe she'd imagined it all. Gripping her bucket of berries, she followed the path to a road, crossed it, then made her way home. For the first time, she found something secretive and menacing about the thick growth of trees and plants that covered the hill. She shivered as the rain increased its tempo.

Chapter 1

Nicole leaned back against the upholstery, ignoring the bright yellow Scottish broom and the wild blackberry bushes disappearing into a tight growth of pine trees lining the highway. She'd once loved this wild, beautiful land that seemed to defy encroaching civilization's attempts to tame it. Now she couldn't bear to look at it.

Her meeting with her sister had been awkward. Marcie had been flushed and late because she'd gotten a speeding ticket on the way to the airport. She was out of breath from rushing from the parking area while clutching her daughter's infant seat in one hand and hanging onto her son with the other. Once Nicole would have known what to say to her sister, but now they were practically strangers.

She noticed but said nothing when Marcie left the freeway. She knew they weren't even close to the base yet, but she was in no hurry to reach it. Curiosity finally triumphed when she felt the car slow. She opened her eyes as Marcie pulled to a stop in front of a florist's or nursery of some sort. The sign on the door showed a row of five squat trees in orange tubs.

"I'll just be a minute." Her sister looked toward her, a hesitant question in her eyes.

"I'll watch them," Nicole answered the unasked question. She didn't mind being left alone for a few minutes with her small niece and nephew. She scarcely knew them, but they were a large part of why she was here today. And waiting in the car on a cool, moist May morning in western Washington was no hardship. It might even give her an opportunity to pull herself together. She hadn't expected the sights and smells to hit her so hard.

Marcie opened her door, then remembered her purse and reached back inside the car for it. Several items spilled onto the seat of the car, and Nicole reached to help her sister pick them up. Marcie jammed a tube of lipstick and her checkbook back in her bag and apologized with the same nervous flutter that had annoyed Nicole so much back when they were teenagers. Marcie was older than Nicole by three years, but it had been Marcie who had followed Nicole about, constantly apologizing over every little thing and annoying Nicole and her friends with her timid reluctance to try anything new or to leave them and go find friends of her own.

Nicole couldn't help shaking her head as she watched her sister hurry toward the nursery. What on earth could she need from a nursery that she couldn't buy cheaper at the PX? That much she remembered from her early childhood; the post stores carried every-thing imaginable, and they were cheaper than the stores off base.

"Truck," her small nephew shouted from the backseat. Nicole looked back to see if he had dropped his toy. Instead she saw he had spotted a large, white truck coming toward them. As it rolled past, she noticed the same logo on the door that graced the nursery. It stopped in front of a closed gate to one side of the building, and a beefy man wearing a cap hurried from the truck toward the same door her sister had almost reached. A premonition of disaster gripped Nicole, and before she could shout a warning to her sister, the two collided.

Reeling, they both stepped back. The man recovered first and, ignoring Marcie, rushed inside the nursery. Marcie stared after him as though dazed. Wondering if her sister had been hurt or if she was just reacting to the man's rudeness, Nicole debated whether she should go to her or stay in the car. Marcie took a step back, looked toward the nursery, then back at the car. She seemed confused, but then gave a diffident little shrug and hurried into the shop next to the nursery.

Nicole stared after her sister. Even with her sister's love for gardening, there was little reason for her to visit a nursery this far from home, but there was absolutely no reason to visit a pet store. Marcie had never wanted so much as a goldfish in her life! She'd even been afraid of the puppy that had belonged to the kids next door at one base where they had lived. Anyway, if her husband had a pet or they'd gotten one for the children, all kinds of pet supplies were available at the PX.

Minutes later, Marcie returned to the car carrying a small plastic bag. Nicole was relieved to see it wasn't the kind that might hold a fish. Her sister climbed behind the wheel, and not for the first time, Nicole wondered if she should offer to drive. Marcie had never been a confident driver; she hadn't even applied for a learner's permit until Nicole had. Nicole didn't offer for the simple reason she felt much too miserable to take the wheel. The past few weeks had been so hectic, she was probably suffering some kind of physical collapse. She brushed aside any possibility her strange feelings were due to the memories associated with returning to Washington and the nagging fear that never quite left her that she might suffer a recurrence of the emotional breakdown that had ended her childhood. As Marcie pulled back onto the freeway, Nicole once more leaned back against the headrest. She closed her eyes and listened in an abstracted way as Marcie launched into an explanation of her purchase.

"I'm not sure it will help, but I heard the soldiers in Iraq are bothered by sand fleas and I thought it might help if I send J.D. a couple of flea collars to put around his ankles . . . and I would feel silly buying them on base." Nicole wasn't sure she wanted to hear more. "I'm so glad you could come. The last three weeks have been just awful. I can't sleep, and every little sound . . ."

Nicole tuned her sister out. Marcie's husband, J.D., had been deployed in April, but Nicole had been unable to leave Utah before graduation. It had taken a couple of days more to close her apartment and put her few belongings in storage. She still wasn't sure why she'd agreed to come; perhaps it was as simple as needing to find closure for a childhood that had gone terribly wrong before proceeding with life as an adult. Then too, she might have said yes because she'd been asked to speak at commencement exercises and been given extra tickets for her family. She'd found something depressing about having no family to give the tickets to. Her mother, who lived in Florida, wouldn't bother to come if she were asked, and with J.D. being deployed and having a new baby, there was no possibility her sister could come. She wasn't sure Marcie would want to come if she could. Then Marcie had called, and it had seemed like the right time to rebuild her relationship with her sister and her sister's family, so she had agreed to stay with her for a few months.

She heard the signal light click on again and knew Marcie was preparing to leave I-5. She didn't have to open her eyes to know her sister's car was climbing the short exit ramp leading to an overpass, and just beyond the overpass would be armed guards waiting to check the IDs of anyone entering Fort Lewis. Twelve years had passed since she was last on a military base, but all the details came rushing back now.

A sound in the backseat had her opening her eyes and turning to look at the two children securely strapped into car seats. Three-year-old John David grinned back at her, and warmth crept into her chest. He pointed a chubby finger at an array of yellow ribbons fluttering from the overpass.

"See! For Daddy." He pointed to the yellow streamers and a large poster that read "Support Our Troops." She certainly supported the troops, especially Marcie's husband, or she wouldn't be here, she thought as she checked on the occupant of the other car seat. The baby had fallen asleep minutes after leaving Sea-Tac Airport where Marcie had come to meet Nicole's flight from Salt Lake. Tiny Lexie slept with one small fist resting against her mouth and damp curls sticking to her rosy cheeks. A frozen spot inside Nicole seemed to be melting.

A measure of peace filled her heart as she watched the sleeping baby. Marcie and the children were the reason she'd agreed to return to Fort Lewis. She treasured the single brief visit her sister's family had made to her apartment in Utah the year before, and she longed for the closeness of family they represented. *If only they lived anywhere but here.* She immediately closed off painful memories. She was no longer an imaginative child. She was an adult and her sister needed her help while her husband was deployed. She could give up a summer to become friends with her sister, get to know her nephew and niece, and be there for them while J.D. was at war. And she would put painful memories aside.

She wished she might have invited them to stay with her in Utah instead of coming here, but her apartment was too small. Besides, she'd planned to give it up following graduation. As soon as she found a job, she'd rent a new apartment and get her furniture out of storage. Marcie could have gone to Florida to live with their mother while

J.D. was gone, but staying with Mom wasn't really feasible. Mom and Teddy were living aboard a small boat off the west coast of Florida that was entirely unsuitable for small children. And though Marcie got along with their mother better than Nicole did, she doubted Marcie could take more than a week or two of being around Mom. Thank goodness for Teddy.

Marcie stopped the car at the checkpoint, and Nicole handed her driver's license to her sister to present to the guard along with Marcie's military dependent ID. Even that simple action brought back memories Nicole had struggled to leave behind and filled her with a sense of being trapped. She could be on base with her sister, but since she wasn't a military dependent herself she would be unable to shop or even come and go as she pleased without Marcie accompanying her.

Seconds later, the car was moving along a paved road, taking them in the opposite direction from what Nicole had expected. Instead of following a curve around a steep, heavily wooded hill that she still saw in infrequent but persistent nightmares, they turned west toward American Lake and Puget Sound.

Nicole straightened and took her first real look out the car window. They weren't entering Main Post but had crossed over to North Fort. Her sense of gloom began to lighten. Marcie had never mentioned that her home was in North Fort Lewis—or Nicole had shut out her sister as she always did whenever she talked about the military base where she and her husband lived. She'd almost forgotten the base was divided by the I-5 corridor, and the smaller area northwest of the freeway was almost a separate entity from the main base on the other side of the interstate highway.

Trees lined the road Marcie followed as far as Nicole could see. Washed with spring rain, their beauty was one more painful reminder of the past. Trees could be found near the places she'd lived while attending college, but they were different from these. She'd grown to love Utah's forested canyons, and she could pretend this forest held the same beauty, she told herself. As long as she didn't have to return to that part of the base where her world had fallen apart, she'd be all right.

She never understood how Marcie could marry a military man and subject herself to live again the kind of life they and their mother had struggled so many years to put behind them. Of course, J.D. was great, and she was glad her sister had found him. She just wished he'd chosen any career other than the army.

Their mother had warned Marcie that J.D.'s career would place Marcie in the same nightmare she had endured while her father had been in Iraq during Desert Storm and reminded her over and over how hard military life could be on a marriage. It was the one time Nicole could remember that Marcie had stood up for herself against her mother. In spite of her mother's dire warnings, she'd married the young soldier who had swept her off her feet. Now J.D. was somewhere in Iraq while Marcie struggled to cope with loneliness and two small children on a military base far from family and friends. When Nicole accepted her sister's plea to come stay with her, she had made up her mind to help her sister handle her husband's absence better than their mother had. But now she wondered what had made her think she could cope with returning to this place.

Since the breakdown Nicole suffered when her father disappeared, she'd forgotten much about those early years, but she thought she hadn't hated military life as a child as much as Mom said she had. She clearly remembered that Marcie had complained about leaving her friends behind each time they were transferred. Her sister had hated starting over in new schools and making new friends. As a shy teenager, Marcie had wanted the same kind of home as some of her friends from the off-base high schools she attended. Nicole knew she hadn't been bothered by those things, no matter what Mom said, but Marcie was three years older. In the normal course of things, perhaps by the time she'd turned fourteen, things like that would have mattered to her too. She'd never know, because their nomadic military life had ended when she was eleven, only a few months after their father returned from the Persian Gulf War.

Marcie rolled down her window and breathed in deeply. The action interrupted Nicole's hesitant trip down memory lane. All Nicole's carefully built defenses shattered as her sister spoke, releasing a floodgate from the past. She tried to withdraw to that place in her mind that had protected her all these years.

"Remember how we used to do this when we were kids, roll down our windows and just breathe? Two years in Texas and a stint in New Mexico made this place seem like heaven." Marcie laughed before going on. "I can't look at a blackberry bush without remembering you with streaks of juice on your face and arms the summer we lived here." She knew returning to Fort Lewis had been a difficult decision for Nicole to make and sympathized with her. The events of that long-ago summer had been traumatizing for both of them, but her younger sister had been hit the hardest. When J.D. got his deployment orders, she'd hesitated to drag Nicole back to the scene of so much hurt, but she couldn't cope by herself, especially with a new baby. J.D. had encouraged her before he left to invite Nicole for an extended visit. He had no family other than her and their children, and he valued family highly. He thought it was time for the sisters to renew the closeness they'd shared as children. After some thought, she'd discovered she wanted that too. Besides, she was almost consumed with guilt for the part she had played in Nicole's breakdown. She glanced toward Nicole and sensed her withdrawal. Had she made a terrible mistake?

She thought of her mother's telephone call two nights ago. "Try to get Nicole to see a doctor," her mother had urged. "She still isn't over Greg's disappearance. It just isn't normal for a twenty-three-year-old girl to cut men out of her life the way she's done."

"Mom, Nicole is perfectly fine. Many women today don't marry until they're a lot older than Nicole is, and she's been busy with school." She'd tried to dissuade her mother from pursuing the topic. Her mother's constant reminders of the breakdown Nicole had suffered all those years ago got on her nerves. It almost seemed like she was still trying after all these years to justify her decision to send her youngest daughter to a mental institution. Nicole had been fine since she'd been released from the institution eleven years ago, and none of them needed a steady barrage of verbal reminders of that difficult time.

"What about that strange church she joined?"

"I joined that church too," Marcie had reminded her mother. "And so did you and Dad. You went to church with us every week until he left with his unit for the war."

"Yes, dear. But J.D. is a Mormon, so you had to join."

"Mom! We all joined the Church long before Nicole's illness. I didn't have to join, and I didn't join because of J.D." She'd had this discussion with her mother numerous times. "I became a Mormon because the Church is true." She wanted to add, *I thought you did too, and you might have handled Dad's absence both during the war and after if you'd stayed active,* but she knew it would just start an argument. Sometimes she thought her mother had selective memory loss when it came to the past, especially where her sister or the Church were concerned.

"Last time she was down here, she was looking at a gruesome web site on that computer of hers that listed descriptions of corpses. That's not normal."

"Mom, she had to take a number of medical classes to get her degree. She was probably doing homework. It doesn't mean she's crazy. Her breakdown is far in the past and was understandable." Even if Mom's suspicions were true and Nicole was checking to see if their father had died since he left them, she could understand that. Marcie, too, found her father's disappearance unfinished business, but she'd come to terms with it and no longer dwelled on it. Not that she thought Nicole did either, but she really didn't know her sister that well anymore—if she ever had.

Marcie was disappointed that Nicole didn't make a move to open her window. She'd hoped the pine-scented air would revive the good memories rather than stir the painful ones of that long-ago time. It wasn't only her nervousness about being alone that had prompted her to invite Nicole to live with her while J.D. was deployed. She'd been nervous herself about returning to Fort Lewis when J.D. first told her of the assignment, but instead of reminding her of all she'd lost, it had in some strange way comforted her by reminding her of even earlier, happier times. She would feel much less guilt if Nicole could find that same comfort.

Nicole didn't want to remember anything about the time she'd lived at Fort Lewis. The tragedy that severed their family had made everything before feel like a lie. Marcie and their mother hadn't believed her twelve years ago about the murder she'd witnessed. Neither had the psychiatrist Mom had taken her to. He'd told Mom that Nicole was suffering from a pre-adolescent fixation on a father absent too long from her young life because of the war. He said she'd made her father a hero in her mind, a superpatriot. When he'd left them and the army mere months after returning home, her mind had been unable to accept his desertion. In her grief, she had blamed herself, inventing an elaborate illusion that removed blame from her father and transferred it to her own wounded psyche.

In time Nicole had allowed herself to believe this explanation, but she'd been unable to completely overcome the mental aberration that continued to haunt her, though she took pains to hide it. She never spoke of the guilt and grief or pseudomemories, but as she stared out the window at the lush countryside, she couldn't stop the pictures that had been blocked so long from running through her mind, pictures of a young girl browned by the Texas sun exploring forest glades, breathing in the rain-scented air, and practically running wild. Dad had just returned from the war, and there were exciting new things to see and discover everywhere she looked.

Spotting a thick tangle of blackberry bushes beside the road, her stomach roiled. The berries she'd once prized so highly nearly nauseated her now. It had been spring when she and her family had arrived at Fort Lewis and late summer when she'd discovered the blackberries. They were everywhere—along the roads, covering vast fields, clinging to hillsides, and filling forgotten hollows. Mom had complained about Nicole's scratches and stained clothing, but she'd turned the berries into pies, cobblers, and jam that tasted like heaven.

Nicole had known nothing about her parents' marital problems or that Mom had threatened Dad with a divorce just before that last field trip to Yakima, over on the other side of the state. Fort Lewis soldiers frequently went there for training exercises, which sometimes lasted several weeks. Mom never liked Dad to be away, but Nicole hadn't noticed that this absence particularly agitated her. They'd all known it was nothing like the months he'd been gone to war. It wasn't until Dad disappeared that she learned Mom had wanted Dad, after twenty years in the army, to retire so their daughters could finish their schooling in one place. Mom had figured that with the income from a civilian job to supplement his military retirement pay, they could buy a house in a nice neighborhood. Nicole had been surprised to learn Mom wanted a house of their own and to be able to shop in more fashionable stores than the PX. Mom considered the PX nothing more than a warehouse-style discount store, but it was all they could afford on her husband's military salary. Dad was equally adamant about staying in the army. The only quarrel Nicole remembered was one over Mom's reluctance to attend church after Dad returned from Desert Storm.

It seemed ironic to Nicole that her mother still didn't have the stable life she'd claimed to want. Her husband, Teddy, could afford a home, but he preferred to live on a small yacht he'd bought and refurbished in opulent style.

Marcie slowed down as they approached a new housing development that looked much like any middle-class suburban neighborhood, except the houses were triplexes instead of single-family homes. Marcie pulled into a detached garage. As she and Nicole began unloading the children and Nicole's bags, Nicole couldn't help thinking of the double carport that had separated their house from the next one on the Main Post where she and her family had lived that summer years before. Her sister's townhouse was much newer and more modern than the house near Miller Hill, a place she'd called Bear Mountain.

Hoping that living on a different part of the huge sprawling base and keeping busy would dull her memories, Nicole hurried to release the children from their car seats and help Marcie carry them and her luggage into the house. The house was a pleasant surprise. Instead of the cold tile floors she remembered, a comfortable carpet covered all but the kitchen area, and Marcie had shown excellent taste in selecting furnishings.

Mom had never shown much interest in caring for the houses and apartments where they had lived, but she had liked cooking and baking. That ended after they left Fort Lewis. Before, Nicole remembered that Mom had spent long hours in social activities and with friends while their father was away, leaving Marcie to tend to the house and her younger sister. After Mom moved them to Florida, she'd paid little attention to the upkeep of their apartment and took no interest in social activities or the Church.

Marcie's taste in furnishings and flare for color went a long way toward raising Nicole's spirits. She could do this. She followed her sister up the stairs with John David bouncing between them, chattering happily. Her confidence grew when she felt his small hand clasp hers.

"This room will be Lexie's when she's ready for it," Marcie explained as she walked through an open door into a small bedroom. "For now, I like having her crib in the master bedroom with me."

The room was simply furnished with a single bed, nightstand, and bureau, but Nicole scarcely noticed. It was the view from the window that caught her attention. A tree-lined lane began almost directly outside where a misty rain had begun to fall. The trees were huge and tightly packed, leaving little room for sky or sunshine. They appeared dark and filled with forbidding secrets. A flash of color appeared on the lane then was gone, swallowed up by the thick, dark foliage. She felt a scream begin deep inside her and cut it off sharply. She'd trained herself a long time ago not to scream or cry, not to do anything that would label her crazy.

A surge of anger had her stepping back from the window. She'd experienced this anger once before—on the day she'd heard her mother's next-door neighbor call her crazy and no one, not even her mother, had refuted the hurtful label. The months she'd spent in a psychiatric hospital and her frequent appointments with a child psychiatrist added up to a label she'd found unbearable. The hurt and anger had gone deep as she realized home was no different from the institution where she'd been imprisoned for almost a year. She'd found a way to survive in that place and eventually to leave it behind her. She could be strong again.

Gaining her freedom from the hospital had required letting that long-ago incident in the forest go and pretending she accepted the doctor's version of the events surrounding her father's disappearance. Living with her mother and sister again required more of the same pretense. It also required hiding all the hurt, anger, and distrust her mother's betrayal had heaped on her grieving heart. Eventually she'd no longer been certain what was real.

Nicole's lips tightened in anger now—anger at herself. She hadn't behaved well since Marcie met her at the airport. Her own doubts and fears were crippling her ability to help her sister. They'd been crippling her life for years. She was tired of pretending, tired of believing what someone else wanted her to believe. One fact remained, her father was gone. Either the things she'd witnessed were real or imagined, and it was time she found out which. She'd let the incident color her thoughts and attitude too long. She couldn't change the images that came to her mind from all those years ago, but she could face them. Starting today, she was going to find out one way or another what happened to her father.

She was no longer a child, and she didn't have to be afraid or allow one frightening memory to determine the course of her life. No one had made her come here, though she believed Dad would have wanted her to be here for her sister. Marcie and her children were her family, and both Dad and the Church had always stressed the importance of family members supporting each other. She would be of no use to her sister if she moped around letting the past or her imagination make her moody and miserable.

There was only one way to face her fears and move on. She had to accept this place without any pretense—and she had to look for the truth. She opened a suitcase and reached for a well-worn pair of jogging shorts. She did her best thinking, and sometimes her most soul-searching praying, when she ran. Fort Lewis was a runner's paradise, and she would run every possible road and trail. When she was familiar with the base once again, she would visit the hill where it all began. From there she would begin a search for her father.

* * *

Braedon welcomed the rain. Coming from southern Utah where rain was considered an infrequent blessing and where, when it did rain, the gullywashers were accompanied by thunder and lightening, this Washington rain was a novelty. It made running easier too. He sucked his lungs full of the moist, oxygen-rich air and continued up the strenuous course he'd set for himself.

Active duty at an American military base, safely within his own country with most of the conveniences of home, hardly seemed worth all of the fanfare his Reserve unit had received from the local media when they were called up. He wasn't eager to go to war, yet it seemed almost a betrayal of his mom and brothers to be merely a couple of states away enjoying beautiful scenery, jogging every day, eating good food, and relaxing in front of a TV most evenings while they were struggling to run the ranch without him.

His family viewed the sacrifice as necessary so that he could fight for his country, but this wasn't combat duty. It was merely filling in for other soldiers who were the ones doing the fighting. Something about that bothered him, even though intellectually he knew he was doing essential work for internal security. Still, it was nothing but inconvenient to be on active duty when there was so much needing his attention at home, especially after the years his mom and brothers had shouldered so much of the burden while he served a mission, attended college, then served four years in the full-time army.

At least this deployment had rescued him from his family's matchmaking. As the oldest of four brothers, but the only one still single, getting him married seemed to have become the family project. He couldn't count the number of young women he'd dated over the years, but the last few years his interest in marriage had waned. He hadn't met one woman he'd wanted to spend an entire year with, let alone all eternity. It seemed to him he'd only met two types of women, and neither appealed to him. There were the career women who were exciting to talk to but who had no interest in running a home, and there were the homebodies without a thought in their heads beyond baking bread and teaching Primary. Perhaps that was an exaggeration, but not by much.

Braedon descended the path he was following to a narrow road. A half dozen young people in their late teens and early twenties, dressed much as he was in running shorts with brightly colored reflector belts crossing their dingy gray army PT shirts, passed the spot where the trail merged with the road a short distance ahead. He didn't often encounter other runners on this road, as it was some distance from the more popular jogging trails. He knew at a glance that the runners were not accompanied by an officer, and there was nothing official about their exercise. The off-duty soldiers were laughing and teasing as they ran, obviously enjoying a workout that was mostly social.

He was well aware that to stay in shape, soldiers did a lot of running, sometimes with heavy training packs on their shoulders, but these runners weren't burdened by gear and seemed to be running simply as an excuse to be together. Being a lieutenant and almost thirty, he didn't want to make the group he assumed to be mostly enlisted privates uncomfortable by joining them, so he slowed to allow them to get ahead. They were soon out of sight, though their laughter lingered behind them as he emerged from the almost hidden trail he'd been following and stepped onto the road. As he did so, he nearly collided with a runner wearing a lime green tank top with black running shorts and no regulation PT belt.

He clutched the runner's shoulder to prevent them both from falling as she too scrambled to avoid careening into him. Instead of immediately releasing her, he forgot his workout, the cluster of runners a short distance away, and stared like a starstruck rock star fan. He was holding onto the most beautiful woman he'd ever seen. Before he could find his voice, she stepped away from their near-collision, abruptly shaking off his hand. She looked past him to the road where the laughter of the group of runners had faded away. He didn't think she was part of the group, since she wasn't dressed as the off-duty soldiers were, but she had probably been following them for the slight security the group afforded her.

He couldn't take his eyes off her. To call the woman pretty seemed an understatement. She had long hair that appeared at first almost black, then he realized it was the darkest red he'd ever seen. She also had green eyes and was tall and athletically thin with sun-warmed skin he suspected she'd gained far from the Pacific Northwest. He was surprised she didn't laugh off the incident but continued to appear shaken. There was a slight tremble to her rigidly stiff body, and her eyes remained wary and dilated as they slid past him.

"I'm sorry," he told her. "I should have checked more thoroughly before barging onto the road."

"My fault," she murmured, her long legs already beginning to propel her in the direction the other runners had disappeared. She'd taken several loping strides before Braedon realized she was leaving. She took four more steps before it sank into his head that he didn't want her to go. He wanted to know her name and much more. He sprinted after her, hoping she would talk to him if he ran beside her.

Braedon found catching up to her wasn't easy. Her ground-eating stride made it clear she wasn't a novice at running. When at last he matched his steps to hers, he glanced sideways and smiled. She didn't return the smile.

"Do you think maybe we could start over if I promise not to run into you again? My name is Braedon Morgan."

"I'm not military. I'm only visiting." She pulled a few steps ahead.

Lengthening his stride and making every effort not to pant, he pulled even with her once more. She didn't even glance at him. He had the distinct impression she was attempting to ignore him. He hoped he wasn't vain, but it had been his experience that most women upon casual meeting were eager to further his acquaintance. He'd learned long ago that being six feet three inches tall with dark, curly hair and blue eyes, as well as possessing a range-rider's physique, were assets which generally garnered more attention than he was comfortable with. The more this young woman ignored him, the more intrigued he became, but half a mile farther down the road, he began to slow his steps.

He wasn't the sort to push himself where he wasn't wanted. If the girl wasn't interested in getting to know him, he'd accept that, reluctantly perhaps, but he hadn't reached the age of twenty-nine without learning that not every young lady who caught his attention reciprocated the attraction. He wondered if she was engaged or married. A girl that attractive was unlikely to be single. He didn't see any rings on her fingers, but that didn't always mean a woman was unattached. And even if she were, she wasn't interested, so it was time to bow out. Still, he found himself wondering if she were the career or home type.

"Perhaps I'll see you around." Taking her rebuff with good grace, he slowed his steps further and turned toward a trail that veered into the dense growth beside the road. He'd only taken a few steps along it when a high-pitched scream made the hairs on the back of his neck stand up. Quickly retracing his steps to the road, he caught a glimpse of the runner moments before she barreled into him once again.

His arms closed around her, and he staggered as he attempted to keep them both upright. He tightened his grip and held her while she gasped incoherently and struggled to escape his hold.

"It's all right. I'm not going to hurt you," he assured her. For just a moment, she tucked her head against his shoulder as though she would rest it there, then she twisted to point behind her. Looking over her shoulder to see what had frightened her, he saw what looked like a bear coming down the dirt road toward them.

Chapter 2

"Whoa!" Braedon backed up several steps, drawing the woman with him. "It's just a cub. I don't think he'll hurt us." Though the young bear might be harmless, it didn't look old enough to be on its own, and its mama would be anything but harmless if she considered them a threat to her baby.

"Back up slowly," he whispered. "If we run, he might think we're playing or start bawling for his mama."

Taking care not to make any sudden movement, he lowered his arms until he could grasp one of her hands. Her fingers laced through his and gripped hard. Keeping himself between the woman and the bear, he took a step backward, then another. She stepped back with each of his steps, but the cub was gaining on them. Braedon searched his mind for a way to discourage the young animal's approach. Stooping, he picked up a small rock.

"When I throw this," he whispered, "start running back the way we came." He released her hand and took aim. Drawing back his arm, he prepared to lob the projectile toward the bear. A shout stayed his hand.

"Yo! Look at that!"

"What is it?"

"A bear!"

"Wow!"

"I want to see it!"

"Did you find the lady who screamed? Oh!" The group of runners looked at the cub, then down the path to where Braedon and the woman stood. The woman inched closer to him, and her hand gripped his again.

The cub halted, glanced behind it to the group of runners who had turned back to investigate the scream, then toward Braedon and the woman who stood trembling beside him. Releasing one squawk, the cub darted toward the thick growth of brambles beside the road. In seconds he was gone.

"Aw, he's leaving."

"All right, soldiers, let's move it before junior's mother shows up to chew us out for disturbing her baby." Braedon took charge. Without releasing the hand tightly gripping his again, he moved toward the young soldiers before anyone could suggest following the cub. Almost as one, the soldiers pivoted and began jogging back down the track they'd been following. They were more subdued now than they had been earlier, no doubt due to his presence.

They'd traveled almost a quarter of a mile before the woman whispered, "Thanks."

"Thank them." Braedon gestured toward the young soldiers who were setting a smart pace before them. "We would have probably been fine, but their showing up to scare the cub away certainly improved our odds."

"I know. As soon as we reach the main road, I'll thank all of them." She didn't attempt to free her hand, and Braedon was surprised by how easily they ran together, their linked hands proving no obstacle to speed or balance.

On reaching the busier road the group hesitated, and Nicole stepped away from Braedon before calling out, "Thanks everyone. That little bear really startled me."

"Glad we were nearby," someone called back.

"Hey, I'll be glad to save you from a bear any day," another offered.

"He was kind of cute, wasn't he?" a female soldier added, laughter in her voice.

"What unit are you in?" a tall young man asked. "We're headed for Burger King on Main Post if you want to join us."

"Thanks, but I'm not military. I'm just visiting, and my sister will be expecting me back soon," she told them. Her words both encouraged and concerned Braedon. If she wasn't enlisted personnel, he'd have no problem with the military by trying to see her again, but if her visit was of short duration, he might not get a chance to get to know her better. He couldn't believe how disappointed he felt at the possibility of not seeing her again.

The group of runners turned toward the gate leading to Main Post, and she turned slowly toward the tall man beside her. She didn't know what to say. Earlier she'd rebuffed his interest almost to the point of rudeness. She wanted to apologize, but she didn't want to encourage him. She knew instinctively that he was military and an officer, just as those young privates had known. She also knew he was interested in her and that he hadn't hesitated to put himself between her and the bear, but she had an ironclad rule against dating anyone in the military.

"I'll be all right now," she told him. "If the mother bear were coming after us, she would have already done so."

"Probably, but I'd like to run with you for a ways. I think we're headed the same direction anyway." He smiled, showing a faint dimple in one cheek. She had to remind herself she wasn't interested.

There wasn't much she could do other than gracefully accept his offer, and as they ran, she couldn't help noticing how evenly matched their strides were. She didn't often run with a partner because she usually found she had to slow her steps in order to stay together. She wished she hadn't noticed. There were a lot of other things about this man she wished she hadn't noticed either, like how tall he was or how blue his eyes were. Especially, she wished she hadn't noticed how much his calm, take-charge style reminded her of her father. Dad had always seemed to quietly evaluate a situation, then take charge without a lot of fuss. Suddenly she felt flustered; she'd never compared any man to her father before.

"If you're going to run while you're visiting your sister, you ought to pick up a PT belt." Braedon mentioned the reflector belt that was required gear for runners and bikers on base, hoping to start a conversation. This woman intrigued him, and he suspected he would always regret it if he failed to make an effort to become better acquainted with her.

"You mean one of those bright orange strips you and all those kids are wearing? My sister probably has one of J.D.'s around I can borrow. She said he ran or rode his bike every day before he was deployed."

"How long will you be staying with your sister? Until her husband comes back?" He hoped to gain a little more information.

"Yes, unless I get one of the jobs I applied for back home. Oh, this is where I turn off." She cut toward a road leading into a new housing area.

"Hey, you never did tell me your name." He tried once more.

"Nicole." She waved and kept running. He watched until she slowed her steps then walked toward the last house on the right. She never looked back before opening the front door and disappearing inside.

Braedon picked up his pace again. He hadn't learned a lot about the mysterious lady, but it was enough to go on. Even if he weren't an experienced investigator, it would be a simple matter to find her brother-in-law's name. He already knew he was a non-com simply from discovering where she was staying, since military housing is assigned by rank. He'd just make running past the house part of his routine tomorrow. Her brother-in-law's name and rank would be on a plate beside the front door. And if he were lucky, Nicole would be setting out for a run too.

Nicole. He liked the sound of it.

* * *

"Did you have a good run?" Marcie looked up from dinner preparations as Nicole entered the kitchen after her shower. Nicole had changed into jeans and a T-shirt. Now she gathered her wet hair into the scrunchie she held in one hand, forming a hasty ponytail.

"I saw a bear." She saw doubt on her sister's face before it was replaced with the bland expression Nicole knew well. Mom and Marcie had perfected that expression years ago. Since returning to live with them following almost a year in a private sanatorium, she'd discovered any mention of anything unusual brought first skepticism, then that bland "that's nice" look to their faces. In the intervening years, it had appeared on any occasion when either of them thought she was imagining or exaggerating the slightest bit—and any time she mentioned her father. It annoyed her that they still saw her as an imaginative child, or worse, as mentally unstable.

She wanted to say, "No, I didn't imagine it, and no, I'm not crazy," but she'd learned long ago that it was better to say nothing about their skepticism and instead continue as though she hadn't noticed the reaction.

"The bear was just a cub, but it startled me," she went on. "A group of enlistees came over a hill and scared it away. We all left the area as quickly as possible in case its mother showed up."

"If you're sure . . . Bear sightings should be reported," Marcie began hesitantly.

"It's all taken care of." There was a forced breeziness to her voice. "One of the men said he'd report it." She took care not to mention Braedon Morgan by name, but she had heard him tell the younger soldiers not to worry about reporting the sighting because he would do it.

"I want to see the bear." John David entered the kitchen, his favorite blanket trailing behind him.

"Too late, sweetie." Nicole scooped up the sleepy-eyed toddler. "He's gone now. Besides he was a long way from here, and I'm not certain I could find the road again, even if I wanted to."

"Do you think he found his mother?" The little boy continued to worry about the bear.

"Yes." She tousled his nap-disheveled hair. "He hurried into the bushes like he knew exactly where to find her."

"You should have taked me."

"I went too far for your little legs." She hugged him, then set him on his booster seat.

"My legs are getting big." He thrust them out for her inspection. "Daddy says I can run races and get prizes just like you."

"In a few years," Marcie reminded her son of the rest of his father's prediction.

"I can hardly wait. You'll be stiff competition." Nicole buckled the little boy's safety harness and scooted him closer to the table. The action reminded her of Braedon's advice about running with a PT belt. She turned back to her sister.

"Did J.D. leave a safety vest or reflector belt around here I can borrow next time I run?"

"Oh, I'm sorry. I should have thought of that." Marcie set a hot casserole dish on the table and turned toward the refrigerator.

"Wearing one is mandatory anytime you run or cycle on base. J.D. and I ride bikes quite often, so there are several hanging beside our bikes in the garage. Help yourself to one next time you run."

Marcie set the milk on the table before seating herself near her small son, who immediately folded his arms and squinched his eyes shut. Nicole took the chair opposite them.

"Will you ask the blessing, John David?" Marcie asked.

Nicole smiled at the simple prayer the boy asked, especially when he added, "Help my daddy come home to play Power Rangers with me."

After the first few bites of the casserole, Nicole asked, "Did you hear from J.D. today?"

"No, I checked my e-mail as soon as I got the kids down for their naps, but there wasn't anything." She sounded discouraged.

"Perhaps you'll get something tomorrow," Nicole attempted to cheer her sister. "He's only been gone a few weeks."

"I didn't really expect anything," Marcie admitted. "He called when they reached Kuwait, and I knew he wouldn't be able to call or use a computer while they're on the move. He said they should reach the area where they'll be based sometime this week. It's just so hard not knowing exactly where he is and if he's safe. I can't bear to watch the news anymore."

Nicole sympathized with her sister, knowing how close Marcie and J.D. were and that Marcie had never liked being alone. She felt a twinge of guilt for all the times she'd run off and left her sister to her own devices while they were growing up.

A wail from upstairs reached their ears, and Marcie started to rise.

"No, finish your dinner," Nicole insisted. "I'll get her. I'll even change her diaper." Matching action to words, she dashed up the stairs to retrieve her small niece. Minutes later, she returned, carrying the smiling baby who stared up at her with round, fascinated eyes as Nicole whispered nonsense to her.

"I'm surprised you got her to stop crying." Marcie gave a little laugh as she pushed her chair back and reached for the baby. "Usually nothing stops her screaming until I feed her, and since her nap was late today, I expected her to really tell us about it."

"She's a little angel." Nicole touched Lexie's nose with the tip of one finger before handing her to Marcie.

"No, it's you. You always did have a magic touch with babies. You should be married and have a couple of your own." Marcie settled in a comfortable chair with the baby in her arms before reaching for the hem of her shirt.

Nicole turned away. She loved babies, and Marcie's children were rapidly becoming the biggest joy in her life. But she didn't expect to ever have any children of her own—not that she didn't want them, but she just couldn't see herself ever getting married. She wasn't comfortable around men, and she had some trust hang-ups. She rarely dated. And few of the men she had agreed to go out with in the years since she'd turned sixteen had inspired her to accept second invitations. She had a few male friends, but she kept them friends by never dating them. Her undergraduate roommates had put a great deal of effort into finding the perfect match for her, but though most of their choices had been perfectly nice young men, she'd found something lacking in each of them. She'd realized a long time ago that she was the problem.

"Oh, that reminds me, is there someone you forgot to tell me about?" Marcie's teasing voice interrupted her thoughts. Instantly a picture of Braedon Morgan flashed through her mind, and she felt a strange little jolt.

"What do you mean?" she hedged.

"You received a call this afternoon while you were out running," Marcie went on. "He didn't leave a name or number, but just hung up when I said you were out."

"I applied for a couple of positions that should be available this fall or early next year. I put your phone number on the applications." She knew her answer disappointed her sister.

Marcie settled deeper in her chair and adjusted the baby to a more comfortable position. She didn't know what to make of Nicole's bear story. It could have happened the way she said, but it had been some time since there had been a bear sighting on base, and even then, the bear had been on Main Post, not North Fort. She hoped bringing Nicole back to Fort Lewis hadn't been a mistake. She'd never forgive herself if coming back caused Nicole to suffer another breakdown.

She listened to the teasing play between her son and sister and wished the call her sister had missed had been from a male friend and not a potential employer. Or was she being selfish? She had found a completeness in her marriage that she wanted her sister to enjoy too. Only when her sister was happy and well would she believe she had a right to the peace and happiness she found with J.D. and their children.

She smiled thinking of J.D. They'd met at a singles dance where she'd gone strictly to keep an eye on Nicole, who had just turned eighteen. Though members of the Church most of their lives, Mom had become bitter toward the Church after Dad disappeared, and Marcie had lacked the courage to attend meetings or activities on her own. After Nicole was released from the "home," she had insisted on attending church, and Marcie had been charged with the responsibility of accompanying her. At first she'd felt sorry for herself, then she'd found something she hadn't even known she was looking for. She would be forever grateful to her sister for a persistence in attending church each Sunday that had rewarded Marcie with a testimony of the gospel.

The first thing Marcie had noticed about the handsome stranger at the dance was his height and the way he stood and walked. He reminded her of Dad. Even though he claimed it was because she was the prettiest girl there, she'd never known why he singled her out for a dance, then another, and another. She wasn't surprised to learn he was a soldier from a nearby army base. Unlike Nicole, who rejected everything about military men and military life, Marcie found that being around J.D. returned the sense of security she'd felt as a child. Besides, how could she help falling in love with a man as confident and caring as J.D. Duran?

Worry interrupted her thoughts. Why hadn't she heard from him? Was he safe? How safe could anyone be in a country torn apart by war? She loved everything about being a peacetime soldier's wife, but somewhere in the back of her mind she'd known since the day she'd fallen in love with him that someday he'd go to war, leaving her alone. Still, she'd been unprepared for his departure and the loneliness of her days—and especially the nights—without him. *Please, Father, keep him safe,* was a constant prayer in her heart.

What if she became as obsessed as her mother or had a breakdown like her sister? Who would care for her children if J.D. didn't come back and she fell apart? An odd thought crossed her mind. She hadn't wanted her mother's help through this time of fear and loneliness. Why was that? It was her sister she was turning to, the same younger sister who had challenged her in sports, restored her faith in God, and who had flown by herself all the way from Florida to Utah to attend the college of her choice. Nicole was the strong one, the one most like Dad, the one she would trust with her children if she and J.D. were unable to raise them—even if she did think she saw a bear this afternoon.

Chapter 3

J.D. had been caught in a snowstorm once while skiing in the backcountry of Colorado. The whirling snow had blinded him, making him afraid to move for fear he'd fall over some precipice. The windswept sand brought back that same loss of orientation. He couldn't see the enemy, but he knew they were out there, possibly mere feet away.

Placing his hands behind him flat against the baked clay, he edged his way along the wall of a structure that might be an ordinary village home, but the intelligence he'd gathered earlier suggested it was a terrorist base. He'd been following a white-robed figure toward this place when the sandstorm struck with a ferocity that made him wonder why anyone bothered living in such a disagreeable place.

His fingers brushed against an indentation, and he knew he'd found a window aperture. He explored its outline and counted the number of bars behind thick shutters. Reaching under the swirling robe he wore, he found a small device. With the tips of two fingers, he lodged it between the shutters, closed to keep out the blowing dust and possibly to protect the privacy of the men who were sheltered inside. One more foray beneath his robe produced another small object, which he inserted in his ear.

Crouching low to avoid detection should there be a break in the sandstorm, he strained to hear. At first the only sound was the shrill, abrasive hiss of sand striking the window shutter and metal bars, then came a man's voice. The words were indistinct, but he wouldn't have understood them anyway since he only understood a few words in Arabic. They were enough, however, to identify the speaker as the man he'd followed from a café off the square, a man suspected of being a link between Saddam Hussein and loyalists intent on preventing the formation of a new Iraqi government.

A second voice revealed the presence of another Iraqi. The wind made identifying his accent difficult, but it appeared he wasn't a native to this northern region. With the large number of Muslim terrorists sneaking across the border from other countries to create chaos in the name of Saddam Hussein, the Taliban, Osama bin Laden, the Baath Party, al Qaeda, and every other Islamic extremist group, he could be anybody. The first voice became louder, and when the second responded in kind, the sergeant's lips stretched in a grim smile beneath the scarf he wore to keep the blowing sand out of his mouth. There was no question the tiny recorder would pick up the words, and hopefully they would be of use to Coalition forces attempting to end terrorist attacks and create order.

Suddenly a third voice erupted in his ear with a well-known American expletive followed by rapid, guttural sounds spoken so low they were indistinguishable as words. One thing he knew, the speaker was American educated, possibly even a fellow countryman. It was time to get back to his partner and signal for the raid to begin.

* * *

Braedon barely made it through the chapel doors before they closed at the conclusion of the sacrament hymn. He hated being late, but responsibilities on base had kept him longer than anticipated.

He found a seat between two families with small children on the back row, and the moment he felt the crunch of dry cereal, he knew he'd made a mistake. He recognized from elders quorum the young father on his left who was sitting beside an attractive blonde, but he suspected the woman on his right, who seemed to be alone, was the wife of a soldier either on duty or deployed.

It wasn't until the deacons were returning to their seats to sit with their families that he noticed two women with a couple of small children seated half a dozen rows in front of him. One woman's hair was a deep, dark red, but the other's was even darker, almost black in the subdued lighting of the chapel. It reminded him, as if he needed a reminder, of the woman he'd met four days earlier. Nicole. He hadn't been able to get her out of his mind. He'd begun jogging in the late afternoon in the vicinity where they'd met, even though he usually ran in the mornings. But all without catching a glimpse of her.

The woman with hair like Nicole's lifted an infant to her shoulder and began to gently pat its back. Braedon felt a stab of disappointment. A toddler with dark curls leaned over the bench, and the woman with the lighter hair tugged him back to her lap.

"Oops!"

A commotion to his right distracted his attention. He glanced down to see a river of liquid spreading along the bench between him and a sobbing toddler who held a bottle in one hand and the nipple section in the other. The toddler's mother snatched a cloth from her shoulder in a frantic move to stanch the flow. The baby on her lap began to scream and wave his arms and legs, sending a plastic bowl of cold cereal flying to the floor and into the juice puddle.

Braedon could see there were only two honorable choices. He lifted the baby from the startled woman's arms and walked out the door to the foyer. The mother could do the cleaning. As he passed the soldier on his left, he noticed the soldier had armed himself with a diaper or something similar and was aiding in stanching the flow of apple juice before it could reach his family.

Becoming aware of dampness on his arm just where it supported the little guy's well-padded behind, he wondered if he'd made the best choice after all, though the baby's screams had stopped abruptly once the chapel doors closed behind them. The baby looked around and even smiled. Raising one sticky hand, he patted Braedon's face.

"Like that, huh?" Braedon whispered. "You were just looking for a good excuse to cut church." The baby giggled.

Braedon sighed. At least he could still hear the speaker. He paced around the small space, pausing to read announcements posted on a bulletin board and examine a few trophies. He nodded to parents who were also pacing the entryway with rebellious infants and toddlers. A few times, the baby made halfhearted squirming motions as though he wanted down, but he didn't push the issue, and Braedon hung on. He'd learned the hard way not to turn his nephews or niece loose when he'd been roped into hall duty back home, and he had a hunch this kid would be nothing but trouble if he were turned loose on the floor.

He heard the chapel door open, then close softly, and wondered if the harried mother of the baby was coming to fetch junior. He turned just as a familiar voice asked, "Yours?"

"What?" Startled, he stared straight into the eyes that had haunted his thoughts for four days. Nicole stood before him, wearing a green dress that made her eyes appear more green than hazel. Her lips curved in amusement as she gave him a quick once-over, making him aware of his wrinkled, damp shirt and sticky face.

About the time he gathered his wits enough to realize she'd asked him a question concerning the baby in his arms, he noticed she too held a whimpering infant. She lifted it smoothly to her shoulder and swayed slightly as she patted the little girl's satin-covered back. The miniature con artist he held made a lunge for a fistful of lace and ribbons.

"No, you don't." Braedon pried the dress loose from the baby boy's grasp and offered his tie instead. Turning back to Nicole, he said, "I never saw this guy before in my life, and I've been expecting someone to come looking for him for the past twenty minutes."

"Oh? He's lost? Perhaps you should ask the bishop to make an announcement." She made a motion as if to return to the chapel.

"No, he's not exactly lost." Braedon lost no time explaining how he came to be holding the baby.

"Well, that explains why you have a wet streak down the side of your pants and Cheerios stuck to your shirt. I even see a few Cheerios in your hair, what little bit of it Uncle Sam has permitted you to keep." Nicole laughed, and Braedon found himself chuckling too.

"And your little bundle?" Braedon indicated the tiny girl now sleeping soundly against Nicole's shoulder.

"My sister Marcie's baby." She continued a slight rhythmic sway as she talked.

The chapel doors suddenly burst open, and two little boys emerged, followed by a surge of people.

"I'm so sorry." The baby's mother hurried toward Braedon, towing the toddler. She was trailed by a couple of slightly older children. "Peter, Paula, now you hurry off to Primary." She motioned to two other children who immediately scampered through the throng toward the hall. "I meant to come get Paxton, but by the time I got Perry's mess cleaned up, sacrament meeting was almost over. I'm just so grateful for your help." She reached for her youngest, and after freeing his tie from young Paxton's clutches, Braedon cheerfully handed him over.

"Wave good-bye to the nice man." The young mother took her son's hand and made a waving motion with it. *Thank you,* she mouthed again before turning to make her way down the hall.

Braedon turned back to Nicole to see that the other redhead had joined her with the little boy he'd seen earlier. Nicole made introductions, though Braedon suspected that for some reason she wasn't anxious to tell her sister they'd met a few days earlier. And was he mistaken seeing a look of relief on Marcie's face when Nicole mentioned his role in the bear episode? He wondered what that was about.

"Would you mind showing Nicole where the Gospel Doctrine class meets?" Marcie asked him. "I'll join you as soon as I get John David settled in class."

Nicole didn't like the speculative look in her sister's eyes, but she meekly accompanied Braedon down the hall to the Relief Society room where the Gospel Doctrine class met. It would have appeared boorish to insist that since most LDS meetinghouses were practically identical, it wouldn't take a rocket scientist to find the Relief Society room. She had little choice but to sit beside him, but she had no intention of encouraging this man who made his interest in her all too clear.

Braedon couldn't believe his luck. He'd not only found his intriguing mystery woman, but she was a member of the Church. And after her sister caught up to them again just as class started, she'd stood up and introduced Nicole as Nicole Evangart. So now he knew her last name as well as where she was staying. He'd already learned that Marcie's husband, Sergeant J.D. Duran, was with Special Forces somewhere deep in Iraq.

He leaned back, feeling good about sitting beside Nicole. Though he made an effort to focus on the lesson, he was constantly aware of the slim figure on the next chair. The teacher was well prepared and sometimes humorous, but Braedon found his attention torn. He regretted when the lesson ended and it was time to leave for priesthood meeting. Reluctantly, he rose to his feet, wishing there was some way to prolong their time together.

"Brother Morgan," Marcie caught his attention, "I put a pot roast in the oven this morning. Would you like to come to dinner?"

This was his lucky day, though he didn't dare look at Nicole's face for her reaction to her sister's invitation. "I'd be happy to come." He smiled back at Marcie. "And call me Braedon."

"Would one o'clock be okay?"

"Perfect." He turned toward the door.

"You might need our address." Marcie's voice held a hint of laughter.

"I already have it." His eyes met Nicole's for just a second before he left for priesthood meeting with a smile on his face and a quick, "See you later," directed toward both young women.

Nicole knew what Marcie was doing. She was playing matchmaker. It wasn't the first time someone had played matchmaker for her, but it hadn't bothered her as much before. This time the object of the little game was too attractive, made her too aware of his presence, and he was military. She didn't want to hurt Marcie's feelings, so she wouldn't say anything, but she'd have to be on her guard every minute. Somehow she'd have to find a way to discourage Braedon Morgan and let Marcie know she didn't appreciate her help.

* * *

Marcie's house seemed much smaller with Braedon sitting across the table from Nicole. His manners were impeccable, and Marcie beamed when he praised her roast. John David was so delighted to have a male visitor, he chattered nonstop.

"My daddy is a sojer!" he proudly informed Braedon.

"I know," Braedon addressed the little boy. "And I know you miss him very much."

John David nodded his head in solemn agreement. "Mommy misses him too. Lexie is too little to miss Daddy."

"I'll bet he likes getting letters from you." Braedon went on talking to John David. Nicole found her mind drifting to the time her father had been away at war and to the many letters she'd written to him. It had been a highlight of her young life when she'd received hastily scrawled notes back from him instead of the usual postcript on her mother's letters.

"I can't write letters good," John David explained. "But I draw lots of pictures for Daddy, and Mom mails them to him."

"That's great."

"Would you like more roast?" Marcie asked him.

"Yes, thank you." Braedon accepted the platter. "I'll have to admit, I'm partial to beef, and this is as good as any roast my mother ever prepared from our own beef."

"Oh, do you raise cattle?" Marcie asked. Nicole disguised her curiosity about his answer by cutting up John David's meat for him, even while she berated herself for being interested in anything the man said. She usually didn't have to pretend a lack of interest in men, but there was something about this man that managed to slip past her guard.

"My family owns a ranch in Utah. Dad passed away four years ago, just two months after my youngest brother, Kendall, returned from his mission. Another brother, Cameron, and I run the ranch now."

"I thought . . . Aren't you military?" Marcie looked from Braedon to Nicole, then back to Braedon. Nicole was almost as puzzled as her sister. She couldn't help wondering why Braedon had given up living on a ranch to serve in the army. She gave up all pretense of being uninterested in his answer.

"Reserve," Braedon clarified. "My unit was activated in April. I joined ROTC while in college, so Mom helped Cameron with the ranch until I finished my time with the army after graduation. None of us expected me to be called up again a little more than a year after being discharged. When I learned my unit was being deployed, I thought we were heading for Iraq. Instead we were assigned to Fort Lewis."

"Why did you take ROTC if you planned to ranch?" Marcie asked.

"Growing up, Dad taught me a deep respect for America and to value liberty. For a while, I toyed with the idea of a career in the military. That's why I signed up for ROTC. But as much as I liked the army, I discovered my heart is in the canyons and meadows of the ranch that has been in my family for four generations. After my required service was over, I joined the Reserve, thinking I could serve my country and still manage the ranch." He chuckled. "Fort Lewis just isn't my idea of wartime duty. I sometimes think I'd be contributing more to the war effort if I were home raising beef for the guys over there to eat."

"So your brother is running the ranch while you're here?" Marcie asked.

"Yes, Cameron is in charge. Kendall and Steve both live nearby and promised to give him a hand when he needs help. Cameron's wife, Lynette, is the best cowhand we've got, though their three-year-old son thinks he is, and Steve's four-year-old twins are just as sure they are. Kendall and his wife have a ten-month-old daughter who will probably turn out to be the true winner."

Marcie laughed, and Nicole joined in. She couldn't explain why her heart felt lighter, and she was suddenly glad Marcie had invited Braedon to dinner. She glanced at him from under her eyelashes. He appeared to have gotten even better looking during dinner.

When they finished eating, Braedon insisted on helping Nicole clear the table while Marcie settled the children for naps. It only took moments until the dishwasher was loaded, then Nicole turned toward the living room.

"Nicole," Braedon stopped her with a gentle touch to her arm. "I've looked all week for you every time I went running. Would you consider another run together?"

"I usually run in the mornings. The day we met I had just arrived in Washington. Flying leaves me feeling cramped, so I was just getting the kinks out by running that afternoon." She attempted to stall him, though she wasn't sure why. It was a technique she used often to deal with men who seemed interested in her.

"I usually run in the mornings as well, but early. I have to be finished before regular PT so I can man a listening station while the other guys in my unit work out. I only run in the afternoons the days I'm not assigned to the listening station. Would five be too early?"

Nicole could think of no graceful way to refuse. To her surprise, she really didn't want to say no, but she'd have to make certain he didn't expect to run with her on a regular basis. She was a competitive runner, and altering her training schedule to accommodate someone else's speed and style could impact her preparedness for her next competition.

At five the next morning, she finished her warm-up routine just as a pickup truck parked in front of Marcie's house. Braedon was behind the wheel.

"Ready?" he called as he leaped from the driver's seat and trotted toward her.

"Sure." She set off at a fast walk down the street. He hurried to catch up. "Do you need to warm up first?" she asked as her conscience kicked in.

"No, I'm fine. Several of the guys I live with have early duty too. They do calisthenics each morning with me, so I'm ready to go." She began to jog as they neared the road leading to the beach and then to run. They ran companionably for several miles, and she was glad he seemed content to let her set the pace. He didn't make conversational demands either. A few miles into the run, she began to relax and enjoy an exchange of casual banter. Near where they had seen the bear cub, he suggested they turn back.

"I have to report for duty by six fifteen," he said by way of explanation.

"All right," she agreed without slowing her steps, but she did turn back the way they'd come. A few blocks from Marcie's house, she slowed to a walk to allow them both a brief cooling-down period.

As they approached Braedon's truck, he asked, "Same time tomorrow?"

"No, Marcie and I will be swimming later in the day, so I probably won't run." She felt a twinge of regret in spite of the fact she'd made the appointment with Marcie primarily to avoid the possibility Braedon might assume she would run with him again tomorrow.

He didn't press the point or ask about the next day, and she wasn't sure how she felt about that. She did decide to shift her running time to a little later in the morning just as a precaution.

* * *

Nicole returned to the house from a two-hour run a few days later just as Marcie and John David were sitting down to breakfast. John David was standing on his chair reaching for a cereal box as she walked through the door.

"Look, Aunt Nicole," he announced. "Fruit Loops!"

"I try to keep cold cereal, especially the sugary ones, to a minimum around here," Marcie said in a cross between resignation and apology. "But we got up late, and John David loves the stuff, so I gave in this time." Nicole laughed. She knew Marcie was concerned about her children's diet.

"Sounds good to me." She winked at her nephew. "I'll take a quick shower and join you," she promised as she made her way up the stairs. When she returned, she carried Lexie cradled in one arm.

"Look who's awake," she called.

"Good morning, pumpkin." Marcie reached for her daughter and snuggled her for a moment.

Nicole slid onto a chair beside John David in time to intercept his reach for the nearly empty milk jug. She poured the last bit onto the bowl of cereal the little boy had already prepared for her. She wasn't a fan of sugary cereals, but she couldn't refuse her nephew's generosity.

"You don't have to eat that stuff," Marcie told her. "There are other kinds of cereal in the cupboard."

"It's okay." She dug her spoon into the brightly colored cereal. A bowl of almost straight sugar wouldn't kill her just this once.

"Do you like it?" John David beamed with pleasure as Nicole swallowed a spoonful of cereal.

"Fine," she answered as noncommittally as possible. In her own apartment, she would have settled for orange juice and toast, with a banana or perhaps a poached egg. Though she was committed to a healthy lifestyle, she certainly understood the appeal of sweetened cereal to a little boy. Seeing her sister's anxious expression, she hastened to reassure her.

"As long as cereal like this is a once-in-a-while treat and not everyday fare, it won't hurt him. Or me." She smiled to convey understanding. "A bowl of cold cereal doesn't make you a bad mother." She changed the subject. "What's on the agenda for today?"

"I need to go shopping. I'm out of everything. That's the last of the milk, and there's no juice or fresh fruit. We're almost out of diapers too. As soon as I finish feeding Lexie and get John David dressed, I'd better run over to the commissary." Nicole got the impression her sister wasn't looking forward to the shopping trip.

"I'd do the shopping for you, but without military ID . . ." Nicole let her voice trail off. She understood why only those who were either military, military dependents, or military retirees could shop on base, but it limited how much she could help her sister. "Would you like me to watch the kids while you go?"

"I want to go," John David spoke up. "I'm a good shopper." Marcie pulled a face that only Nicole could see.

"We can all go," Marcie decided, and she sounded more enthused. "That is, if Aunt Nicole is willing to go with us." She turned to Nicole. "John David really does like to help, and it will give you a chance to learn where everything is. The shopping and service areas of the base have expanded some since we were kids."

Nicole wasn't sure she wanted to become reacquainted with the business center of the base, but she'd have to sooner or later, so it might as well be this morning. If she was going to conquer her aversion to everything from her old life and find out about her past, she had to start somewhere.

"Okay, John David and I will clear up breakfast, then go upstairs and see what we can find for him to wear." She stood to begin clearing the table. John David carried his precious box of Fruit Loops to the cupboard before taking Nicole's hand for the trip up the stairs.

By the time she and her nephew were ready, Marcie had the baby dressed in a one-piece jumper and had found her purse and keys. John David led the way to the detached garage, where Marcie showed Nicole how to buckle the children into their respective car seats. John David provided unneeded driving directions to his mother all the way to the commissary, and it occurred to Nicole that Marcie was a much better driver than she had given her sister credit for.

The commissary and the Post Exchange were both large, sprawling buildings with huge parking lots. They reminded her of the box stores that had become popular recently around the Salt Lake valley. Nicole vaguely remembered shopping for groceries at the commissary and the PX for school clothes with her parents when she was a child, but she hadn't been interested in such activities then and, she realized now, had forgotten a great deal. In some ways, it wasn't much different from shopping at any large supermarket, though it was more structured with arrows painted on the floor to keep traffic moving in one direction. It was more crowded, too, than the Albertsons store where she usually did her grocery shopping.

Marcie placed Lexie's infant seat in the shopping cart, and John David walked beside Nicole with his hand in hers. He chattered with enthusiasm as they walked, and it soon became obvious he saw his role as a tour guide. Nicole knew military families got a break on grocery store prices, and she noticed prices were a little better in the commissary than in her store back home, but there wasn't as much difference as she'd expected to find. That was another reason, she decided, for avoiding involvement with an army man. The pay wasn't too great, and the perks didn't make up the difference.

Braedon is only a part-time soldier. She tried to block out the reminder. She wasn't interested in dating or marriage, so why did thoughts of Braedon keep popping into her head? And why had she found herself missing him this morning? After all, they had only run together twice.

"This row is where the cookies are," John David announced, releasing his grip on her hand to skip ahead. Nicole found herself weaving between carts and dodging people as she hurried to catch up. Even in a military store, it wasn't a good idea to allow a child to take off on his own.

"Excuse me," she murmured as she slipped between a young woman wearing BDUs and an older couple pushing a heavily laden shopping cart. At last she knelt beside her nephew.

"You were supposed to keep hold of my hand," she delivered a light scolding, remembering how difficult she had once found adult rules. She also recalled how often she had escaped restraining hands.

"I forgot." He dropped the package of cookies he held to look around for his mother and baby sister. Nicole looked too, and was relieved to see them coming down the aisle toward them. She never knew what caused her to lift her eyes higher. A man at the far end of the row was just turning the corner. She caught a glimpse of a profile that brought goosebumps to her arms. It couldn't be! He was older, but . . .

"What's the matter?" Marcie caught up to her and John David.

"Maybe nothing . . ." she started. She couldn't tell Marcie what she'd seen. Her sister would call her mother, and they'd both demand she see a shrink. At best, they'd begin doubting her sanity again. "I just thought I saw someone I know. Excuse me a minute." She hurried toward the corner where the man had disappeared. She ignored the glares coming from shoppers as she moved against the flow of traffic.

There was no sign of the man when she reached the end of the aisle. She checked each remaining row and scanned the checkout counters without seeing him, then returned to the back of the store where she'd caught a glimpse of him. He was gone.

Her legs trembled as she made her way back to Marcie. She paused to take a deep breath and willed her hands to stop their nervous flutter. She'd imagined the whole thing, she told herself. It was probably just someone with a similar face. *But maybe it was real. Maybe it was all real.* What if she really had seen her father killed all those years ago?

No, she had to get control of herself. She hadn't seen anything twelve years ago, and she didn't see a murderer's face today. She was through being afraid of the past. Starting today, she was going to visit every place associated with the time when she'd lived on the base. And on their way back to her sister's house, she'd ask Marcie to drive past the house on Holly Street where they'd lived that summer. Perhaps that was the real reason why she'd felt compelled to come here. She needed to put the old ghosts behind her, and she couldn't put off doing so any longer.

Chapter 4

Nicole averted her face as Marcie drove past Miller Hill. She kept her eyes focused on the left side of the road, noting that the trees in the subdivision looked larger around the elementary school. Pulling into the housing area, she felt a mixture of emotions, but she refused to let herself shy away from seeing the street where she had once lived. Marcie slowed as she approached their former home. Nicole tried not to let her sister see how much the sight of their old home bothered her.

She picked out the house easily. It hadn't changed much, though the nameplate next to the door no longer read M. Sgt. Evangart. Some other sergeant lived there now. Other children played on the playground behind the houses, and a white SUV instead of her mother's Datsun was parked in the carport. The flag flying in front of the house told her that the soldier who lived there was somewhere far away.

Memories she'd struggled to suppress streamed through her mind, and she could see the day she'd arrived at the house. Mom and Marcie had been in the Datsun while she and Dad had pulled in behind them in Dad's Jeep. They'd slept in sleeping bags on the floor for almost a week while they waited for their furniture to arrive, but it hadn't mattered. She'd seen it as an adventure, and she was so happy her father was back and they were together in this beautiful place, nothing else mattered.

She and Dad had hiked and ridden bicycles as often as his schedule allowed that summer. Mom and Marcie had accompanied them to the beach at Tolmie State Park and to the zoo at Point

Defiance. She'd fallen asleep at night to the soft rumble of Dad's voice and Mom's light laughter from the next room.

When Dad was busy or away for a day or two during those first few months, she'd coaxed Marcie into accompanying her as she'd explored the base. Marcie had gone with her a few times, but she met a few teenagers in their new ward and was soon more interested in shopping or hanging out at the pool than exploring. Often, while Mom was away and Marcie was distracted by her new friends, Nicole had slipped away by herself. It was then that she'd discovered the blackberries. The fat, juicy fruit ripened in abundance on the thick brambles that seemed to grow everywhere. Their sweet goodness had been a happy addition to that golden summer.

Sometimes time distorts memories, but she knew it was no distortion reminding her they really were happy that summer. And not just her, but Marcie and Mom and Dad. Yes, when she forced herself to remember, she did recall that her parents had argued too. But even seeing those arguments now from an adult's perspective, she didn't believe they were the sort that could drive her father to abandon them. Mom was the flighty, emotional parent, not Dad. It made less sense today than it had twelve years ago that he would just walk out on them.

"Seen enough?" Marcie asked. "This area is in the middle of a renovation phase. As a pair of houses become vacant, Housing is having them modernized. It may take a couple of years, but eventually this area will be like new."

Nicole nodded her head, hearing without really absorbing her sister's words. She was glad they'd driven down the street and paused near the house that had once been theirs, and she was glad that the happy memories had come to mind first. Looking back as an adult at the child she'd been, she felt sympathy for the little girl she used to be, the one who had adored her daddy and been terrified as the days passed and he didn't come home. She recalled trying to tell her mother what she had seen and not understanding why Mom didn't call the MPs. Staring out the car window as Marcie restarted the car and pulled away, she could almost see the little girl she had been, walking alone all the way to the building where the military police reported for duty and got their orders. She was amazed at the courage exhibited by her younger self.

At first, no one had listened to her, then a tall young man with rabbity teeth had escorted her to an officer's desk. The captain listened without interrupting as she told him about seeing a man in civilian clothes shoot a soldier she believed was her father. The captain asked her a few questions, but he actually didn't say much. After a few minutes, he drove her home and asked to speak to her mother. At first her mother hadn't wanted to talk to him, then she'd sent Nicole to bed. Nicole heard the murmur of their voices for almost an hour, but she hadn't been able to make out the words.

The next day, Mom had taken her to see the horrible doctor who tried to make her think he was her friend. He asked a lot of questions about her father and about the men she saw in the woods, but something didn't feel right. He seemed angry, and she suspected he thought she was too young to know what she'd seen.

She'd been forced to see the doctor four more times, then one day she'd thrown a heavy ashtray at him. He'd called her mother, and Mom came for her. Mom and Marcie packed a few things, then Mom drove all night and the following afternoon until they reached a home in California for disturbed children. Nicole never returned to the house on Holly Street. When she left the home ten months later, she joined her mother and sister in Florida.

"Nicole, are you all right?" From the tone of her voice, Nicole guessed it wasn't the first time Marcie had asked.

"I'm fine," she quietly assured her sister. "I was just thinking how that summer was the end of my childhood."

"I'm really sorry," Marcie looked nervous, as though she still wasn't comfortable talking to Nicole about that time or the events that had led up to it. "I've always wanted to tell you I thought Mother was too impulsive when she took you to that place."

"It's water under the bridge now." Nicole shrugged her shoulders. She didn't want to discuss that painful, lonely time in her life.

"You and Dad were so close. She should have given you more time. And she shouldn't have forbidden us to talk about Daddy." Marcie's words hinted at a resentment Nicole hadn't known her sister shared.

"Did it bother you that Dad and I were close?"

"No," Marcie assured her. "What I resented was Mom's assumption that she was the only one with a right to grieve for Dad. She was always jealous of the time he spent with us, and that jealousy carried over to refusing to allow us to miss him when he was gone. J.D. said the pain might have lessened for both of us if we'd been allowed to talk about him. When J.D.'s parents died, his grandparents encouraged him to talk about them and remember all the fun times they'd had together. He said it helped him feel closer to them as he grew up."

"I thought you didn't want to talk about Dad."

"Mom said mentioning Dad could cause you to have a relapse. I didn't dare cause you more trouble. When J.D. and I were dating, I told him all the things I could remember about Dad and it helped. I thought it might help you too, but I didn't dare disobey Mom."

Nicole turned to see the sadness on her sister's face. How foolish she'd been; she'd never given a thought to her sister's grief. Of course Marcie and their father had loved each other, even though their relationship had been different from the one she and Dad shared. A sudden picture of Dad dancing with Marcie on the tile floor of the Holly Street house flashed into her mind. The music had been loud and their movements fast, not at all like the soft, barely moving dance Dad and Mom shared minutes later when Mom changed the tape for one of her favorites.

"I'm sorry too," Nicole reached across the short distance between her and her sister. "Being apart, I guess I forgot you were grieving too." They smiled at each other in a sad kind of way just before Marcie pulled into the garage behind her house. They would talk more later, but it was a beginning. A quiet assurance filled her, telling her she'd made the right decision. It was time to revisit the past and put it to rest.

Looking into the backseat, Nicole saw that both children were asleep.

"With any luck, we can get them into their beds without disturbing them," Marcie whispered. A few minutes later, she was tiptoeing down the stairs after depositing John David on his bed. When the phone rang, both women lunged for it before it could awaken the children.

"Hello," Marcie spoke into it in little more than a whisper, then turned to hand the receiver to Nicole. Surprised, Nicole took it.

"Nicole, this is Braedon." An unfamiliar warmth filled her at the sound of his voice. "I've only got a few minutes, but I wanted to see if you would run with me again tomorrow morning."

She meant to say no, but she remembered there was one more place she needed to visit before she could put the past to rest, and she didn't want to go there alone. Braedon was the perfect person to accompany her.

* * *

Braedon whistled as he laced up his running shoes the next morning. He was looking forward to running with Nicole. He'd almost decided she wasn't interested and, for the sake of his pride, he should just forget about her, but he hadn't been able to resist trying one more time. He was glad he had. Life was definitely looking up. He wondered where she wanted to run. She'd made that a stipulation—that she pick their route. That was okay with him. He didn't like running on sand, but he'd even take her to Solo Point and run on the beach if that was what she wanted.

He was glad Cameron wasn't around. His brother would tease him unmercifully if he knew how hard Braedon had fallen for Nicole. They'd both sworn as teenagers that they wouldn't marry until they were at least thirty, but less than a year after Cameron returned from his mission, he met Lynette, and four months after that he married her in the St. George Temple in spite of Braedon's barrage of teasing. Cameron would jump at the chance to even the score. Braedon wasn't sure what was happening to him. He'd always been the cool one when it came to women. He'd been the one who backed off when he suspected a woman's feelings might be involved and she might get hurt if he continued to see her. Now here he was, chasing after Nicole like she was the only woman on earth. Unfortunately, he had a sneaking suspicion that for him, she *was* the only woman on earth.

He grabbed his wallet and headed for his truck. Not many of the temporary soldiers on base had their own transportation, but he'd been allowed to bring his truck. Rank had its privileges, even if he was merely a second lieutenant.

Nicole was in the front yard stretching when he pulled up in front of her sister's house. Her hair was pulled back in a ponytail and she wore no makeup. Instead of the shorts she'd worn when he'd first met her, she wore gray flannel sweats and an oversized, faded-red T-shirt with a bright orange PT belt hanging loosely around her waist. On her, the outfit looked great. Before he could set the brake and walk around to open the door for her, she opened the passenger door herself and climbed in.

"Good morning," he greeted her. She smiled back before reaching for her seat belt. He wondered if he made her nervous or if she was a little shy of all men. Her smile hadn't looked too steady to him.

"Where to?" he asked as he lifted his foot off the brake.

"Main Post," she responded. "Just beyond the main gate there's a place where you can pull off. I'd like to run north of there."

He knew the spot she meant. There was a steep hill that offered more challenge than the miles of almost flat roads and trails that covered most of the base. He'd run there before and found the hill more like the steep trails he was accustomed to back home, but the thick brush was a nuisance.

"Miller Hill. I run on hills like that and steeper back home," he told her.

"I used to run on the canyon roads near Cedar City myself," she said. "It's a good place to train. For the past two years though, I've run in the canyons east of Salt Lake."

"You're from Utah?" he asked in surprise. It hadn't occurred to him that she came from Utah too.

"Not originally. I was an army brat, and my father was based in Texas and New Mexico during most of my childhood. I've lived in California, Florida, and Kansas too. I went to college in Cedar City for my undergraduate degree, then transferred to the U for my master's," she told him.

"My family's ranch is northeast of Cedar City. I can't believe we had to come all the way to Washington to meet." He laughed and she joined in.

"Ever run any marathons?" he asked after a few minutes, remembering the way she ran.

"Yes, I've run St. George and the Days of '47 as well as some of the lesser-known runs," she said. "How about you?"

"I haven't gotten to compete as much as I would have liked, but I've run St. George a couple of times. We'll have to compare notes and see if you were one of those runners who left me in the dust when I did compete," he suggested as he stopped at the guard station where they both had to show ID.

Once on Main Post, he went back to something she'd said earlier. "You said you went to the U for your master's. In what field?"

"Hospital administration. Turn left here." She pointed to a side street.

It was only a short distance to a spot where Braedon could park. Again Nicole didn't wait for him to open her door and was already intent on doing warm-up stretches when he rounded the hood. Propping one foot on a rock, he began his stretching routine as well.

All his efforts to start a conversation as they began the uphill climb met with distracted replies. He'd felt she was warming to him in the truck, but now he didn't know what to think. In spite of her extensive warm-up routine, Nicole appeared tense, and she moved more slowly than he had expected. He wondered if her encounter with the bear cub had left a residual fear of running on brush-lined off-road trails. The track they ran on looked to have once been a road, but not much of one. All that remained were the parallel ruts a four-wheel-drive might possibly be able to follow. He moved a little closer to Nicole, hoping to lend her reassurance. Instead of welcoming the move, she countered by once again widening the distance between them to the distance that had separated them before.

Was he the problem? Was she afraid of him or of men in general? Surely if she were nervous about being alone with him, she wouldn't have chosen such an isolated place to run with him. Perhaps she was only accustomed to running alone and felt a need to have space between herself and another runner.

A bird landed on a branch a few feet ahead, and Nicole cringed before continuing on. The sudden chatter of a squirrel brought a jerky motion of her head as she turned in its direction. When the path narrowed, forcing them to run single file, she chose to lead, and Braedon became aware that the seemingly effortless stride he'd observed before was gone, and the higher they climbed and the more dense the undergrowth became, the more skittish she seemed to be. Several times she almost stumbled.

Underestimating her proximity to a tree branch, her hair caught on a twig. Before he could reach to help, she jerked her head, pulling herself free, but loosening her ponytail and leaving behind several strands of her long hair. The band that had held her hair high on her head now sagged nearer her shoulders. Her hand shook as she pushed the loose hair behind her ears and continued running. A few minutes later, the path crossed a track that looked like it too might have once been wide enough for an all-terrain vehicle, but the only sign of recent use was the imprint of bicycle tires. She turned onto the track.

By now Nicole's movements were almost a stagger. Several times she glanced his way as though assuring herself that he was still with her. When she wiped the back of one hand across her eyes, he knew his earlier speculations were wrong. She wasn't afraid of him, but something was definitely upsetting her.

"Nicole," he spoke her name quietly, not wishing to startle her. "Are you okay? If you aren't feeling well, we can turn around and head back to the truck."

"I'm okay. I just have to . . ." She stumbled, falling to her knees.

"Are you all right?" He rushed to her side. Dropping to one knee, he reached toward her to examine her scraped knees. To his complete shock, she threw herself into his arms with tears running down her cheeks. Teetering on the balls of his feet, he struggled to balance himself while tightening his arms around her to keep her from falling. He drew her head against his chest, and she trembled and hunched closer. Her body shook with the depth of some emotional pain. Helplessly, he patted her back and searched for something to say. When no words came to his mind, he simply continued to hold her while she cried great, gulping sobs.

After several minutes she tried to pull away, but instead of letting her go, he merely shifted to a sitting position and settled her across his thighs, pulling her more comfortably against his chest. Lifting one hand he tangled his fingers in her hair, heedless of the elastic band that slipped from her hair and fell to the forest floor.

"Nicole, what is it? Are you hurt?"

"No." She wiped her eyes and tried once more to sit up. Braedon helped her to a sitting position but kept his arm around her. He followed her gaze around the trees and noticed the blackberry bushes that formed an almost impenetrable thicket around the area where they sat except for on the roadlike trail. Above them he could see through the thick canopy of trees that the blue sky had been replaced with clouds and a light mist was falling, though it scarcely made its way through the thick foliage to the ground. Nicole shivered.

Concerned, Braedon asked, "Are you cold? Do you want to start back?"

"I really am crazy. It's all as real as it was then." Her words were almost inaudible and filled with a sadness that touched his heart and made him want to shelter her from whatever was causing her such pain.

"You're not crazy." His hand brushed through her hair as he turned her face toward his own to better see her eyes. "Something or someone hurt you. I wish you'd trust me enough to let me help." Instinct told him that something unusual had happened and that something was connected to this place or a place much like it. Her tears weren't those of a woman who cried easily or used tears to get her own way. Some trauma had prefaced her outburst. He waited, steeling himself to be patient until she made up her mind whether or not to confide in him. He couldn't begin to guess how much time passed while he held her, but holding her felt right, and he found he could be patient.

"I owe you an explanation, though I usually don't tell anyone." An element of determination in her voice suggested she'd made a monumental decision. She brushed her hair back with both hands, then wiped away the wetness on her cheeks. Her voice was stronger now and seemed edged with anger, making him fear she was about to tell him she had been assaulted, but when she began to speak, her words were far from what he expected.

"I lived here on this base when I was a child. It was wonderful until something happened and my father never came home again." She didn't look at him as she spoke, but he watched her face. There was both sorrow and purpose written there.

"Was he killed in battle?" If she'd lived here as a child, her father must have been associated with the military. He was surprised by the strong emotions he continued to see pictured on her face. It was as if her grief were new, though her father's death must have occurred a long time ago if it was while she was a child.

"He returned from Desert Storm without a scratch," Nicole refuted his assumption. "And shortly after his return, he was transferred here. I loved Fort Lewis and had a wonderful time discovering everything possible about my new home. Then one day, Dad left for a two-week training exercise and never came back. Officially, he's still listed as AWOL. We couldn't miss him as we had while he was at war, and we couldn't take flowers to a cemetery and formally say good-bye as we might have had he died or been killed in action. Without Dad serving in the army, Mother, Marcie, and I had to leave here."

"That must have been rough." Braedon sympathized with Nicole, but deep inside he felt both relief that she hadn't been victimized by some predator and disgust for a man who could walk out on his duty to his family and country. "Did you ever hear from him?"

"Not a word, but I never expected to." She lifted her chin and stared at the top of a tall tree. "What I told you is what I'm supposed to say. For a long time I believed it, but coming here today convinced me that the desertion story is a lie. You see, I saw two men kill him. They and I are the only ones who know he's really dead."

"Dead?"

"Murdered!" Mingled with her anger was fear. "I saw them kill him. He died right here!"

"Here, at Fort Lewis?"

She pounded a clenched fist against the ground. "They shot him right here on this very spot where we're sitting."

He started and looked around as if he expected gunmen to suddenly appear. While he tried to absorb her words and make sense of them, she continued. "What I saw supposedly never happened. A doctor here on base and my mother both said I imagined it. His body was never found, and the official story is that I was only an imaginative child traumatized by my father's long absence in the war followed by his desertion."

"You mean you saw someone kill your father, but no one believed you?" She heard the incredulity in his voice and for a moment thought he believed her and was surprised that no one else did. Then she realized he was like everyone else. It was *her* story he found incredible.

"That's why I was locked up for ten months in a home for mentally disturbed children." The old anger flared, fueled by the disbelief she heard in Braedon's question. She'd wanted to discourage him from pursuing a relationship with her, and she supposed her words had accomplished that goal. Only, picturing Braedon turning away from her didn't feel as though she'd won anything. He continued watching her with an expectant expression in his eyes. She couldn't prevent the rest of the story from exploding out.

"After a time, I stopped believing it myself, and they sent me home." Her words turned flat and bitter. "After all, with the tight security on a military base, how could someone hide or carry away a body? What was the motive? And didn't I know my parents were having marital problems?"

"You don't really believe that you imagined your father's death, do you?" Braedon asked, then hurried on before she had a chance to respond. "I think you convinced everyone, including yourself, that you believed the official version. No doubt it made life easier for you, but now something has changed. You're through pretending. What happened to change your mind? Was it coming here?"

Nicole leaned forward, and Braedon released his hold on her. Wrapping her arms around her knees, she rested her chin on her knees and remained silent for several minutes. He reached forward to massage the taut muscles between her hunched shoulder blades. When she spoke, she didn't turn to look at him.

"There's been no relief from the memories since I returned here. Yesterday I was at the commissary with Marcie, and I saw a man there I thought was one of the two men with my father twelve years ago. Then we drove by the house where we lived, and I remembered how happy Dad was to be home. That memory was like opening a tightly drawn blind, expecting to see black clouds and discovering bright sun instead. I saw my father clearly for the first time in years. He was a man who took responsibility seriously. He wouldn't leave us, and he wouldn't desert the army. He loved us—I know he did. The most important things in his life were his family, the Church, and his country. Denying what I saw is a denial of who he was."

"People change. It's not unheard of for a man's values to change under the duress of war." She sensed Braedon was playing devil's advocate rather than trying to change her mind.

"I know. But he didn't change. He was the one who tried to help me understand that my mother had a difficult time while he was away. Mom's talk about leaving the army and settling in one place was her way of letting go of the pressure that had built inside her while she waited and worried. Even that last morning when she threatened to leave because he was going away for field exercises was only her way of telling him she missed him when he had to be away."

"What exactly do you remember?" Braedon asked.

She'd never really told anyone except the captain at the MP station what she'd seen on Miller Hill that day. She hadn't trusted the doctor at Madigan Regional army Medical Center enough to tell him the whole story, and the one at the children's psychiatric hospital was so busy finding explanations for her mental state that he didn't really listen to her. Mom hadn't allowed her to even finish her story when she'd tried to tell her about what she'd seen, and she'd forbidden her to tell Marcie.

The psychiatrist at Madigan hospital had asked too many questions, and her answers had seemed to make him angry. After talking to him, Mom had completely turned on her. Telling Braedon was a risk she wasn't certain she wanted to take, but if there was a chance that talking about the past might help her clear Dad's name, she had to take that risk. At least Braedon wasn't a doctor who could order her locked up if he decided she was crazy.

"I had just turned eleven," she began. "Fort Lewis was a magical place to me, doubly so because Dad was home. I loved searching for blackberries and picking big buckets of them for Mom to turn into cobblers and pies." At some point in her narration she wound up leaning back once more against Braedon, and his arms circled her as she described the events that had changed her life forever. Twelve years had passed, but in her mind, the events had stayed as clear as though they had happened yesterday.

"I didn't tell mother for four days," she brought her story to a conclusion. "I was afraid she'd punish me for wandering so far away when she'd warned me not to. But when Dad didn't come home the night he should have, or the next day when everyone else in his unit did, people started saying that he'd gone AWOL. I knew my father hadn't deserted. He'd never do that. I became convinced that the man who had been killed here on this hill was my father. I was consumed with grief and guilt, which must have made my story even more questionable."

"Why guilt?"

"It occurred to me that if I'd gone for help immediately those men might have been caught and that a doctor could have possibly saved my father."

"I think you know that he was already dead before he was taken from this hill." Braedon spoke slowly, as though he were dissecting her story bit by bit. "From what you've told me, I suspect you were also keenly aware of your own precarious position." She started to nod her head in agreement; she had known it was too late the moment the man wearing the pale blue shirt pulled the trigger. Then it sank in. Braedon believed her. At least he was seriously considering the possibility that she had witnessed something terrible that day. It was enough to start tears flowing again, though this time they slipped silently down her cheeks. Someone finally believed her.

"Stand up." He placed his hands under her arms and urged her to her feet. She struggled to rise. For a fleeting moment, she wondered if she'd been wrong and Braedon didn't believe her, that he'd had enough of the crazy lady and was anxious to be rid of her. His words cleared up that misconception.

"Okay, show me where each of the three men stood." Startled, she glanced at his face and saw he was serious. Something inside her soared with relief and gratitude, causing her to hurry to obey his instructions. Taking a few steps farther along the track, she almost disappeared from view where the track suddenly dipped back down. She stopped, then turned back toward Braedon.

"The men came this way," she pointed to where the trail disappeared into the trees in the opposite direction from which they'd come. "I was picking blackberries in the thicket opposite where you're standing. There's a curve in the track, and it heads down toward the main road, so I didn't see them until they were almost directly in front of me." She walked back to where he stood. "Dad was walking between the other two men, and his face was turned away from me toward the man in civilian clothes. When they stopped here, Dad's back was to me, and the other two men turned to face him." She demonstrated their positions.

"Why didn't you call out to him?"

"I wasn't supposed to be here. Mom had told me not to leave the play area."

Braedon nodded his head as he accepted a child's reasoning. He gathered twigs and placed them in each spot she indicated, then stood back to stare at the spots he'd marked. She watched him with a faint tremor of excitement. Was there anything he could tell her from the positions of those three men after all this time? She'd gone over and over each movement in her mind so many times without learning one iota more than she'd seen all those years ago.

"Now show me where you were." He tilted his head and gave a dubious look at the thick blackberry bushes. "In twelve years they've likely grown a great deal." There was hesitation in his voice.

"They don't look much different now from how they did then. They completely filled the area east of the path just as they do now, then thinned out and disappeared where the trees grow close together. I suspect new bushes replace old ones on a regular basis. I remember following a steep, narrow trail that twisted and turned up the hill from the road below until I had almost reached this track. I stopped to fill my bucket just over there." She pointed to a thick clump of bushes a short distance behind him that seemed to be one edge of the blackberry patch. "The path I was following circled the bushes, then crossed the track by that tree." She walked to the tree, then disappeared behind it.

Braedon hurried to catch up to her. When he reached the tree, he found the indentation of an old trail that had been worn deep in the past leading up from the road. He'd run here several times and had never noticed the almost overgrown trail. He followed it, lifting tree branches out of the way as he slowly worked his way upward. Remembering the barriers he'd seen at the bottom of the hill along the paved street, he guessed that when Nicole was a child, there had been no concrete barriers, and the path had been used on frequent occasions by adventurous children. He had to crouch to follow the trail of bent grass where Nicole had passed.

Taking care to avoid pricking himself on the sharp thorns of the thicket blocking his way, he ducked beneath a long sweep of willow-like tendrils. There he found Nicole crouched in what appeared to be a path made up of pebbles or small rocks. He'd wondered how even a child could hide in a dense blackberry thicket, but now he knew. A trail created by runoff water and renewed with each heavy rainfall passed beneath the thicket, leaving a path similar to a narrow creek bed. He hadn't been certain whether the story she'd told him was memory or imagination until this moment, though something had urged him to believe. Her mention of a facility for disturbed children had made him hesitate, as had his knowledge of berry thickets. But now he knew it could have happened just the way she'd told him. A shiver ran down his spine.

He dropped to all fours and worked his way toward her. She glanced at him, then without speaking moved closer to the spot he'd marked on the trail. He could see the place where he and Nicole had sat a few minutes earlier. It was approximately fifteen feet away. He felt satisfied that her story was possible, but there was one more thing he needed to check.

"Stay here," he whispered, then wondered why he was whispering. She nodded her head, and he began to retrace his steps.

Once back in the clearing, he stood in each place he'd marked earlier and asked, "Can you see me?" Each time she indicated she could and told him which position he occupied. Peering toward the bushes, he strained to see her. Even knowing she was there, he couldn't glimpse her through the thick foliage. Finally he knelt as the uniformed man must have done to heft a heavy body from the ground to his shoulder. A small patch of dull red caught his eye, and he felt coldness in the pit of his stomach. Might the uniformed man have seen a bit of color that day that didn't belong to the berry thicket? If so, why had he kept quiet all these years?

Chapter 5

Marcie scanned her e-mail while listening for the kids to awaken and want their breakfasts. She listened, too, for Nicole to return. With a sigh of disgust, she deleted a string of junk mail. "Now there's something all those anti-everything nuts can protest, and I'll grab a sign and join them. Spam is definitely an invasion of privacy," she muttered as she deleted several more trash e-mails. She'd have to get Nicole to show her how to change her settings so junk went straight to the trash bin.

Thinking of Nicole, she glanced at her kitchen clock. Her sister was later than usual. Before she could start worrying though, she remembered Nicole was running with Braedon this morning. *Nicole is an adult and she runs every morning, no matter where she is,* she reminded herself. *I shouldn't worry about her. It's just that she's been a little strange since she arrived. What if being back here brings on another breakdown?*

Her thoughts made her uneasy. Their trip past the house where they'd lived that summer and the closeness she'd felt to Nicole when they'd talked had started her thinking about her father. Greg Evangart had been a larger-than-life kind of man. He was six feet four and wore his sergeant's stripes with pride. She remembered her parents had argued that summer over Dad's reenlistment, but she suspected Nicole was right and that not even Mom had believed Dad would leave the army. *But Dad* did *leave—not only the army, but Mom and Nicole and me. Or had he? What if Nicole really had seen him die?* Now Marcie was the one being fanciful. She tapped on the mouse, trying to force the computer to download faster. She knew there had been an investigation. *But it had been more than a week later, and there had been a number of rainstorms before Nicole told her story.*

As new mail came into her e-mail box, a name on the screen caught her eye, then another. A smile broke through her thoughts, and she clicked on the sender name J.D. Duran. She could worry about her sister or read an e-mail from her mother anytime. A message from J.D. took precedence over everything!

** *

By tacit agreement, Nicole and Braedon walked slowly back to Braedon's truck, their run forgotten. Finally Braedon asked, "Did you ever try to find him?"

"No, why would I? Even when I thought I had accepted everyone else's version of my father's disappearance, I think deep down I knew better. It would have been a waste of time to search for him. Besides, the army searched. The army doesn't give up easily on soldiers who desert."

"That's not what I meant." Braedon pulled a long stalk of grass that had gone to seed and decimated the head as he walked. "What I meant to ask was if a search had been made for a body."

"Mom said an army detail searched all over this hill, and the soldiers were advised to watch for a disturbed area that might conceal a body everywhere they went on base." She flipped her straggling hair over her shoulders and searched futilely in her pocket for an elastic band.

"Here." Braedon handed her the one that had fallen to the ground earlier. He watched her wrap the band around her pulled-back hair. "It's a shame to scrunch all that gorgeous red hair into a ball like that," he said with real regret.

"My hair isn't red!" He was surprised by her vehemence.

"It sure is," he attempted to tease her. "When the sun strikes it, it looks just like a fire I saw once smoldering along a ridge at night."

"My hair is too dark to be considered red," she argued.

"Not by me." He lightly touched her bunched ponytail.

Nicole walked more quickly, and he wondered if he had offended her. He'd never figured out why some women dyed their hair red and natural redheads did everything possible to deny the color. Nicole's hair fascinated him. He'd seen dark hair with red highlights before, especially on Hispanic women, but her hair wasn't like that. Hers was simply a deep, dark red, as close to black as red hair could get.

"All right, then as far as you know, the search was limited to the base?" He resumed their earlier discussion.

"I think so, but Mom hustled me off to that home so fast I never had a chance to find out how extensive the search was. She wouldn't talk to me about it, and on doctor's orders, no one was allowed to mention my father or any details of the case to me. Mom and Marcie have maintained that silence all these years." Her voice wobbled at the end, and her steps looked none too steady, so taking her elbow, Braedon guided her to a fallen log. He sat beside her as she continued. "A few days ago was the first time Marcie mentioned Dad to me in all these years. I think it was really hard for her, but in the few minutes we talked, we were closer to each other than we've been at any time since we were children."

"That's good. Marcie's memories may provide some clue that will help you in your search."

"She and Mom will try to stop me." She worried her bottom lip between her teeth in a nervous gesture.

"You're not a child anymore, Nicole." He pitched his voice low, reluctant to risk antagonizing her, but her story intrigued him, and he felt a need to get the answers he could see she needed. "They can't stop you. And it seems to me that as an adult, you have a responsibility to do some checking, whether it upsets them or not. You need to find out if the army still has a file on your father's disappearance. And if it were me, I'd be checking with every law enforcement agency for three hundred miles around to see if any unexplained bodies showed up anywhere about the time your father disappeared."

Nicole was speechless. Never before had anyone offered a single suggestion for unraveling the mystery of her father's disappearance.

"I've been thinking about that," she admitted. "But I don't want Mom or Marcie to know I'm looking for Dad. Every time I even mention him, they start worrying, and Mom begins checking into suitable programs to enroll me in. I know she can't send me to some institution again, but I am concerned about upsetting them."

"Maybe she's the one who needs a suitable program," Braedon muttered under his breath, but Nicole heard him and rocked back as though she'd been struck. He'd voiced, even if it was mumbled under his breath, a suspicion Nicole had harbored for some time. She supposed she should defend her mother. After all, Braedon didn't even know Mom, but she couldn't help the delicious feeling that swept through her as she began to see him as an ally.

"How good are you with a computer?" Braedon's forehead wrinkled as he took a stub pencil and a scrap of paper from his pocket.

"Not too bad," she admitted.

"Okay, here are some web addresses for you to try. Unidentified bodies generally make the news, so start with the newspapers." He began scribbling. "I'll find out about the earlier investigation. I'd like to know if it was limited to this base or if the surrounding area was searched as well."

"Everyone told me it would be impossible to smuggle a body off the base." She pressed her lips together and shook her head slightly, then lifted her chin as though challenging him to contradict her. "Even as an adult, I still don't know what would be so hard about it. If those men had a car concealed in the trees at the other end of this trail, no one would have seen them enter it or hide someone in the trunk. And although IDs are checked coming onto the base, the MPs don't normally check vehicles leaving."

"Right. I was thinking the same thing, and I suspect the two thugs you saw did just that. The risk was too high to chance being seen if they buried or hid the body on base."

"I did do a feeble missing persons search once." Her admission sounded hesitant. "I didn't follow up on the links to John Doe bodies, but I will now."

"It won't be easy." Braedon followed an impulse to place an arm around her and give her a quick hug. "I can tell your memories and the uncertainty about your father's disappearance still cause you grief. My father always said that if something from the past comes frequently to mind or affects what I do today, I should examine it thoroughly. If it's a good memory, I should be grateful for it, but if it's a bad one, I should get to the bottom of it and take care of it. He was a big believer in facing fears. Finding out what happened to your father is something you need to do. If you don't, it won't ever give you rest."

"I think I've finally reached the point where I have to know. If my memory is faulty, I'll have to deal with that. But if I really saw my father killed, I owe it to him to clear his name." Nicole rose to her feet. "We'd better be getting back. Marcie will worry if I'm any later."

"Yes, I need to get back too." He stood and walked beside her to his truck.

Back at her sister's house, he reached across her to open her door. "Good luck with your search," he told her. She scrambled out, then turned.

"Thanks for believing me," she said so softly he barely heard the words over the motor of his truck.

"One more thing," he said. "Be careful. Once you start searching, you never know who or what you might stir up."

* * *

J.D. awoke from a sound sleep. As was his habit, he listened carefully before opening his eyes. He soon became aware it wasn't danger but a noisy soccer game that had awakened him. He cracked his eyes open and looked around at the interior of the two-man tent he shared with a specialist from his unit. They'd opted to share quarters since neither man smoked or used the kind of language most of the men in the larger tents used as a kind of bravado. Specialist Cassaday wasn't a Latter-day Saint, but he was a religious man, a devout Southern Baptist, and sometimes the two engaged in discussions, which J.D. always found a way to end before their conflicting views could result in an argument. That was one thing they agreed on; they wouldn't risk their friendship by letting their religious differences create the kind of hate and distrust they saw every day in the war-torn Middle East.

Rolling over, he pulled himself to a sitting position and checked his watch. It was early evening here, which meant the day was just beginning back home for Marcie and the kids. Actually, it was just beginning for him too. He usually slept through the heat of the day and went on duty at night. Tonight he and his squad had one of his least favorite tasks to perform.

A wave of homesickness swept over him. When he'd decided to make the army his career, he'd known it would mean separation from his family at times, but his parents were gone, and he'd been single and in love with adventure back then. Since meeting Marcie, and even more so since John David was born, he found being away from home more difficult. Now he had a daughter he scarcely knew. She'd been only a few weeks old when he'd been deployed, and she'd probably be walking by the time he saw her again. He ached to be home watching her grow.

Forcing himself to shake off his longing for his family, he looked toward his roommate, who was still asleep. Sometimes he envied Cassaday. The guy could sleep through any noise, even Howitzer or rocket fire, but some inner alarm always seemed to alert him if danger was headed his way. Then he was instantly awake and alert. He was the kind of man the western heroes J.D. had grown up reading about would have called "a man to ride the river with."

If he hurried, he could eat something and stop by a tent belonging to a National Guard intelligence unit from Utah before he had to check in. The guard unit had a much more powerful computer than the ones most of the soldiers used to e-mail home. They'd given him an open-ended invitation to stop by to send instant messages to his wife. And tonight seemed like a good time to give it a try.

The sun was almost down, but the temperature was still well over a hundred degrees when he stepped outside his tent. He and Cassaday had plenty of uncomplimentary things to say about the tiny air-conditioning unit in their tent, but he never failed to appreciate its feeble efforts when he stepped outside.

It didn't take long to eat. Not only was the food none too appetizing, but he never ate much before a mission, and tonight's promised to be one requiring steady nerves. In minutes, he was poking his head into the tent that housed the computer he wanted to use. Only one soldier was present, and he was dressing for tonight's exercise. In answer to J.D.'s query he waved him toward the computer.

While waiting for his log-on, he glanced again at his watch. Almost ten in the morning back at Fort Lewis. Marcie was probably busy with the children now and had long since given up on hearing from him, but for once luck was with him. A small bell sounded, and he was so startled to find her online, he nearly forgot to click on the icon to let her know he was there too.

Hi, honey! he typed into the message box.

Sorry, came back a quick message. *This is honey's sister.*

Feeling both embarrassed and disappointed to discover Nicole was online instead of Marcie, he sent her a quick hello, then she excused herself to call Marcie to the computer while she took over with the children. He didn't know his sister-in-law well, but what he did know, he liked. Both his wife and her mother described Nicole as emotionally fragile, but he didn't buy it. He suspected there was more to that mental episode she suffered as a child than had ever been told. In his estimation, Nicole was smart, savvy, and as emotionally solid as a rock. He was glad she'd agreed to stay with Marcie while he was away.

Marcie was almost trembling with excitement when she sat down at the computer. Though she couldn't hear her husband's voice, it was wonderful to type messages back and forth. He assured her he was fine and getting enough to eat, but he wouldn't object to a care package or two.

What I really want is pictures, she read on the screen. *See if Nicole knows how to use my video camera. If not, send me a photograph every week of you and the kids. I don't want to miss any of their growing up.*

Okay, she typed back. *Do you know yet when you'll be coming home?*

Afraid not.

Marcie told him all the news she could think of about the children, her new calling to teach Relief Society, and that Nicole had met a young reserve lieutenant from Utah. They chatted for several minutes more before he had to go. When he signed off, sending her his love, she stared at the screen for several minutes, both elated by their brief conversation and disappointed that their chat was over.

J.D. had called her once from Kuwait, and though they had exchanged a couple of e-mail messages and a letter with two-week-old news, this was the first time they'd been able to chat. Thank goodness Nicole was doing some research this morning and happened to be online at the right time.

Her mind was beginning to return to the world around her when the screen she stared at suddenly came into focus. Nicole wasn't job hunting. A shiver slid down Marcie's spine as the information on the screen began to make sense. She was looking at a list of unclaimed bodies in Washington State dating back twelve years. Suddenly she felt sick. Nicole was still delusional! After all this time, she still believed she had seen their father killed.

Marcie's hands began to shake. What should she do? She'd have to call Mom. If Nicole was ill again, did she dare leave her alone with the children? If only she'd seen this before J.D. messaged. He would know what to do. Slowly she rose to her feet.

"You're through already?" Nicole poked her head in the room to ask. "I thought you two would chat for at least an hour."

"We would have, but he had to report for duty." She tried to make her voice cheerful.

"What's the matter?" Nicole came closer. " I expected you to be on cloud nine. Has something happened to J.D.?"

"No, I am . . . I was." She motioned toward the screen. "What's all this? I don't mean to pry, but I couldn't help seeing . . ."

"Sit down, Marcie. We need to talk."

"The children?"

"The children are fine. Lexie fell asleep, and I put her in her crib. John David is playing trucks on the kitchen floor."

"Okay, but you know I'll have to tell Mom." She tried to sound stern, but she could see Nicole wasn't concerned about her threat. She had changed in some way, and that frightened Marcie more. It was almost as though she were once again the brash, daredevil little sister she had been so long ago.

"You can tell Mom if you want to, though I don't see why you would want to interrupt her new life. It's taken her all these years to stop expecting Dad to walk through the door any day. I think this marriage might actually work out." Nicole pulled another chair closer to the computer chair Marcie had sunk back onto. "But before you call her, you might as well know the whole story."

"Mom told me you had some kind of vision of someone shooting Daddy."

"It wasn't some kind of vision. Mom never listened to me, and she didn't let me talk to you then. But she's not here now, and I'm going to tell you what happened. Think back to that summer. Mom and Dad weren't about to get a divorce. They were crazy in love. Mom is the one who had some kind of breakdown, not me. She couldn't believe me, because if she believed me, she'd have to admit Daddy was never coming back to her."

Marcie stared at her sister in numb shock. What she said made more sense than she wanted to admit. She was the one who had been with Mom that first year, and she'd heard her cry for hours on end, had watched her frantic chase from one beauty salon to another so she'd be beautiful when Greg returned. Marcie had listened, too, to her mother's angry accusations concerning her youngest daughter. Gradually she became aware Nicole was still speaking.

"Braedon went with me back to that place. As soon as I saw it, I knew I hadn't imagined any of it. I didn't see the face of the man who was shot, but everything else about him matched Dad. If Dad had reason to believe something terrible had happened to me, he would never have given up looking for me, and I'm not going to give up looking for him. I'm going to find him and clear his name."

"It's been so long. There's no way you can prove anything now," Marcie protested. "It's better to put it all behind you."

"I can't. Not until I know. Braedon believes I did see something that day, and he's offered to help me."

Marcie was unsure what to say. Nicole's own story was much different from what her mother had told her. It sounded plausible, and if it were true, Dad hadn't abandoned them. The mere possibility lifted a piece of the burden she'd carried so long. Still, her sister had been seen by at least two psychiatrists . . .

She listened without saying anything, and she felt real regret that she couldn't tell her sister she believed her. But if her story were true . . . it changed everything. When Nicole finished speaking, Marcie continued to say nothing until the silence felt awkward.

"If you can't accept what I told you, will you at least promise to think about it?" Nicole finally asked. Marcie nodded her head. For some reason, she wanted to put her arms around her sister and cry. To her surprise, it was Nicole who reached out. The sisters clung to each other and wept until their tears turned to hiccups.

"I don't not believe you," Marcie finally managed to say.

"I know." There was sadness in Nicole's voice, but Marcie had the distinct feeling she really did understand.

Marcie put off calling Mom. She couldn't get Nicole's story out of her mind, and she sensed there was something to it. But she wasn't sure she could dismiss everything Mom had said or all their mother had passed on from conversations with Nicole's doctors. If she called her, Mom would doubtless fall apart and demand Nicole see another doctor. She might even fly out here, and right now with J.D. gone, she wasn't sure she could handle one of Mom's visits. She'd been looking forward to telling their mother that Nicole finally had a man in her life, but now with Braedon encouraging Nicole to search for their father, she suspected Mom wouldn't approve. She wasn't sure how she felt about Braedon right now. If only she could talk to J.D. about it.

Chapter 6

A thin manila folder lay open on the scratched metal desk where Braedon sat. It had taken several days to obtain the file, and it appeared to be far from complete. The tag on the side indicated the case was still open but not currently active. The report was thorough enough, he thought as he read through the file he'd finally unearthed in a back storage room, but it appeared to have been sanitized. The information he'd gained through computer sources was also frustratingly vague. About the only thing he'd discovered for certain was that Master Sergeant Greg Evangart had been in the army nineteen and a half years when he disappeared. That alone set off alarms in Braedon's head. He'd never heard of a non-com sticking with the military that long, then leaving just months shy of being able to claim retirement benefits.

He read on, whistling softly to himself. The sergeant's record was impressive, if impersonal. He'd seen duty briefly in Vietnam, where he'd served as a young but highly skilled Ranger. He'd been decorated for valor and had taken advantage of educational opportunities after the war, which led to his rapid advancement in the army. He could have gone to officers school but chose to stay with the enlisted men he led. Quite clearly he was liked and respected by his unit and by the officers he served under. Again in the Persian Gulf War, his record was spotless, and he'd received several commendations and a bronze star.

With increasing frequency, Braedon discovered sections of the record missing or inked out and marked classified. That wasn't unusual for someone working in Intelligence, and Braedon was beginning to suspect Intelligence was the direction Evangart's career had taken him. Not everything from before Desert Storm had been converted to computer files, but he was surprised by how little information he could find concerning Evangart when he turned from the paper file to electronic files. Even though Braedon's intelligence classification was high and his area of expertise gave him access to materials that were off limits to most people, he discovered when he tried to access the missing portions of the record that his clearance wasn't high enough to learn anything about the blank periods in the man's records or to discover what, if anything, he was working on at the time of his disappearance.

He turned back to the folder spread across his desk. At last he came to an account of Master Sergeant Evangart's disappearance a few months after transferring to Fort Lewis. Eagerly he read that the sergeant had left the Yakima training ground early on the final day of the exercise with another sergeant and two specialists. Sergeant Tim Malen had sat with him in the backseat of a Jeep driven by Specialist A. E. Poursaid. The fourth occupant was Specialist Shad Fahim. Both Malen and Fahim claimed they were dropped off at their off-base homes before reaching Fort Lewis. Malen was quoted as saying that Evangart slept through most of the trip. Fahim backed up this assertion by adding that Evangart woke up only as the younger soldier was exiting the Jeep and that Evangart had decided to move to the front seat beside Specialist Poursaid.

Poursaid had been interviewed too. He claimed he hadn't seen Evangart after parking the Jeep at the compound where he had transferred to his personal vehicle. He had also indicated that several individuals had been hanging around the compound waiting for the soldiers who were returning from exercises at the Yakima training facility. A few of those individuals had been located, but none of them had been able to state unequivocally that they'd actually seen Evangart arrive or depart.

Braedon tapped the papers spread across his desk with the eraser end of the pencil he held in his hand. He'd do some checking on all three of those men, see where they were now. He picked up the next paper to discover a letter from a psychiatrist, Air Force Captain Jason Detford, who was part of a research team at Madigan hospital. It gave a sketchy account of the story Nicole had related to him. The doctor's written version didn't vary substantially from the story Nicole had related to him, though it left out details she'd shared with Braedon. It proved the doctor had listened to her story better than Nicole thought. The report concluded with a request for careful handling of the child's mother, who appeared to be on the verge of both physical and mental collapse.

The letter was followed by several pages detailing a search of Miller Hill. The final page in the file was again a report from Captain Detford.

> *It is my recommendation that the child, Nicole Evangart, be placed in a psychiatric ward. She has become violent and is unable to reconcile herself to her father's desertion. Though an intelligent girl, she has deluded herself into believing her father would return to her if he could by creating a highly plausible fantasy in her mind to explain his absence. Mrs. Evangart is unable to handle the child, and continued insistence by the girl that M. Sgt. Evangart is dead only increases the strain the woman is undergoing. I fear she may lash out physically at her daughter. Further exposure to her mother's animosity can only harm the child; therefore, I recommend Nicole Evangart be committed to the Barkdale Home for Children in Barkdale, California.*

Braedon grimaced in distaste. Ambiguous rubbish. It appeared to him the wrong person was the psychiatrist's patient. Nicole had told him about launching an ashtray at the man she'd found so odious. Thinking of the lovely young woman he'd become enamored with, he couldn't imagine her becoming so frustrated that she'd throw something, but he suspected she'd had good cause. He wasn't sure why, but the ashtray story amused him. He'd always had a soft spot for women who fought back when the going got tough. He suspected the feisty child was still hidden somewhere inside Nicole, and he looked forward to discovering that part of Nicole's personality.

Gathering up the papers, he stacked them neatly before returning them to their file folder. He slipped the notes he'd made into another folder and added the folder to his personal files. He hesitated a moment, then tore a page off his desk calendar. On it he wrote the names of the three men who were known to have seen Nicole's father last. His next free time would be spent seeing how much he could discover about each of them.

He had business on the other side of the base in thirty minutes, but before picking up his beret and leaving his office, he reached for the phone.

Marcie answered, and when he asked for Nicole, he had the unmistakable impression a cold front had moved in.

"She's busy." Marcie offered no explanation.

"I'll only keep her a minute." He kept his voice pleasant, and after an awkward pause, she agreed to call Nicole to the phone. Her reluctance puzzled him, especially when Nicole's voice sounded sunny and warm when she greeted him. He'd gotten the definite impression earlier that Marcie approved of his interest in her sister.

Braedon and Nicole chatted easily for several minutes, then he suggested they meet early Saturday morning to compare notes.

"There's a place some of the guys have been telling me about," he told her. "I don't know whether we can run or not, but bring your hiking shoes. We can talk while we hike."

Nicole agreed. When she hung up the phone, she turned to see her sister's troubled face. "You're going out with him, aren't you?" Marcie's voice was almost accusatory.

"Yes." Nicole raised a questioning eyebrow, then added with a smile. "What happened to the big sister who has been trying since the day I arrived to interest me in a certain lieutenant? Have you decided Braedon isn't hot enough?"

Marcie flushed. "Oh, Nicole. It's not Braedon. He's certainly attractive enough and has all those other qualifications I hoped you'd find in a man, but . . ."

"Hmm, would that be returned missionary, college graduate, owns his own car, and has a good job?" She repeated the litany of qualifications she'd heard her sister mention numerous times.

"Be serious. It's this business about Dad, and you know it. Braedon is encouraging you to dig into the past. If you have another breakdown, I'll never forgive myself for not watching you more closely."

Nicole stood still, feeling waves of shock followed by anger. "Marcie, you have no responsibility to watch me. I'm neither a child nor a lunatic. I'm almost twenty-four years old and have been looking out for myself for a long time."

"Oh, I didn't mean it the way it sounded." Marcie began to cry. "I love you, and I worry about you, that's all."

Nicole sighed and placed her arms around her sister. Marcie was three years older, but in some ways, Nicole had always felt older. As children, Nicole had taken the lead in the games they played, and after her sojourn at the hospital, Nicole had discovered her sister was even more shy and introverted than before. Now a suspicion began to grow in her mind.

"Mom made you watch out for me all the time I was growing up, not just when I was a child, didn't she? That's why you spent more time with me and my friends than with your own." Her mind leaped to the present, and she couldn't help wondering if Marcie's plea for help was merely a continuation of her sister's lifetime charge to look after "poor Nicole." "Was it your idea or Mom's for me to come here?" She could see Marcie's shock at the blunt question.

"I wanted you to come."

"But it was Mom's idea."

"She suggested it. But Nicole, you know I don't like to be alone."

Yes, Nicole knew how frightened Marcie was of being alone. Though she had been given a bedroom of her own in their mother's apartment, Marcie had shared their mother's room while Nicole was away. After her return to the family, their mother had insisted the sisters share a room, though there was a third bedroom not being used. Marcie had been adamant about preferring to share a room with Nicole to being alone. At the slightest sound or clap of thunder, she would jump from her bed to Nicole's and bury her head beneath the blankets.

Mom and Marcie had clung to each other for years after Dad disappeared, until Marcie met J.D. at a ward singles activity. Then Nicole had witnessed the only stormy confrontation between Mom and Marcie she could recall when Marcie had declared that she loved J.D. and was going to marry him because he made her feel safe.

Safe had seemed an odd criteria for marriage, but Nicole had to admit that marriage to J.D. was good for Marcie. She was far stronger and more independent than she'd ever been before in her life. And whether or not she realized it, she was managing very well on her own while she waited for her husband's return.

In fact, she was doing much better than Mom, who was on her third marriage since Dad. It was only after Marcie married J.D. and Nicole had been notified of the scholarship to attend college at Southern Utah University that Mom began accepting invitations to go out with a few men she had met at work. Nicole had wondered more than once if her mother might have rushed into marriage with each of her husbands simply to avoid being alone.

Nicole's temper cooled as she realized Marcie was merely following a lifetime habit. "You don't really need me here." She took her sister's hands. "I've noticed how all the wives on this street support each other while their husbands are gone. You have friends both on base and in the ward. If you invited me here because you're afraid that now I'm through with school I'll somehow fall apart, you're wrong. I'm not unbalanced. I acted like a child that day in Major Detford's office because I was a child. I'm an adult now, and I never throw ashtrays at anyone anymore, no matter how much they might deserve it." She smiled, hoping for an answering smile from her sister. "If you invited me here to look after me, I assure you I can look after myself. I've been doing it since the day Mom took me away from here."

Marcie wiped her eyes and faced her sister. "I should have leveled with you to begin with. My reasons for asking you to come are a little complicated, but not what you think. When Mom learned that J.D. would be away for at least a year, she was adamant that I should move in with her. I love Mom, but I don't want to live with her again. Even though she's married to someone else, she's still mourning Dad, and she's drifted away from the Church. Ted is a good man, but he sees nothing wrong with drinking beer and coffee. They watch movies I don't want my children exposed to, and they have almost nightly poker games. Her current lifestyle and vocabulary are not the examples J.D. and I want for our family. I don't want John David and Lexie to be the way we became either—afraid to laugh or have fun. After Daddy left, we had no one but Mom. J.D. and I believe an extended family is important, and our children should have more family than just their parents, but J.D.'s family is all gone. All we have is you and Mom."

"I guess I'm the lesser of two evils." Nicole couldn't completely erase a hint of sharpness from her voice.

"I didn't mean it that way," Marcie protested.

"Actually, I'm surprised I qualify as family. Mom banished me from the family twelve years ago." Nicole struggled to keep the bitterness that had grown over the years at bay. Braedon's suggestion that her mother was ill had gone a long way toward easing her resentment, but old hurts disappear slowly.

"I'm sorry for so much," Marcie said. "When Mom suggested I invite you here so I wouldn't be alone, she said that now you're through with school you're alone too, and that with no one to watch over you, you might have problems again. I thought having you here would keep her off both our backs and give us a chance to get to know each other again." She turned away and sat down heavily on the sofa. "I guess I forgot how Mom dramatizes everything and always expects the worst. She's never let me forget that I should have been watching you that afternoon when you wandered off. Before you arrived, she warned me several times that I had a responsibility to make certain you don't have another breakdown. I guess I took her instructions to watch over you too literally. I apologize for that."

Nicole took the few steps to the sofa and sat down beside her sister, placing her arms around her. She didn't say anything, only held her while she sat with her head bowed. Silently she asked Heavenly Father to help her know what to say. After a few moments' silence, it was Marcie who continued speaking.

"When J.D. told me we were being transferred to Fort Lewis last year, I was really scared. I didn't know if I could handle coming here, but in a way it helped me. I began to remember that I was shy as a girl, but I wasn't always afraid of my own shadow. I found myself thinking of the fun things we did that summer, and I felt more at peace. J.D. encouraged me to talk about Dad and the summer we lived here. For me, this became a healing place. I thought that coming back might help you the same way."

"It has helped," Nicole assured her sister after only a slight hesitation. "But not in the way you expected. It's made me realize my memory isn't faulty and that I really did see someone killed. I feel certain the man killed was Daddy. I wish you could understand that finding out what happened to Dad is something I have to do."

"You can't accept that he's gone and he's not coming back?" There was a pleading expression in Marcie's eyes.

"No, not without knowing I've done all I can to clear his name. Dad would never just let it go if he saw something tragic happen to one of us."

"You're right," Marcie admitted with reluctance in her voice. "That's what was always so hard to understand. Dad had such strong feelings about us being a forever family. Once he told me that was what gave him the courage to fight, knowing that no matter what happened, we would all be together again someday. That's why his leaving never quite made sense to me."

"When you called, asking me to come, I hesitated at first because we've practically become strangers," Nicole said. "Then I remembered he used to say, 'Stand by your family. God and country and everything else will work out if you do.'"

"I remember that, and I used to think we were one of those families we learned about in Primary that would be together forever. After Dad disappeared, though, we fell apart as a family. Mom even stopped going to church. I did for a while too, but when you came back, you insisted on going every week, and Mom made me take you to keep an eye on you."

"I didn't know that. I thought you wanted to go to church." Attending church had been one of the few bright spots in Nicole's teenage years, and she had assumed her sister felt the same way.

"After a while I did, but at first it was guilt and Mom making me go. Sometimes I think guilt tore the three of us apart even more than Dad's absence. Mom blames herself because her jealousy got out of control and she argued with him, threatening to leave him if he went away again. You've blamed yourself all these years for not being able to save him, and I've felt responsible for not being enough for Mom or for you. It was my fault you were sent away too. If I'd been watching you, you wouldn't have been on that hill, and you wouldn't have seen whatever you saw." Marcie wiped at a tear that slowly slid down her cheek.

Nicole couldn't help smiling as she hugged her sister. "Just being able to talk with Braedon has helped me a great deal in beginning to forgive myself. I was a child. There was nothing I could have done to save Dad. Now it's my turn to remind you that I was an impossible child. There was no way you could have kept me from hunting berries that day, so it's time to let that guilt trip go."

Marcie smiled as though remembering something. "You're right. You were pretty impossible." Tears turned to laughter as they remembered Marcie's futile attempts to keep track of her little sister.

"Mom heaped too much responsibility on you because she couldn't control me either. Face it, sister dear, I was a brat." Nicole's laugher rang out with almost forgotten abandon.

"You said it," Marcie concurred. This time both sisters wiped away tears of laughter. Marcie paused, and her expression sobered. "You will stay, won't you?"

"Yes, at least until I have to fly back to begin my new job—and if you understand you're not my keeper."

"You got the job you wanted as assistant administrator at a new hospital?" Marcie picked up on her sister's reference to a job.

"Yes, the job offer was in this morning's mail from the Valley View Medical Center in Cedar City. I won't start until October, but I'd like to go back a little early to find an apartment and get my things out of storage."

"This calls for a celebration. I'll fix something special for dinner." Marcie stood and began rummaging through her refrigerator. "What time is Braedon coming? You're not planning on going out to dinner are you?"

"He's not coming until Saturday morning. And we're only going hiking, though he did mention lunch afterward."

"Well, give him a call. Tell him dinner will be at 6:30."

* * *

J.D. had long since learned to wait. Patience had been drilled into him early in his career, and a dozen seasons of duck hunting with his grandfather before that had taught him the danger of the slightest cough or gesture while on lookout. Waiting motionlessly with a sniper's rifle, only his eyes moved, following a ribbon of pockmarked pavement that stretched between Baghdad and Tikrit. The nearby road had been the scene of two ambushes in recent days, and it was his job to make certain the terrorists didn't get a third strike or get too close to the American base.

With midnight just past, the temperature was still hovering near the hundred mark. For an Idaho farm boy who had most recently hailed from the cool Northwest, he couldn't help seeing the Iraqi desert as one huge, overheated litter box. It was hard to believe these were the same hills that were once grazed by Abraham's flocks. He looked forward to the day he'd step off a plane in Seattle, watch the windshield wipers on his old Subaru dash water every which way, then splash through the rain as he ran across his driveway to the house. He didn't dare let his thoughts go any further. If he thought about Marcie and his kids, he wouldn't be able to keep his mind on the job at hand. Daydreaming could cost his life—or someone else's.

Slowly he visually sectored the landscape, examining each shape and shadow with minute care as he watched for any variation from his last scan. The night was still and lit by a billion stars. He couldn't see Cassaday, but he knew precisely where he hunkered down, waiting. Within a mile of where he crouched were four other unseen soldiers, silently watching and waiting. Behind him was an airfield that had once belonged to the enemy but now served as a major military base for the United States. A long row of UH-60 Blackhawk helicopters stretched along the nearest runway. Somewhere on the far side of the long strips of tarmac was the tent where he would attempt to sleep through the stifling daytime heat a few hours from now.

Stars began to fade on the eastern horizon, telling him morning was near. But he knew better than to relax his vigilance. His eyes swept the slowly lightening hills, making grotesque shapes of rock formations, and he noted without alarm two military Humvees leaving the base. A new day was beginning. To his left, a Jeep left a hangar to make its way across the tarmac toward one of the waiting Blackhawks.

The Humvees left the checkpoint, turning toward Baghdad. He watched their progress from his vantage point, scanning the road ahead of them for any booby trap he or his men might have missed. All appeared clear.

Where darkness and soft starlight had covered the land, there was suddenly light. Having watched the slow arrival of the sun over mountaintops most of his life, he was always amazed by its abrupt arrival in this Old Testament land. With the sun came a rapid acceleration in the temperature, and he allowed himself a fleeting longing to strip off his uniform and protective gear for a few luxurious moments in a cold shower.

He was aware of the recently arrived Blackhawk crew readying the big chopper behind him. He noted a few more vehicles on the road and scrutinized each one. Any one could hold an ally, an innocent family journeying to visit relatives, or a terrorist. In the terrorist's twisted mind, it didn't matter if his victims were American or Iraqi. He was willing to blow up himself and anyone else he deemed an enemy of his brand of Islam. Roadside bombs and suicide attacks were major threats to those who sought peace. Far too many American and British soldiers had lost their lives to such attacks.

Out of the corner of his eye, he caught the slightest of movements. Instant recognition flashed a message to his brain. As the pilot of the Blackhawk revved his engine for takeoff, a man with a shoulder-mount rocket launcher pointed his weapon toward the spot where the Blackhawk would rise above the desert floor. J.D. opened fire with his M-16/203. A ball of fire shot skyward as his rapid fire met its target. The nearby assault rifle in Cassaday's hands joined the barrage he was laying down. He and his men had not been the only ones silently waiting through the night for dawn to come.

Wriggling on his belly, he moved closer, then paused, waiting for gunfire or movement to reveal the enemy's location. All was quiet. Either he hadn't been seen or there was no one left alive in the nest he'd stirred up. *Don't think about it!* he gave sharp orders to himself, forcing himself to feel neither guilt that he'd almost missed seeing the launcher in time nor regret that he'd taken the enemy's life. He was a soldier trained to save lives. He was good at his job; the Blackhawk crew was proof of that.

Without seeing or hearing them, he knew his men were following, moving from shadow to shadow as they covered him and kept up their surveillance of the surrounding area. In the distance, he was aware of a Bradley Linebacker rumbling into position. He dropped behind a rocky outcropping and let the armored tank pass him. Holding his position, he waited, though he didn't need the Bradley crew to confirm what he already knew. The danger was past—for now.

Chapter 7

Marcie watched Nicole walk down the sidewalk beside Braedon. There was no question they looked good together. At five feet ten inches, there weren't a lot of men significantly taller than her sister, but Braedon was almost half a foot taller. They were both athletic with sun-bronzed skin and dark hair, though Braedon's lacked the deep red gleam that made Nicole's hair unique. There was a kind of electricity between the two that had Marcie biting her lip with concern.

Nicole had gone to great lengths to convince her that she was quite capable of living a solitary, independent life. She knew that was true, but ever since Marcie had fallen in love with J.D., she'd wanted her sister to experience the joy and happiness she'd found in marriage. She suspected Braedon was the man who could fulfill and complement Nicole's life—or he could hurt her more than anyone else ever had, even their father. She couldn't bear thinking of Nicole being hurt again.

Wrapping a curl around one finger, she twisted it just as she'd done as a child. She'd seen Nicole stuff a sheaf of papers into her backpack before leaving, and she suspected those papers had something to do with the search she had begun for Dad. *Why can't she let it be? Dad's gone, and whether he's dead or alive, he's not coming back. Stirring up the past could be dangerous. If she's right, and the men she saw kill Dad learned she saw them, they might kill her too.* She clapped her hands over her ears much as John David did when he wanted to pretend he didn't hear her.

A strident sound penetrated the barrier of her hands, and at first she thought she'd imagined it. Then she recognized the ring of the telephone. Feeling foolish, she dropped her hands and ran to answer it. Just as she reached for it, she hesitated. *What if?* There had been an awful lot of those pesky calls lately where she'd run to answer the phone only to discover no one was on the line. She had the uneasy sensation this had happened once before. *Could the caller be one of the killers?*

"I'll get it," John David shouted as he came down the stairs.

"I've got it." She scooped up the phone, disgusted with herself. She was scaring herself with fanciful thoughts, and John David's shouting had probably awakened Lexie. A thin wail floated down the stairs right on schedule.

"Hello," she practically shouted into the phone.

"Hi, honey."

"J.D.!" She didn't know whether to laugh or cry at the sheer pleasure of hearing her husband's voice.

"I want to talk to Daddy!" John David tried to grab the phone. She turned away from him, and he began to cry.

"Sounds like you've got your hands full." J.D. sounded choked up.

"I do, but unless this is only a two-minute call, how about talking to John David a minute while I go get Lexie?"

"Put him on," J.D.'s deep voice rumbled, "but hurry back."

"Okay." She handed the phone to her son. "Talk to Daddy for a minute while I get your sister, but when I get back it will be my turn."

He nodded his head as though accepting her terms, and she dashed up the stairs. "Hi, Daddy," she heard her son say. Seconds later she was hurrying back down with the baby in her arms. Settling herself in a chair with the baby, who stopped screaming when she began to nurse, she reached for the phone. After a lengthy pause, John David handed it to her, apparently following his father's instructions.

"I miss you so much, J.D." Her voice caught as she tried to speak.

"And I, you," he returned. "How's everything going?" She caught him up on all the antics of the children and the changes in their ward and neighborhood. After a few minutes, she told him about Braedon and Nicole's search for their father. He'd known from the start about her father's disappearance and her sister's breakdown, but now she explained it might not have happened quite the way she'd been told.

"I don't know what to do," she said. "Mom's afraid Nicole is about to have another breakdown, but I don't see it that way. When

Nicole told me what she saw that day twelve years ago, I could see it might have happened the way she said. But if it did, then she was angry when she threw that ashtray, not crazy. She had a terrible temper when we were children, but now she controls her emotions so completely, I worry that she won't be able to love anyone again the way she loved Dad."

"Sounds like she might have something going with this Lieutenant Morgan," J.D. said, reading between the lines of all Marcie had told him.

"Yes, I think he's interested in her, but she's reluctant to get involved. I think her experience in that institution, losing Dad, and becoming estranged from Mom has left her leery of attachments." She shifted the baby to her other side. "J.D., if she didn't have a breakdown and really did see Dad killed, she was treated terribly. I couldn't stand it if she lived in that place for almost a whole year for no reason."

"Honey, whatever happened, that part of her life can't be undone or changed."

"I know, but I think it's my fault no one believed her. There's something I never told anyone, not even Mom." She started to cry.

"Hey, babe, don't waste our phone call crying when I'm not there to kiss you better."

"I've been getting a lot of phone calls lately that when I answer, there's no one there. A little while ago I remembered another time when we got a lot of those calls. Shortly after Dad disappeared, I picked up the phone three or four times in a row to find no one there. Then it rang, and when I said hello, a gruff voice, like someone trying to disguise his voice, said, 'Keep your mouth shut or you'll be sorry.'" The baby started to whimper, and Marcie realized she was holding her too tightly.

"Why didn't you tell anyone?" There was puzzlement in her husband's voice.

"I didn't think it had anything to do with Dad or Nicole." She gulped, then struggled on. "I thought it was . . . There was a girl I hung out with at the pool . . . I walked in on her and her boyfriend a few days before . . . They got really angry, and I promised my friend I wouldn't tell her mother, and the boy said if I told anyone, he'd make me wish I hadn't . . . Anyway, I thought it was him threatening me again, but now I'm not sure. What if the caller was one of those men, and he thought I was Nicole?" She hiccupped as she struggled not to burst into tears.

"Don't cry, Marcie, honey. It may have been just as you assumed at the time, but I think you should tell Nicole and the lieutenant what you told me. If there's a chance it was one of the men Nicole believes she saw, they should both be alert to the fact that at least one of the men involved knows they were seen. Now, let's talk about something happier. I've only got a couple more minutes."

"I'm sorry, I didn't even give you a chance to tell me what you've been doing or find out when you're coming home."

"I can't exactly talk about what I've been doing, you know that. But I can tell you it's way too hot here. Some guy in another unit rigged up air-conditioning for the tent I share with Cassaday. The guy brought some other interesting items over here with him too. I don't know how, but he managed to bring the computer I used to chat with you a few days ago and a microwave oven. Do you think you could send me some brownies and popcorn?"

Marcie's tears changed to laughter. She knew all about her husband's sweet tooth. "I think I can manage that," she told him. "Would you like a bunch of candy bars too?"

"Uh, no. No soft candy, especially chocolate. It melts and is nothing but goop by the time it gets here. I've seen some of the packages a few guys have received. Brownies are about the only chocolate that seems to work. I've got to go now."

"All right. I love you," she responded. "Be careful."

"I love you too, and I'm always careful. Don't worry about me. I'm good at my job, if I say so myself. I'll e-mail you soon and call again in a week or two. God be with you."

"And with you." The line went dead, but it was a moment or two before Marcie could rouse herself to return the receiver to its base.

* * *

As Braedon wove his way through the outskirts of Tacoma, Nicole realized where he was taking her. They'd been so busy telling each other about their respective research projects, she'd forgotten to question where they were going.

"Point Defiance! You're taking me to Point Defiance, aren't you? I remember visiting the zoo there. Actually I guess it's more aquarium than zoo."

"You've been there before?" He sounded a little disappointed. He took his eyes from the road for a moment to send her a questioning look. She grinned back at him.

"Dad took us there one time. I loved watching the big fish, especially the sharks, up close and personal through the glass." He smiled with a touch of relief as he focused once more on the road and the Saturday morning traffic moving around them.

"I thought we could hike the trail first as we compare notes, then finish up at the zoo for lunch on the restaurant deck overlooking the water." She smiled her approval of his plans. Point Defiance held happy memories for her, and she leaned back against the headrest, savoring one of those days when all was right in her world.

Braedon stopped as the light ahead of them turned red. Through half-closed eyes, Nicole noticed a small house completely surrounded by flowers. There was no lawn, only flower beds. Baskets of blooms hung from the house eaves and from poles and arches spaced all through the yard. It was a riot of color. She opened her mouth to draw Braedon's attention to it just as the light changed to green again. She felt the pickup begin to move, then a movement caught her eye.

"Braedon!" she screamed as a heavy dump truck bore down on them. Tires screamed, and the light truck Braedon drove skidded sideways. Several horns blared as Braedon fought the wheel and forced his vehicle up onto the sidewalk just as the larger truck sped by.

Then it was over. Cars resumed their orderly rush to and fro, the traffic light changed again to red, and the dump truck disappeared down a side street. Braedon glanced both ways before pulling back onto the street.

"Did you see the license plate on that truck?" Nicole finally asked.

"It was too covered with mud to read." Braedon's voice was flat, and Nicole couldn't bring herself to ask if he harbored the same impression she did. The dump truck hadn't seemed to her to be out of control. There had been something deliberate about the way it charged straight for them. Had she imagined it, or had that truck been waiting for them?

Putting the melodramatic thought behind her, she leaned forward, watching for the turnoff. In minutes, they were pulling into a parking lot almost hidden from the road by a thick growth of trees. Almost as though they had made an agreement not to speak of the near-accident, they reached for their backpacks and exited the truck. Braedon locked it and shouldered his backpack. Nicole walked around the truck to stand beside him, and they began their hike in silence.

An hour later, Nicole and Braedon sat side by side on a bench beneath a clump of large pines overlooking Puget Sound. The sun was out, creating a shimmering effect on the water. Boats, large and small, plied the waters, sending ripples of white rushing toward the rocky coastline.

"That's all I found so far," Nicole said, pointing to a page she'd drawn from her backpack. "Just three unclaimed bodies in Washington and Oregon with gunshot wounds. There were also two bodies that washed up on shore, one in Washington and one in Oregon, within a year of Dad's disappearance. No cause of death was listed for either one, though both were male and presumed drowned."

"We'll have to contact the various agencies involved to see if DNA samples were taken and what specific data they have. The gunshot victims will be the easiest, so let's start with them," Braedon outlined a plan of action.

"All right, but it all just seems so gruesome."

"I'll make the calls," Braedon offered. "Do you think you can talk Marcie into going in with you to have DNA samples taken? It's like having your throat swabbed for a strep test. It's not difficult or painful. Soldiers routinely have DNA samples taken now before they're deployed to make identification easier should they be killed in battle."

"I'll try to convince her to go with me, but she's still having a difficult time accepting that Mom might have been wrong about what I saw. She wants me to just forget about it."

"From what I read about your father, your version is the only one that makes sense," Braedon told her. "A lot of your father's military record is classified, but I didn't see anything that would lead me to believe he could be a deserter."

"I never knew if anyone even looked for him. I told my story at the MP office and to the shrink Mom took me to, but no one ever approached me with questions, and no one answered the ones I asked. Don't you think that was odd?"

"Not necessarily," Braedon countered. "Children are often unreliable witnesses. I've learned there was an investigation by the post MPs, then it seems to have been dropped. It struck me that the search for him wasn't as intense as it should have been, and I wondered why. After thinking about it, I've decided there might have been a good reason."

"Why would they have stopped?" Nicole stood up and faced out toward the sound. She didn't want him to see how much his words upset her.

"That's what I've been thinking about." Braedon rose to his feet and stood beside her. "Do you know what your father did during the years he was in the army?"

"He was a Ranger in Vietnam. After that he traveled a lot and trained other soldiers. I don't know exactly what he trained them to do, but he was an excellent shot. I remember he had a velvet case full of medals, and there was a whole row of tiny bars that hung on chains beneath his marksmanship award on his dress uniform."

Braedon stared at her for several minutes, and she could read the indecision in his eyes.

"You found out something you don't want to tell me, didn't you?"

"I'm not certain I've drawn the right conclusion, but if I have, there may be a solid reason why we shouldn't dig any further."

"I don't care what you found. I need to know. My father's abrupt departure from our lives changed my family in a terrible way, and I don't believe any of us will be free to live normal lives until we find out what really happened and why."

Braedon took her hands and led her back to the bench where they had been seated earlier. "All right, I'll tell you what I'm thinking, but remember it's only a guess." He fiddled with the papers she'd given him for a few minutes then began. "Your father was temporarily assigned to other units at times, but he never really left Intelligence.

Much of his military record is classified, but from what I know of the type of work he did, it's likely he sometimes worked undercover. I suspect someone much higher up the chain of command than the local MPs took over the investigation and knows your father is dead and possibly why."

"But wouldn't they have told Mom?"

"I don't know. I suppose it would depend on whether or not knowing would endanger her or you or your sister."

"That would explain a lot, I suppose." She stared out at the broad expanse of water. "If Mom knew he sometimes worked undercover, that would explain why she continued to hope he would return."

"It could also be the reason," he wrapped his arms around her and rested his chin against the top of her head, "why she went to such great lengths to keep you from telling anyone what you saw. She may still believe there's a risk to you."

"I can't believe she had me locked up in that place for almost a year to protect me." Anger surged through her, and she pulled away from Braedon to pace across the lookout point. "Every conclusion you've drawn is logical, but something in here," she struck her fist against her chest, "tells me protecting me had nothing to do with anything my mother did or said. It doesn't make sense either that the army would keep her husband's death from her all these years. Even if there were security reasons for not telling her immediately, I would think they could've invented a car accident, a fire, or some such thing a few months or years later so she could get on with her life."

"You're right, there are holes in that theory," Braedon conceded. "Still, there may be elements of truth as well, so let's not close our minds to the possibility."

"All right, as long as you understand that what I've started, I mean to finish. I'm going to follow up on those unclaimed bodies."

"Even if it's dangerous?"

Nicole's mind flashed back to the dump truck, but she didn't hesitate. "Yes. I can't live with not knowing any longer." Without announcing her intention, she began running. There was something comforting in hearing his footsteps following hers along the forested trail.

Gradually her steps slowed, and Braedon pulled even with her. Running seemed to have eased her tension, and they walked companionably, pausing frequently to admire the view. On returning to the parking lot, he asked if she would like to visit the zoo before having lunch.

"I think you'll like it. Not long after we got to Fort Lewis, several of the guys in my unit decided to do a little exploring, and we wound up here," he told her. "It's not a large zoo, but it has some interesting exhibits."

"I know," she smiled at his suggestion. "I loved the aquariums when I came here with my family. They've probably been expanded since I saw them."

"Yes, they're pretty neat. I'm not terribly familiar with sea life, so it was my first experience seeing sharks and whales." He took her hand and led her to the admissions gate.

The trail led them first to a barnyard zoo, where they briefly watched children petting goats and feeding ducks before they hurried on to the aquatic area. They didn't linger at the well-lit upper pool either, making their way to the lower level where a huge expanse of glass revealed numerous sharks.

"Look at that!" Braedon pointed to a long, sleek shark, then one of another variety. Nicole gave an exaggerated shudder.

"Too many teeth for me!"

"The better to eat you with, m'dear." He mimed the shark's huge grin.

Acting almost like children, they exclaimed over the fish and practically ran from one display to another as they viewed creatures ranging from tiny sea horses to mammoth whales.

As they emerged into the sunlight and stood blinking to restore their vision, the sensation that they were being watched made the hairs on the back of Braedon's neck prickle. An instant picture of a huge truck bearing down on them came to mind. He hadn't shared his impression of that frightening incident with Nicole, but there had been something about it that had left him feeling uneasy. He'd had the distinct impression there was something deliberate in the way it seemed to target his much smaller truck. Slowly, to avoid revealing his awareness, he let his gaze roam in a seemingly casual perusal of the area. Everything looked normal, but it was impossible to examine all the many trees and buildings someone might hide behind.

"I'm starved. Let's go eat lunch." Nicole touched his arm.

"You don't want to see the rest of the zoo? I understand there are some wolves . . ."

"I've seen wolves running free in Yellowstone." She tightened her grip on his arm. Was it his imagination or had she too sensed someone watching?

"One lunch coming up!" He wrapped an arm around her shoulders to steer her toward the restaurant with its deck jutting out toward the water. If asked, he wouldn't have been able to explain the relief he felt at the sight of the huge throng of people seated on the deck and making their way up the long flight of stairs.

Chapter 8

Braedon was waiting outside the ward meetinghouse when Marcie pulled into the parking lot the next morning. As soon as he spotted her car, he hurried forward to help free John David from his car seat while Nicole picked up the infant carrier and Marcie collected the visual aids she'd brought for her Relief Society lesson. He'd learned his lesson—no more last-minute back row for him. He followed the two women to a padded bench midway in the chapel.

When sacrament meeting ended, Marcie took John David to Primary in spite of his protests that he wanted to stay with Braedon. Nicole carried Lexie, and Braedon couldn't help thinking there was something right about sitting next to Nicole through Sunday School, and he even found himself admiring the picture the three of them made. Nicole looked awfully good with a baby in her arms. He almost groaned at the direction his thoughts were taking him, and he was glad his brothers weren't around to witness how the mighty had fallen.

Following the block of meetings, Marcie once more invited Braedon to dinner.

"I'd love to come," he responded, "on one condition."

Both women looked at him, and he could read the question in their eyes. "You let me take you to dinner tomorrow night."

"Not tomorrow." Marcie rushed to explain. "A group of wives whose husbands are in Iraq meet once a month for a joint family home evening. I promised to be there and take dessert."

"That lets you off the hook for tomorrow." He grinned as he turned to Nicole. "What are your family home evening plans?"

"Well, there's a singles group I've been invited to join . . ."

"I'm single. Does that mean I can go along?"

"Far be it from me to try to stop you." To his delight, she blushed.

"That's another thing I like about redheads." He picked up a lock of her hair and twirled it around one finger. "They turn such lovely colors when teased."

"I'm not a redhead!"

"Are too." He closed Nicole's door and spoke to Marcie. "Drive carefully. I'll be right behind you, and we'll settle later on a date I can take you all to dinner."

Dinner turned out to be much like the previous time they'd shared Sunday dinner, with John David excited by the attention he received from Braedon, and Marcie doing a little matchmaking. After dinner, she put the children down for naps and suggested Braedon and Nicole watch one of the new LDS movies she'd recently ordered online.

Nicole was surprised by how natural it felt being with Braedon. On Monday night, they attended the singles group family home evening and ran together almost every morning that week. On Saturday, Braedon took them all out for pizza.

He had duty the next Sunday, and she and Marcie spent a lazy afternoon catching up on each other's lives. They didn't talk much about their parents or the past but discussed at length their present plans and goals. Nicole knew Marcie still didn't approve of the search she and Braedon were making for Dad, but she seemed willing to step back and see what happened. That was progress, Nicole supposed. Unfortunately, the search involved long, tedious hours on the computer or telephone with few results.

* * *

They were well into July when a change in Nicole's voice one morning alerted Marcie that the telephone call she'd just answered was different from the others. She suspected the hope and excitement she heard concerned their father and found herself waiting expectantly to catch a few crumbs of information. Realizing she was deliberately eavesdropping and her own heart was pounding, she faced the fact that she hadn't put aside hope of finding their father any more than Nicole or their mother had.

Stunned, she sat down heavily. Did she expect their father to walk in the door one day as their mother did? She shook her head, answering her own question. No. Somehow over the past months, she'd entirely changed her thinking about her father's absence. She faced what she'd always known deep inside—Daddy was dead, and Nicole was right. The only way to find closure was to find his body.

"That was the police chief in Port Angeles," Nicole announced after hanging up the phone. "He wants me to examine some pictures and go over some evidence he has of a body that washed up there a short time after Daddy disappeared. He said there are indications the victim died of a gunshot wound before being placed in the water."

She stepped into the front room and hesitated a moment before hurrying to her sister's side. Kneeling, she touched Marcie's wet cheeks. "I'm sorry. I should have been more tactful."

"No, it's not that." Marcie brushed away the tears with the back of her hand. "I think I just grew up a little bit, and it hurt in a way. You're right about finding Daddy. We have to know."

Nicole hugged her sister for several minutes, then asked, "Do you want to go with me?"

"No, take Braedon. He'll be of more use to you than I could ever be." She shuddered. "I might be convinced Daddy really is dead, but I don't think I could bear to look at pictures of dead bodies." She paused a moment, then added, "You'd better plan on a two-day trip if you're going to Port Angeles. On the map it looks like a two-hour drive, but between the weather around the rain forest and the narrow, twisting road, it usually takes much longer. Besides, if you and Braedon go that far, you might want to take a ferry to Vancouver Island. It would be a shame to be so close and miss the Butchart Gardens."

* * *

Marcie awoke one morning a few days later feeling disoriented. Her first thought was for the baby, then she heard the sound again. Frantically she searched the nightstand beside her bed for the phone. A tissue box dropped to the floor with a soft plop, and papers rustled.

By the third ring, she had located the receiver and jerked it to her ear, praying the ringing hadn't awakened Lexie. She couldn't help the note of wariness in her voice as she said hello. By the illuminated dial of her alarm clock, she could see it was a little after two in the morning.

"I'm sorry, honey. I know it's the middle of the night there, but I have to call when I get an opportunity."

"J.D.!" She sat up straighter, cradling the phone against her face. "I don't care if it's the middle of the night. I'm happy whenever you get a chance to call me."

"I'm sorry I woke you, but I needed to hear your voice."

"Is something wrong? Are you hurt?" She hoped she didn't sound as panicked as she suddenly felt. J.D. didn't sound like himself.

"No, I'm not hurt—at least not the way you mean. I-I shot someone last night . . . a woman."

Marcie was quiet for a moment, absorbing his words. It didn't make sense to her. "I didn't think Muslims allowed women to serve in their armies."

"She wasn't a soldier, at least not the usual kind."

"But she must have been firing at you." Marcie was quick to defend him.

"No, she wasn't. I know men have died because of my actions in combat, but the woman . . . she was just walking toward the soldiers at the gate. The translators told her in her own language to stop, but she kept coming."

"How awful." Her heart ached for him, but she never doubted he had a valid reason for the action he'd taken.

"I kept hoping she would stop . . . She was just an ordinary woman wearing a long scarf over her head . . . I kept thinking I couldn't shoot someone who was just walking toward me . . . I waited . . . too long." His voice broke. "I fired. Those were my orders, and there was a huge explosion. She was carrying explosives strapped to her body under her robe. Two of the sentries were injured. It was my fault. I should have fired sooner, but I didn't want to kill a civilian."

"Oh, J.D., I'm so sorry. But if you hadn't shot her, those sentries and maybe others would have died."

"I know that, and when I decided to become a soldier I thought I had dealt with the spiritual ramifications of taking a life in combat.

But I wasn't prepared for this. I don't know if God can forgive me for shooting that woman. I was in no danger, and she didn't even have any means of defending herself."

"J.D., you listen to me. Being a woman didn't make her any different from a man who did the same thing. You didn't kill her. She committed suicide. She would have been dead in minutes anyway, along with who knows how many good men who are only trying to give people like her a chance for a better life. It's not your fault if she chose to give up her life."

"I know, but—"

"You wouldn't be the man I know and love if her death didn't bother you, but you have no reason to feel guilty. Concentrate instead on the lives you saved."

"That's another thing . . . I should have fired sooner. Neither soldier is seriously injured, but it's my fault they were injured at all."

"Oh, honey, what you need is a priesthood blessing. I wish some of the other guys in your unit were members of the Church. Would it help if I talked to our bishop and had him e-mail you?" She wished she knew words or scriptures that would comfort him. J.D. was well trained and deeply committed to his country, but he was a sensitive, caring man too, and she didn't know how to help him move beyond the devastating experience that appeared to have caught him emotionally off guard.

"Don't worry about me. I'll be fine. Just hearing your voice helps more than I can say." She heard the emotion in his voice. "And you're right about a priesthood blessing. I told you there's a Guard unit here from Utah. I think I'll stop by their tent. Most of them are LDS, and I attend Church services with them as often as I can."

"I'm glad you have them, but more importantly, you have your own faith to help you through this. I wish I could put my arms around you right now and tell you how much I love you."

"I wish that too, but just talking to you helps. I've got to go now."

"Are you going to be okay?"

"Yes. Don't worry. I'll be fine in a little while. I love you."

"Not half as much as I love you," she whispered with a fierceness she hadn't known she was capable of.

"Sweet dreams," he whispered back before the line went dead.

* * *

Braedon picked up Nicole at noon on Friday to drive to Port
Angeles. He placed her small bag and a picnic hamper in the space
behind the front seat of his truck beside his own overnight bag. Of all
the prospects she'd discovered that might be her father, the gunshot
victim who had been discovered under the ferry docks in that small
resort town sounded the most promising. Braedon had called the
police chief back and gleaned as much information as possible from
him, and he'd faxed a number of documents to him. He wasn't certain
how much more they would learn in a face-to-face visit, but Nicole
wanted to talk to the police chief in person, and Braedon had agreed
to go with her.

A few raindrops hit the windshield as they followed I-5 to
Olympia, but the sun played peekaboo with the clouds as they
turned north once more. He occasionally caught a glimpse of water
through the trees, but they had quite a distance to travel before they
would reach the Strait of Juan de Fuca, which separated this thumb
of land from Canada. Sensing Nicole's reluctance to talk about their
mission, he talked about his own family and the ranch he'd grown up
on. They listened to CDs and exclaimed over the scenery and
wildlife they passed.

Nicole was excited and nervous by turns, but spotting a picnic
area, she remembered she'd packed a lunch. "Let's eat lunch there,"
she said, pointing to a trail leaving the highway.

"I thought you'd forgotten all about your promise to feed me,"
Braedon teased as he pulled the truck onto the narrow road and
stopped in a small, graveled parking area. He grabbed the picnic basket
and followed Nicole down a steep path to a wooden picnic table that
had seen better days. While Nicole spread a cloth on the table and
unpacked their lunch, Braedon turned his attention to the glimpses of
gray water he could see through the trees, watching the choppy water
and waves rippling toward shore.

"It's ready," Nicole told him. He sat down and began filling his
plate. Nicole was still nervous and was hardly touching the food on
her plate. Hoping to help her relax, Braedon told her more about his
family's ranch and his ambition to turn a small segment of the ranch

where his grandfather had attempted unsuccessfully to raise alpaca sheep into recreational property.

"Skiing?" She sounded skeptical.

"No, it's a small valley that's virtually cut off from the rest of the ranch. It's easily accessible from the highway, but that route is twenty miles from the ranch house. To reach the valley from where we graze stock involves cutting through a steep timber area and following a narrow, rocky path along the side of a mountain. It's not readily accessible for grazing stock, but it's a great camping place."

"But if you open it to camping, won't you have problems with trash and environmental damage? Public campgrounds are notorious as litter magnets and consume a lot of tax dollars for their upkeep."

"That's why we want to make it a special-use camping area. We're not concerned with making money on it, but hopefully we can charge the groups using it enough to pay for maintenance and taxes. We could even require them to police the area for trash themselves." He unwrapped a packet Nicole handed him and bit into a thick ham sandwich.

"What kinds of groups do you mean?" Nicole nibbled on a chunk of melon and eyed him speculatively. "Handicapped?"

"The area might be a little rough for those with severe physical disabilities, though I wouldn't rule that out. I was thinking more of family reunions, ward campouts, father and son outings, and educational groups where the organization is willing to pay for a private camping area but can't afford to pay a lot." He expounded on his plan.

"That might work," Nicole conceded. He noticed that a mist seemed to cling to her hair. It rapidly changed to a drizzle, followed by sheets of rain that slanted toward them.

"Let's head for the truck." Braedon began stuffing the remainder of their lunch back in the hamper. She snatched up the plastic cloth and dashed toward the truck with Braedon at her heels. Just steps from shelter, Braedon's foot came down on a trailing corner of the tablecloth. Thunder cracked as Nicole lurched backward, caught up short by his foot on the cloth she carried. Braedon grabbed for her as she stumbled against him. They both fell in a flurry of arms and legs, crushing the hamper between them. On the road above them, Braedon heard the squeal of tires as someone fought a skid on the wet pavement.

"Are you all right?" he asked Nicole while struggling to disentangle himself and set her free. A strangled sound reached his ears. "Are you hurt?"

"N-n-no." Alarmed, he twisted to see her better. Rain plastered her hair against her cheeks, and mud streaked her face and clothes. Again she made a strange gasping noise as she gathered the hamper's remains. Turning so he was on his knees, he reached for her, then rose to his feet with her in his arms.

"Where are you hurt? I'll get you to a hospital as quickly as possible."

"P-put me d-down. I'm fine. J-just so funny."

She was laughing, not crying as he'd supposed. Relief swept over him, but he didn't put her down immediately. Something nagged at the back of his mind, and instead of setting her on her feet, he took the remaining few steps to the truck, opened the door, and set her inside. In seconds he was around the hood of the truck and climbing behind the steering wheel. Pulling the door closed behind him, he faced Nicole.

"You're sure you're all right? Did I knock the wind out of you when we fell?"

She lifted her eyes, and he saw the corner of her mouth twitch. "I'm fine. Really. But you . . ." She doubled over in a fit of laughter again, and he felt himself becoming slightly annoyed. Nicole didn't seem the type to find that much humor in a Three Stooges–style fall.

"Your face . . ." Nicole struggled to stop laughing.

"I know. It's covered in mud and pine needles." He swept a hand across his face to sluice away the moisture and mud, but it came away dripping yellow mustard onto his seat covers. He remembered a mustard squeeze bottle he'd used liberally on his ham sandwich and had obviously failed to close! When he and Nicole had crashed into each other, smashing the remnants of their picnic lunch between them, he must have received the full brunt of the mustard.

Nicole grabbed a tissue box and began wiping at his face. Taking the box from her hand, he wiped at the seat covers. When they were cleaned to his satisfaction, he turned to Nicole and noticed that the soggy, yellow tissue she held also sported a few sliced olives, a chunk of lettuce, and some orange mush that once was probably bread and cheese.

"I don't suppose you want to finish your lunch?" she giggled.

"It appears I ended up wearing my lunch. I must have looked like a real dope." He tilted his head to one side and sniffed as though affronted.

"Well, actually you did look a bit like a sandwich."

"A tasty one I hope," he teased and watched the rosy color creep up her neck and spread across her cheeks. "Want to try a bite?" He leaned toward her. She backed away in mock horror. He reached for her shoulders with both hands to hold her in place. Her eyes sparkled with laughter, then slowly changed to something else as he closed the distance between them. His mouth took hers in a kiss as light as sunshine chasing away the rain.

After a moment, he broke off the kiss, letting his hands trail down her arms slowly before withdrawing them to place them on the wheel. It took considerable effort to keep them from shaking. He started the engine without speaking and, with a quick check for oncoming traffic, pulled back onto the highway. He was filled with an exhilaration like nothing he'd ever experienced before, yet as he checked his rearview mirror, he had an uneasy feeling he was missing something.

She was getting in too deep. Nicole gazed through the rain-streaked window and wondered what was happening to her—and fearing she knew. Braedon Morgan was becoming too important in her life, and now that he had kissed her . . .

Through the trees, she could see a small boat bobbing at anchor. Sky and water seemed to meet in a choppy blur, making it impossible to see across the small inlet the road paralleled. Having lived most of her life in states with plentiful sunshine and where rain is preceded by noticeable clouds, she was continually amazed by the ever-present gray skies that unpredictably spewed rain in the Northwest.

In spite of the rain and gray sky, there was a cozy warmth inside the truck she suspected was attributable more to the man beside her than the truck's heater, which was turned on low.

He hadn't said one word since he kissed her, and she was confused by her own reluctance to speak of it. She should tell him she wasn't looking for that kind of relationship, but there was something about that brief meeting of lips that had somehow changed something inside her. She didn't want a man's career determining where she lived and worked. She didn't want to link her life to a man who could suddenly leave her without answers. Braedon wasn't career military, but belonging to the army Reserve, he was still subject to sudden call-ups. Perhaps she was reading too much into a single kiss. After all, many people kissed without meaning commitment or anything close to it.

She would just pretend it never happened. He hadn't said anything, and neither would she. She'd just imagined that earth-shattering moment when they'd touched. She'd been kissed a few times before, enough to recognize a pleasant moment, and she was losing it if she thought this kiss was any more. It was time to get her thoughts centered once more on finding her father.

She turned to Braedon, intending to ask what time he thought they'd reach Port Angeles, but he chose that moment to glance at her, and she forgot her question. All she could think was she hadn't imagined a thing.

Braedon swallowed unconsciously and forced his attention back to the road, which now angled toward the west. Though the water was not many feet from the road, Braedon couldn't see it for the trees. He'd thought the forest thick on and around Fort Lewis, but this was ridiculous. He'd never before seen such a thick tangle of growth. On the corners, he found lights had been placed along the side of the road under the trees to illuminate where the road passed through the near-jungle. They were driving on the extreme edge of the Olympic Forest, the United States' only rain forest, and it was all he'd ever supposed a rain forest to be.

Accustomed to the wide-open rangeland and the rocky, lightly timbered mountains of his native state, he found the impenetrable forest almost claustrophobic. He hunched over the wheel and tightened his grip. It was midafternoon, but the darkness lent a gloomy aura of approaching night. Water no longer splashed on the windshield, and he wondered if the rain had stopped or if the canopy of trees was too thick to allow it passage.

"This place gives me the creeps," he heard Nicole say.

"I know what you mean," he agreed. "But I've always wanted to see a rain forest, so I'm glad we came this way. It's beautiful and fascinating in its own way."

"If we were visiting the park and hiking some of the trails with a guide, it would probably be different from just driving across the outside edge. I've heard there are beautiful flowers and a lot to see, but I haven't seen any flowers here. In fact it's so dark, I'd get lost if we weren't riding in a vehicle with lights." Nicole peered through the windows as if concentrating harder might enable her to see farther.

Braedon laughed and pointed ahead. "I think we're almost out of the forest. I see a bit of blue, but I can't tell if it's water or sky."

As they left the dark trees behind, they discovered both the sky and the strait offered glimpses of blue, and Braedon found himself whistling. Though their errand might be sober, he couldn't help feeling lighthearted. He wanted to tell Nicole how much he enjoyed being with her and that kissing her had confirmed what he'd suspected for some time—he was falling in love with her. He thought she probably wasn't ready to hear what he wanted to shout from the treetops, so he kept his feelings to himself, though it required real effort. Nicole hadn't said much about her future plans, but he sensed she would hold any long-term plans, especially those involving romance, at bay until satisfied she was neither mentally unbalanced nor that her father had deserted her.

Port Angeles was a larger town than he had expected. Instead of a quaint village, he found a small but busy port city. As Nicole read off the instructions she'd found on the Internet for locating the police station, he found his attention straying from the street where he drove to a large ship anchored not far from shore.

"Look at the size of that thing." He pointed, and Nicole laughed.

"As ships go, it probably isn't terribly big, though it looks enormous to a couple of landlubbers like us. Dad took me to Seattle once to see the ships there. I couldn't see how anything so large and heavy could float."

"I've always had a yen to travel once or twice on the ocean in a big ship," Braedon confided. "I've flown outside of the United States, but I've never been on a ship. Though I've tried waterskiing and ridden in motorboats, I'm not really comfortable on a small craft in deep water. But a cruise sounds like fun."

"When Dad took me to Seattle that day, he promised me that someday we'd hop on one of the ferryboats that crosses to Vancouver

Island and go to Victoria to see some huge flower garden there. We never got to go." There was regret in her voice.

"I've heard of the Butchart Gardens. My mother told me that since I'm going to be in Washington for a while, I should plan to visit the gardens and to take a camera so I can get lots of pictures for her. She's crazy about flowers."

"Look," Nicole interrupted. He glanced quickly where she indicated. "That sign."

He pulled to the curb near the sign and looked toward a building resembling a large warehouse. Next to it, he could see two ferryboats. The closer one appeared to be for passengers only, but cars were being unloaded from the second one.

"We could take a ferryboat from here to Victoria as your sister suggested . . ." Spending the following day with Nicole, riding a ferry to Victoria, visiting the gardens, then finding a romantic seafront restaurant in which to share dinner before starting back seemed like a wonderful idea.

"I've heard there are a lot of things to do and see there."

"How about it? Should I see about tickets?" he asked.

She took so long to answer, he was bracing himself for a refusal when she suddenly grinned. "Let's do it!"

"All right. As soon as we finish at the police station, we'll hurry back here to see if we need to purchase tickets in advance and check on departure times." He put the truck in gear and turned away from the waterfront. In minutes they were at the police station. Nicole pulled some small packets of moist wipes from her purse, and they laughed as they took turns using the mirror to make themselves presentable. Their clothes had dried, and the loose dirt from their earlier spill brushed off easily. The moist towelettes took care of the rest.

Deciding he looked as presentable as he was going to get, Braedon jumped from the truck. Just once he'd like to get Nicole's door open before she did. Hurrying around the back, he saw he was too late. She was already standing on the sidewalk waiting for him.

Something caught his eye. He backed up a step to examine the truck's tailgate better. With one hand he reached out a finger to touch a small hole. He didn't need a ballistics report to know a bullet, probably from a small-caliber gun, had slammed into the metal. It hadn't been there when they started this trip. A shudder ran through him as he remembered a crash of thunder just as he stepped on the trailing tablecloth, causing Nicole to trip and sending them both sprawling into the mud. It was the thunder that had nagged at him. It hadn't sounded quite like thunder and, though there was plenty of rain, there had only been that one clap of thunder. It had rained almost every day since he'd arrived in Washington, and that was the first thunder he had heard. He remembered the squeal of tires and wondered if the shooter had assumed he'd hit his target when he and Nicole tumbled to the ground. Or had the single shot been some kind of warning?

Chapter 9

Braedon was still musing over the bullet hole in his truck when he followed Nicole into the police station. He looked around, then spotted a young woman in uniform seated behind a counter. She was wearing earphones. Seeing the console in front of her, he guessed she doubled as receptionist and dispatcher. He walked toward her.

The woman looked up as he approached, and when he asked to see the police chief, she pointed toward a short hall. He could just see the corner of a heavy oak desk piled high with papers in a room at the end of it.

"Do you have an appointment?" she asked almost as an afterthought.

"Chief Daniels is expecting us."

"Oh." She appeared flustered. "I'll show you to his office." She unhooked the headset and motioned for them to follow her. She led them past the office he'd glimpsed and the heavyset, gray-haired man seated at the desk.

Ushered into an office that was almost spartan in its furnishings, Braedon looked around and felt right at home. The plain metal desk and filing cabinets, a couple of wooden chairs, and some sophisticated computer equipment made the room similar to his office on base. A man he judged to be in his late fifties, with a fringe of steel gray hair surrounding his shining pate, stood to greet them. He seemed to be focusing on Nicole as he introduced himself as Chief Walter Daniels. Braedon introduced himself and Nicole.

"Have a seat." Chief Daniels gestured them toward two straight-backed chairs. Once they were seated, he took his place behind his desk and pulled a manila envelope from his top drawer. Wasting no time, he extended the envelope to Nicole.

"They're not pretty," he told her. "The body had been in the water for several weeks before it washed ashore."

Braedon shifted closer to Nicole as she loosened the clasp and drew out a handful of glossy prints. He saw her close her eyes briefly and take a deep breath before glancing down. He expected her face to turn pale, but she gamely leafed through the photos. Remembering she was preparing to become a hospital administrator, he guessed she had viewed autopsy photos before. He was torn between wanting to examine the pictures himself and watching Nicole. He noticed their host was also watching Nicole closely as she took her time moving from one shot to the next. Several times she shook her head slightly, but made no comments until she finished.

Taking care to avoid marking the photos with fingerprints, she carefully stacked them and returned them to the envelope.

"This isn't my father," she said in a quiet voice as she handed the envelope back to Chief Daniels.

"What are you basing your opinion on?" he asked, not appearing as disappointed as she did. Braedon got the impression Daniels had expected Nicole to refute the possibility the dead man in the photos had been her father. "This John Doe's physical description fits the one your friend here faxed to me." He acknowledged Braedon with a brief jerk of his head in his direction.

"This man was shot in the head. My father was shot in the chest."

"You didn't tell me . . ." The chief scowled at Braedon but didn't appear surprised by Nicole's statement.

"I didn't know," Braedon defended himself. Turning to Nicole he explained in terms as gentle as he could manage. "He may have been shot more than once. If he was still breathing, the murderers may have made certain he was dead by shooting him again before dumping his body in the ocean."

"I thought of that," she said. "Most of the soft tissue in the chest area is gone, which could explain why there's no sign of a chest wound. But . . . The teeth . . . I was so young, and I had forgotten . . . These pictures show this man's lower jaw is almost intact . . . And the teeth are wrong. Dad had a lot of trouble with his teeth. There should have been fillings, and he was missing a molar on the lower right side."

"There were no dental records with the material you sent." Once again the chief turned his disapproval toward Braedon.

Taken by surprise, Braedon couldn't think what to say for several moments. He remembered distinctly seeing a dental chart in Greg Evangart's file. No way could he have neglected to send the simplest means of identifying a cadaver.

"I'm sorry, sir. It must have stuck to the back of one of the other papers and failed to copy when I faxed the papers to you. I'll check on it when we get back." He stood and reached for Nicole's hand. "I'm sorry we wasted your time."

"Sit back down." The police chief waved them back to their chairs. "You haven't wasted my time, and I'll admit I'm intrigued by your story." He returned the packet of pictures to his desk drawer then placed his hands palm-to-palm on his smooth desktop. He looked at Nicole for several moments, as though he were seeing through her, while tapping the tips of his fingers against each other.

"It seems you have a bona fide mystery here. I became a cop because I can't resist a good mystery, so perhaps I can give you a bit of help. I won't press for details, but it appears that either the army slipped up going after one of their own, or for some reason they didn't look hard enough. Now I can think of a few reasons why they might not have looked too hard, but from the little you told me of his previous record, I suspect someone with enough rank to get away with it has done some covering up. Have you two considered the possibility that somebody doesn't want the sergeant found and that person or persons could cause you serious problems if word gets out there was a witness to the killing?"

Braedon considered telling the police chief about the bullet hole in his truck. Instead he merely nodded his head. There was something about the chief that Braedon liked, and he suspected he could trust him, but it was up to Nicole to decide how much to tell the man.

She surprised him by suddenly blurting out the whole story to the police chief.

Only an occasional "hmm" came from the officer as he concentrated his attention on Nicole. When she finished, he turned to Braedon. "How much have you been able to check out?

"We returned to the trail where Nicole witnessed the incident, and everything she described checked out. I located her father's case file and noticed large sections have been classified."

"Not surprising." The lawman brought his steepled fingers to his chin and tapped lightly as though deep in thought. "You know, your investigation might step on the toes of military intelligence. There may be security reasons for keeping the case quiet."

"I don't care," Nicole told him. "I need to know about my father."

"I suspect you need to know, too, whether or not there was a valid reason for being sent to a mental institution," he came back with startling bluntness. "Did you consider the reason you were sent there might not have had anything to do with your mental or emotional state?"

"Yes," Braedon answered for her. "We discussed the possibility she was sent there to keep her from becoming a target."

"The possibility she could be a target may still exist." Chief Daniels's quiet statement sounded almost like a warning.

Nicole turned wide eyes toward Braedon, and he knew she was remembering the dump truck that had nearly run them down. Perhaps he should tell her about the bullet hole in his pickup's tailgate. Together, the two incidents could mean someone was worried about her stirring up the past.

"You need to be careful," the older man repeated. There was an almost fatherly plea in his voice. "The men who killed your father could still be in the area."

This time it was Nicole who stood first. She extended her hand to Chief Daniels and thanked him for his trouble.

"Thank you for listening to us," she said.

"I'll keep your case in mind," the chief told her. "If I hear of anything that might help you discover what happened to your father's body, I'll contact you. In the meantime, be aware that advertising what you're up to is a surefire way to attract trouble."

Braedon placed a hand on Nicole's back as they moved toward the door. "I should have checked to make certain all of the papers copied properly," he began by way of a second apology.

"Strange it should be that one particular document that didn't copy." He had the distinct impression the lawman was trying to tell him something he didn't want to say in front of Nicole. The chief followed them to the door, then reached past them to grasp the doorknob.

"You folks aren't headed back tonight are you?" he asked.

"No," Nicole told him. "We were thinking of visiting Victoria tomorrow."

"Great place, you'll enjoy it. If it's your first trip there, I would suggest you purchase one of the tour packets that are available at most of the local hotels or at the ferry office."

"Thanks, we'll do that." Braedon shook his hand.

"There's a good motel just around the corner, if you haven't already made reservations," the chief told them. Reaching back to his desk, he picked up two small, white cards. "Bernice Roma owns it and is a friend of mine. Give her my card, and she'll find room for you." He handed them each a card. "I'd like to talk to you again before you leave. While we were talking, I remembered hearing about a body that washed up on one of the islands north of here some time back. If you don't mind, I'll make a few calls, then contact you at Mrs. Roma's later this evening."

They agreed, then said good-bye before driving the short distance to the motel Chief Daniels had recommended. Though small, it was clean and attractive, and they were pleased with the rooms Mrs. Roma directed them to. Nicole was glad Braedon was the kind of man who never even broached the subject of sharing a room. There was something comforting in knowing he took his commitment to gospel standards as seriously as she did.

He set her small travel case inside the door and asked, "Half an hour long enough, or do you need a little more time?"

"Forty-five minutes?" she bargained. "I'd like to shower, and I promised Marcie I'd let her know if we decided to wait until tomorrow to drive back. I'm glad she insisted we prepare for a possible two-day trip."

"Okay, forty-five minutes. After my encounter with the mustard, I guess I'd better shower too."

Once inside her room next to the one assigned to Braedon, she showered, then called Marcie to tell her their plans for the following day. After a slight hesitation, she told her sister about their visit with

Chief Daniels and her certainty that the body found in Port Angeles twelve years ago wasn't their father.

"At first I thought Chief Daniels was rather stiff and formal. I suspect he's retired military, and usually I shy away from men like him," she confided while holding the phone with one hand and wrapping her hair in a towel with the other. "But there was something about him that put me at ease, and I wound up telling him everything. It was almost like he was an old friend."

"Are you sure you can trust him? What if he tells a bunch of people there's a woman at Fort Lewis who can identify a killer?" Marcie's concern surprised Nicole. Most of the time she talked as though she still didn't quite believe Nicole, but now she was as full of warnings as the police chief had been.

"I do trust him. I can't explain it, but I know he isn't a threat to me and that he only wants to help. Has something happened to make you think I might be in some kind of danger?"

"I've tried to tell you for the past several days, but I just didn't know how. I guess I was a little afraid you'd think me silly. But J.D. said I should tell you, then he called again because he was having a difficult time with an action he had to take over there, and I've been so worried about him I put off telling you."

"Marcie, just tell me."

"Oh, Nicole, I never associated it with you all those years ago. I went swimming with some friends that morning you wanted me to go pick berries with you. I didn't even look for you when you ran off. When I walked into the changing room, I caught one of the girls with her boyfriend. They . . . were pretty involved, and he shouldn't have even been in the girls' changing room. They were upset, and he threatened to get me in trouble if I told her mother. Then a few days later . . . after Dad didn't come back, and while Mom was driving you to Madigan to that doctor, there was a phone call."

"What kind of phone call?" Nicole spoke with a calmness she didn't feel, but she'd learned a long time ago that Marcie couldn't be hurried. Getting her excited or defensive would delay the story indefinitely.

"It was the way it's been around here lately. The phone rings several times a day, but when I answer there's no one there. That time, I answered, and a voice warned me to keep quiet or something terrible would happen to me. I thought it was Melissa's boyfriend. It only occurred to me since you started searching for Dad that it might have been one of the men who killed him and that he'd found out you saw what happened. When I answered the telephone that day, he could have thought I was you."

Nicole felt goosebumps on her arms. Was it possible? Could there be someone out there who knew who she was and that she'd been hiding in the blackberry thicket when her father was shot?

A knock on the door reminded her Braedon was expecting her to be ready to explore the town and go to dinner.

"I need to go now," she told Marcie. "I'm glad you told me about that call, and I will be careful. I think you should be cautious too."

"I will. Have fun tomorrow. I hope you enjoy Victoria as much as I did when J.D. took me there."

They exchanged good-byes, and Nicole hurried to the door. Seeing the towel on her head Braedon asked if she needed more time.

"Just a couple of minutes," she told him. "Have a seat while I finish." Hurrying to the bathroom, she put her still damp hair in a braid and applied minimal makeup. While she worked, her mind kept repeating Marcie's story, and she found herself wondering about the nuisance calls Marcie was getting now. Were they connected to Nicole's search for her father? And she hadn't been able to get that dump truck out of her mind. She gave the band securing her braid a final twist and stepped out of the bathroom to find Braedon watching the evening news.

"That was fast." He clicked off the television and rose to his feet.

"Sit back down, Braedon. Marcie told me something on the phone, and I've been thinking about the day we went to Point Defiance. I think we should talk where no one might accidently overhear us."

Braedon sat back down, a look of concern on his face. He listened without interruption while she told him about Marcie's phone call.

"She could be right. The message may have been meant for you." Braedon sounded thoughtful. "I'm glad she told you about that call and that you decided to tell me. There are a couple of things I've put off telling you as well."

"Like what? That dump truck in Tacoma?" She sank down on one corner of the bed. "That's the other thing I wanted to talk about. I don't think that was an accident. That truck was sitting at the side of the road like it was waiting for something. It didn't start to move until we stopped for the light, then it shot straight at us."

"I wish I could disagree with you, but I admit I also found something calculated in the way that truck headed toward us. But there are a couple of other things. Ever since the day you told me what you witnessed twelve years ago, I've hesitated to alarm you by mentioning there was a slim chance you were seen that day. I crouched almost to the ground in the place you said was the spot where the shooting took place. Just as I started to stand back up, I caught a glimpse of your sweater through the brush. The soldier who bent to pick up your father may have seen something similar after the shooting. In his rush to get away, he probably dismissed a flash of color as unimportant until he heard rumors a few days later that the missing man's daughter claimed to have seen him killed. If that's what happened, he must have put two and two together and realized you could possibly identify him and the other man."

"That adds credence to Marcie's speculation that the telephoned warning was meant for me." Nicole shivered. "And if our suspicions about that dump truck are true, he's still here and knows I'm back."

"More than that." He reached for the hands she was twisting in her lap. "Someone took a shot at us earlier today while we were running to the truck to escape the rain. There's a small bullet hole in my truck's tailgate."

"No!" She rose to her feet, brushing aside his hand. She paced across the room and back. "Why didn't I hear anything? Even if he used a silencer, I should have heard the bullet hit the truck." She clenched her fists and walked away again.

"We both heard something. I thought it was thunder. Now I wonder if I really heard a shot or a slamming car door, sounds that are nothing like thunder. It was raining, and I thought you might be hurt, so I heard what I expected to hear."

"Did you find the bullet? Can it be traced?" She whirled around to face him.

"I looked but didn't find a thing. It could have fallen out of the truck bed or ricocheted somewhere."

"Do you really think someone is trying to kill me? Couldn't the bullet have come from a careless hunter?" Her voice was softer and filled with pain. There was little color in her face. His heart went out to her.

"I'm not certain anyone is trying to kill you. Both attempts were somewhat clumsy and may have been accidents or could indicate he's only trying to frighten you." He took a step toward her.

"Well, he's certainly succeeded at that."

Braedon closed the distance between them and gathered her in his arms. "Do you want to quit? Are you frightened enough to pretend you didn't see anything?"

"No!" She pulled herself loose from his embrace and looked at him with a touch of defiance. "He's not scaring me away. I have to find out what happened to Dad, but you don't need to help me anymore. There's no reason for you to be in danger."

"There's every reason. I'm not turning my back on the possibility you might be in danger. I'm with you until we get some answers. Besides, there's a soldier, Master Sergeant Greg Evangart, who deserves to have his name cleared."

"Thank you." Rising up on her toes, she kissed his cheek. He pulled her closer for a couple of seconds, then released her with a grin.

"I think it's time we go hunt up some dinner." He enjoyed the flush of color that instantly flooded her cheeks.

"Will you pray with me before we go? I'd like to ask Heavenly Father to protect Marcie and the children and to help me know whom to trust."

Without hesitation, he held out his hand to her, and together they knelt. When she asked him to offer the prayer, he felt both honored and humbled. He poured his heart into the prayer with an intensity he'd given too few times since his mission. Afterward, they both remained on their knees in silent, peaceful contemplation until a firm rap on the door warned they had company.

Their earlier conversation led to an element of wariness as Braedon stepped to the door. A quick check through the peephole showed Chief Daniels on the other side. Mixed feelings assailed Braedon as he viewed their visitor. On one hand, his inclination to trust the lawman was increasing, but on the other, he had a strong impression that Daniels wasn't completely leveling with them. Releasing the chain, he pulled the door open.

"I called a friend up north," Chief Daniels said as he stepped inside and pushed the door closed behind him. "The body he had up there a few years ago isn't a close match. Too short. But he suggested a couple of other possibilities, including one in Oregon. He says the sheriff there wasn't comfortable with the ID made twelve or thirteen years ago. He remembers that something about the fellow who claimed the body was his brother's set off warning bells. He's convinced the guy was lying."

"How would you suggest we check up on that one?" Braedon asked.

"You just get me that dental chart, and I'll do a little checking for you."

"I appreciate the help," Nicole told him. "But I know you're a busy man . . ."

"Don't you worry about it. I told you I enjoy the challenge of figuring out a mystery. There's not much happening around here right now, and I have an assistant chief to handle the tourists if they start giving me trouble, so I've got plenty of time to do a little looking around."

"Chief, there are a few things you should know." Braedon wasn't certain how much he should tell the man. Both threatening incidents had occurred outside the police chief's jurisdiction. Besides, there was something about the lawman's eagerness to help in the search that raised red flags in Braedon's mind. Chief Daniels had seemed to be testing him in some way when he first arrived in his office, and he had the uncomfortable feeling Daniels was not only a little too helpful, but he already knew more about the case than Braedon did, though he couldn't see how that was possible. When he returned to Fort Lewis, running a background check on the Port Angeles police chief would be one of his first priorities. Reluctantly he proceeded. "We were almost the victims of a suspicious accident last week, and today someone fired a shot at us."

"I wondered if you were going to tell me about that shiny new hole I noticed in your tailgate." The chief shook his head in what appeared to be genuine commiseration. "About a .38, wouldn't you say?"

Chapter 10

Morning dawned bright and clear, chasing away the doubts and worries of the night before. Nicole was ready when Braedon knocked on her door. Hastily picking up her small bag, she preceded him to the office, where she insisted on paying for her own room.

It was only a few short blocks to the docks where they found all-day parking for the truck. Nicole decided to leave her bag locked in Braedon's truck and carry only her small shoulder purse with her. Across the street, they could see cars forming a long line to board a large ferry and were glad Chief Daniels had suggested they leave the truck and purchase a tourist package that included the Butchart Gardens, a tour of Victoria, and round-trip passage on the ferry across the strait.

"If you would like to exchange any money, we can do that here," the ticket agent told them after they'd purchased their tickets.

"Won't I be able to use my credit card in Victoria?" Nicole asked.

"Certainly. Most businesses in Canada accept any of the major credit cards used here in the States, but if you want to buy drinks or small incidentals, you'll need cash. Of course, you can exchange your money on the Canadian side if you wish."

Braedon handed him a twenty and received back more than twenty Canadian dollars in return. Nicole decided to do the same. She took a moment to familiarize herself with the paper bills and handful of coins she was given before stuffing them inside her purse. They were the same denominations as U.S. money, but with the current exchange rate, they added up to slightly more. The small exchange of money added to the excitement of their impromptu venture. Though she'd been told her family lived in Germany for two years when she was little more than a baby and she had vague memories of a year in Japan, she felt like this was her first trip abroad.

"It's a little early, but we can board if you'd like." Braedon took her hand and led her out a door to where the ferry waited. Few people were aboard, so they took their time exploring. It wasn't large. The cabin was much like a bus or airplane with its rows of seats, except one end was partially partitioned off for a snack bar and a restroom. A stairway led off the snack area to where the captain and crew piloted the boat. Doors also opened from both ends of the cabin area to allow passengers to go out on deck or climb to an upper deck.

After a few minutes on the upper deck, they climbed back down to visit the snack bar. With small bottles of orange juice and donuts, they made their way to seats in the cabin. Almost half of the seats were now taken, and they hurried to find seats together. As they ate, the remainder of the ferry filled with passengers. Some were obvious tourists, but others looked like business commuters.

Nicole could swim, but she'd never learned to waterski, and she'd never taken her mother's new husband up on his offer of a short cruise along the Florida coast. She really didn't have much experience with boats, so perhaps that was why she found everything about this adventure thrilling, and her heart gave a little skip when Braedon leaned across her to watch through the window as the ferry moved away from the dock and headed for open water. Only a few minutes into their journey, she was surprised to see two seals sunning themselves on a buoy that rocked up and down in the water.

"Want to go back out on the deck?" Braedon asked, and she suspected from his tone that he was hoping she would say yes, which she did. It had been a long time since she'd felt so much eagerness to explore and to discover all life had to offer. And there was something about sharing this adventure with Braedon that added an extra dimension.

It was chilly on deck, and she found herself wishing she'd worn a heavier sweater or brought a jacket. Occasional gusts of spray dampened their clothes but not their enthusiasm. They pointed like children each time they spotted an ocean-going vessel or the occasional large fish that jumped in the water. Even watching Vancouver Island grow larger as they approached was fascinating.

She was almost sorry the journey was ending when the ferry pulled into the Victoria harbor. The momentary twinge of regret was quickly replaced by the sight of a pontoon plane landing in the harbor and her first glimpse of the castlelike Empress Hotel. Cruise ships lined one side of the docking area, and a diverse array of boats, including huge rubber rafts equipped with outboard motors, churned through the water.

Once they left the ferry, Nicole laughed to see a row of double-decker buses like those she'd seen in pictures of London lined up to meet the new arrivals. It took only minutes to discover which one they should climb aboard. They made their way to the top deck where they had a bird's-eye view of the city, complete with a running commentary from the driver below them. Though the buses looked clumsy and top-heavy, she found the ride comfortable and fun as they wove through city streets that reminded her of European movies.

A prickling at the back of her neck interrupted her enjoyment of the view. Casually she turned to scan the faces around her. She recognized a few people on the bus who had also been passengers on the ferry. Port Angeles was a popular tourist town, and she'd learned that many tours of Victoria and Vancouver Island start there, so recognizing fellow passengers from the ferry shouldn't have been surprising, but it reminded her of the reason for their journey to Port Angeles.

A man with a baseball cap pulled low over his eyes sat in a seat several rows back. He'd appeared to be asleep with the cap over his face on the ferry, and she wondered about his seeming disinterest in his surroundings and why he was traveling alone on a tourist bus. Perhaps he lived in Port Angeles but worked on the island. Two young men with backpacks sat in front of him. They might be college students, but they had seemed to show up wherever she and Braedon had gone on the ferry. A slightly overweight man accompanied by a woman with harshly bleached hair sat in the seat across the aisle from her and Braedon. She remembered the way they had nearly tripped a young couple with two small children to beat them to that front seat. They'd been on the ferry as well.

"Do you think whoever shot at us might have followed us this morning?" she leaned closer to Braedon to whisper.

Startled, he glanced around. He'd been enjoying himself so much, he'd let his defenses drop. Keeping his voice low, he asked, "Have you seen anything suspicious?"

"No . . . It was just a feeling we were being watched."

"Perhaps it's just a reminder to be more conscious of those around us. Tourists are often targeted by pickpockets," Braedon reminded her.

She knew he was right, and though he didn't say so, she wondered if he was thinking she was becoming a little paranoid. She couldn't help wondering that herself.

The bus carried them out of the city and into the quaint countryside. In front of nearly every farmhouse was a sign proclaiming something for sale, whether it was produce or fertilizer. The driver explained that most of the acreages were not really farms, but they produced just enough of some marketable product to keep their agricultural status, which lowered the homeowners' taxes.

Once they reached the gardens, Nicole was lost in the beauty around her. Though she'd become accustomed to seeing an array of blossoms in Washington, she was amazed at the profusion of flowers she found in the garden that had once been a quarry. They wandered slowly along the trails hand in hand, stopping frequently for a closer look or to snap a picture.

"Would you like a picture of the two of you together? We could take one of you, then you could take one of us." A young couple stood beneath an arch with their arms around each other.

"Uh, sure." Braedon handed his camera to the young man, then stepped back to Nicole's side.

"Put your arm around her," the young woman coached.

With a shrug of his shoulders, Braedon moved closer and placed an arm around Nicole. "We might as well play along," he whispered. "Besides, when my mother sees the picture, she'll be excited about more than the flowers."

Nicole laughed, and the young man took a couple more shots, then it was Braedon's turn to play photographer. He took one picture of the couple standing beneath the arch, then suggested they move to a small bench where there was less shadow on their faces. This time as he lifted the camera to his eye, a slight movement beyond the couple caught his attention. Perhaps a tourist had paused behind a row of shrubs to avoid ruining someone else's photo, but to him, there had appeared to be something furtive about the movement. Casually, he lowered the other man's camera and raised his own.

Focusing on the background rather than his supposed subjects, he clicked the shutter several times before switching cameras again. After a couple of different poses, he returned the camera.

"Thanks," the young woman smiled up at him. "You probably guessed we're on our honeymoon. Are you too? We're just so happy, and I can tell you are too." She linked her arm through her husband's and walked away without waiting for Braedon's answer.

He glanced at Nicole, noticing a troubled look in her eyes. She'd heard the question, and where he'd found a touch of humor in it, she appeared troubled.

"Look at that fountain. I think I've seen pictures of it before," he said in an effort to distract her. He took her hand and moved toward the famous Sirio Tofanari bronze, *Fountain of the Three Sturgeons.* They admired it for several minutes then moved on to the Japanese Garden. Nicole was quieter than she had been previously, and he was preoccupied by the thicker growth and isolated stretches of walkway in this part of the gardens. It occurred to him that this would be a prime location for an ambush. He took quick steps to catch up to a group of Asian tourists.

The memory of someone lurking just beyond the rose garden stayed near the surface of his mind. Instead of strolling in their former casual manner, he took pains to remain near other visitors as much as possible. But pausing on a small bridge to view a cluster of water lilies, they suddenly found themselves alone. A moment he would have earlier found romantic now seemed fraught with danger. He suspected Nicole's eagerness to follow the path on the other side of the bridge didn't stem from the same stimuli that drove him to be with a larger group of people. Unexpectedly, the path opened onto a wooden dock where a small, blue float plane anchored in a picturesque cove. Just leaving the cove was a single-mast sailboat, appearing as graceful as a bird in flight.

"It's beautiful," Nicole remarked. "Your mother will want to see this spot." Dutifully he brought the camera to his eye and snapped a picture before turning to another path Nicole pointed out after a quick check of the map they'd been given when they entered the gardens. She didn't seem to notice—or didn't mind—when he increased their pace to hurry along the path bordered by water on one side and a thick growth of trees on the other.

They emerged onto a circular path, and Braedon's eyes narrowed when he caught sight of the man with a baseball cap who had traveled with them both on the ferry and then on the bus. He was just stepping onto the circular walkway from a path on the other side of the trees that ran parallel to the one he and Nicole had followed. He considered confronting the man, but then he spotted two more familiar faces. The couple who had sat across the aisle from them on the bus were ensconced on a bench nearby with a perfect view of several trails.

By tacit agreement, they didn't linger over the remaining gardens. A glance at his watch told Braedon they had only half an hour until the tour bus would leave, and Nicole had mentioned a desire to purchase souvenirs for Marcie and the children.

He turned to her. "Do you want to look at souvenirs now?"

She nodded her head, and when they reached the little souvenir store, they found it crowded. That suited Braedon fine since he believed a crowd would provide some security.

The store was full of fascinating treasures, and they wound their way slowly through the throng of shoppers. A jewelry display caught his eye near where Nicole stopped to purchase a collector's spoon for Marcie. He decided to buy spoons for his sisters-in-law and a thimble to add to his mother's collection. Nicole went on to select T-shirts for her niece and nephew and a couple for herself, then she turned to a display of postcards. He took advantage of her momentary distraction to make another purchase of his own.

Turning back to where he'd left Nicole looking at postcards, he couldn't see her. Panic set in as he scanned the small store looking for her familiar dark locks. He didn't believe she would leave the store without him. Even if she'd wanted to visit the restrooms, he felt certain she wouldn't go without telling him.

"Braedon, we need to hurry." Startled, he whirled around to find Nicole, her arms full.

"Where did you go? I looked all over for you."

"I was right here." She looked at him warily, and he glanced down to see a display of stuffed toys in a huge bin and then noticed two small polar bears in her arms. He saw at once why he hadn't seen her. With her head and upper torso in the bin searching for the bears, he'd looked right past her.

"I'm sorry," he apologized with a sheepish grin. "You're not the only one who's a little jumpy. When I didn't see you, I panicked. I was afraid something might have happened to you."

"I'm a big girl. I can take care of myself. I also have good manners and would have let you know if I'd decided to leave without you." Nicole handed the clerk her credit card, wincing at the total.

"Remember, when you get the bill, it'll be less," he whispered in her ear. She silently computed the rate of exchange and grinned, her good humor restored. "I should have bought the red shirt too," she told him as they once again strolled amiably out the door and made their way to the bus. They didn't arrive in time to claim the front seat, but Nicole was pleased to see the family with young children there instead. The seats they found afforded them a great view of the trip back anyway.

The bus let them off on the shore side of the Empress Hotel. It was a picturesque spot with a view of the grand, old Victorian hotel on one side with a backdrop of blue water and a bridge and wharf on the other. They opted for lunch at one of the restaurants along the wharf.

Over seafood salads and long, thin loaves of hot bread, they relaxed beneath a bright umbrella and watched the big, yellow rubber rafts carrying tour groups setting out on their searches for whales. Musicians wound their way between the tables, and the sun glinted off the water. At one end of the wharf was a bridge spanning the water, allowing cars, trucks, double-decker buses, and a steady stream of rickshaws drawn by bicycles to pass over it. Pedestrians frequently paused to brace their arms on the heavy stone balustrades and watch where ships and boats passed beneath them. The real world seemed far away.

Braedon set his small shopping bag on the table and reached inside it. She watched him withdraw a slim box. He set the box on the table with a slight gesture toward her.

"Open it." He smiled and pushed the box closer to her.

She glanced at it, then back at him. Curiosity won out, and she reached for the box. With a finger and thumb she lifted the lid to find a delicate chain bracelet nestled on a bed of cotton. At evenly spaced intervals dangled an array of delicate porcelain blossoms, each one a different variety of flower.

"It's beautiful," she murmured.

"Try it on," Braedon encouraged.

"It looks expensive. I can't accept—"

"I want you to have it as a reminder of a beautiful day." He reached toward her, lifting the bracelet from its box. With deft motions, he fastened it around her wrist, then met her eyes with a twinkle in his. "Besides, it's too late to take it back."

She admired the bracelet for several minutes and pondered what to say. It was beautiful and a perfect souvenir of the garden she had enjoyed so much. More than that, it would always remind her of the man who fulfilled a childhood dream for her. Finally she settled for a simple, "Thank you."

"Finished?" Braedon asked a few minutes later, looking at their empty plates. She nodded. Gathering up their purchases, they made their way up a flight of steps to street level where they hurried across the street to another double-decker bus that took them for a tour around the city.

They remained on the bus for the entire trip, and she found herself relaxing and enjoying the tour. Though Braedon hadn't said anything, she'd noticed the little stunt he'd pulled with the cameras back at Butchart. She suspected he'd seen something she'd only sensed. She wondered if even during their lovely luncheon he'd felt eyes on them as she had a time or two. She also wondered if he meant to discuss whatever he'd seen and if he was only keeping quiet now in an effort not to mar what was an otherwise beautiful day—one of the best in her life.

She thought briefly of her father. He had wanted to bring their family here, and she felt regret that he'd never had that opportunity. As if he could read her thoughts, Braedon's hand settled on hers, and he asked, "You can't help thinking of him here, can you? Because he'd wanted to bring you here, I suppose, in a way, he's part of this place."

"No, not really a part of Victoria, though I recognize my desire to come here was fueled by his desire to bring me. I don't think the old city would have fascinated him the way it does me, and the gardens, as lovely as they are, would have been explored quickly. But watching the seals sun themselves on rocks, running on jagged beaches, searching for whales, and driving a motorcycle on country roads with the wind stinging his face would have brought him a great deal of pleasure."

"The outdoors type," Braedon commented.

"More than that. With Dad it was always more than just being outdoors. He said he never felt closer to God than when he felt the elements on his face and the earth beneath his feet. He climbed Mount Rainier once, and he said that as he stood in the clouds, a gust of wind created an opening that gave him a view that touched him to his soul, much like the moment when we were sealed together as an eternal family in the Mesa temple. He loved challenges, but he said being outdoors renewed him in some way."

Braedon squeezed Nicole's hand but said nothing. For several minutes, they sat quietly, viewing the coastline from a road that curved around a hill covered with beautiful old houses. In that silent action, she found a closeness to another human being she hadn't experienced since childhood.

"Steep hill. Hang on," the driver shouted cheerfully, and the bus swooped down a sharp incline. A few passengers squealed, most laughed, but the brief adventure ended their moment of quiet communion.

"We're almost back to our starting point, and we have an hour and a half before we need to board the return ferry. What would you like to do until then?" Braedon asked.

Nicole considered going inside the Empress Hotel to see as much of it as possible, but the tour driver had mentioned a chocolate factory. She'd like to buy some candy to take back with her, and the quaint shops and streets she'd seen from the bus were intriguing. She'd love to explore them.

"Let's do a little exploring on foot," she suggested. "If we wander down a few streets, we should still have plenty of time to get back to the ferry."

"Okay, but take it easy on the shopping," he teased. "We've already got plenty to carry." He held up his own tiny shopping bag in one hand and her much larger bag in the other.

"Wimp," Nicole teased.

The first shop they entered obviously catered to tourists. They wound their way through aisles of souvenirs without purchasing anything, then moved on to the next shop. They studied everything from art pieces to toys in the various stores as they drifted away from the wharf. Finally pausing on a street corner, they tried to look in all four directions. It was impossible to see far because a crowd of people had gathered to wait for the light to change.

"I don't see that chocolate shop anywhere," Nicole voiced her disappointment. "Marcie has a bigger sweet tooth than even I do, and I had hoped to buy her some specialty chocolates."

"Perhaps we could ask someone in there." Braedon pointed to the store behind them.

"I'm afraid it's too late. We should be starting back."

Braedon glanced at his watch and someone elbowed him. He staggered back, losing his grip on Nicole's hand. Immediately he sought to reconnect, but pressed between them was a short, heavyset woman. Over the head of the stout shopper he shouted, "We've still got time if it isn't too far out of our way."

"Okay . . ." Her response ended in a scream as something hard thumped against her back and sent her flying forward. Instinctively her arms propelled in a frantic gesture to regain her balance, but to no avail. She was falling toward a loud roar and the stench of burning rubber.

Chapter 11

From Braedon's height, he saw a nightmare unfolding. A powerful shoulder struck Nicole from behind then disappeared into the crowd. Braedon lunged forward to catch her. He was vaguely aware of the woman he trampled in the process screaming at him, but all he could see was Nicole falling toward the street where a double-decker bus was bearing down upon her.

"No," he shouted as he frantically shoved at the people in his way.

He caught a glimpse of a hand reaching out of the crowd to grip the back of Nicole's shirt. For what seemed an eon, she appeared suspended in space, then the hand jerked with enough force to send her sprawling backward onto the sidewalk at Braedon's feet. He felt the whoosh of air as the bus passed by and heard the screams and snorts of annoyance as the crowd pushed forward with the changing of the traffic light.

Dropping to his knees, he attempted to shelter Nicole from the crowd pressing toward the street and at the same time check her for injuries. Several bystanders inquired if she were all right or offered to call for an ambulance. He couldn't tell if the person who had rescued her was one of those who continued to linger nearby.

"I-I'm all right." She struggled to a sitting position, and Braedon noticed scrapes on her elbows and the backs of her arms. She sounded winded and dazed. A trickle of blood dripped on her pants from one of the larger scrapes.

"Help me up." She held out her hands to Braedon, and the few people who had paused to offer help drifted away.

"You shouldn't try to move." He attempted to discourage her from standing, but seeing she was determined to struggle to her feet anyway, he bent forward and placed an arm around her. Once upright, she wobbled and appeared unsteady, so he kept an arm around her. He knew that even if she were steady, he couldn't bear to not be touching her. He needed the feel of her slim form in his arms to assure himself that she had miraculously survived, that she was alive. The sight of that bus bearing down on Nicole would haunt his dreams for a long time.

"Someone pushed me." Her voice was indignant but pitched low enough to reach only Braedon. Her anger was somehow reassuring. He felt his own fear giving way to anger also, and he began looking around, wishing he could identify the shoulder that had shoved her toward the street. He had no doubt the shove had been deliberate.

A movement further down the street caught his attention, and he recognized a familiar figure. A man wearing jeans and a baseball cap was running toward the wharf. He glanced back once, then disappeared into a doorway. Braedon's first impulse was to go after him, but the pressure of Nicole's fingers gripping his hands changed his mind. He couldn't leave her to fend for herself.

"Can you walk?" he asked.

"I think so." She took a cautious step, and he suspected she hurt more than she was admitting. When she'd been pulled backward, she'd abruptly sat on the hard sidewalk with enough force to drive the air from her lungs and probably bruise her behind. The instinctive gesture of bracing her arms to catch her fall had left her with deep abrasions.

He was just contemplating carrying her back to the wharf when a voice spoke up, "Sir, bring the lady inside my shop, and we'll find bandages for her arms and something to drink. I've got your parcels, all safe and sound."

Looking up he saw a slender, stooped woman of sixty or so standing in the doorway of the nearest shop, holding the shopping bags he'd been carrying earlier and had since forgotten entirely. He turned to Nicole, and she nodded her head. With his help, she moved gingerly toward the woman and the shop door.

With his arm around Nicole, Braedon didn't notice the name of the shop or the bright display windows until he stepped past the woman. Then he did a double take. Had he bumped his head?

Surrounded by a platoon of nutcrackers and a forest of evergreens covered in twinkling lights, he'd stepped off the street on a July afternoon straight into a Christmas wonderland.

"Here you go, miss." The woman handed Nicole a cup of water, which she drained slowly while looking around. Her face lit up in pleasure at the array of ornaments and lights surrounding her.

"You have a Christmas shop!" No longer sounding frightened, Nicole was looking around in wonder. "When I was a little girl, my father took us to see the *Nutcracker* in Austin. Then for Christmas that year, and each year after, he gave my sister and me nutcracker dolls. I've bought a few more since then, but I've never seen such a wonderful display as this before." Slowly she moved toward the nutcrackers. She fingered the uniform of a figure dressed in the red coat of a Canadian Mountie.

While Nicole looked at the nutcrackers, Braedon returned to the front of the store. From beside a six-foot nutcracker guarding the entrance, he examined the street. Everything had happened so quickly, he had no idea how he and Nicole had become separated or who might have been close enough to push Nicole into oncoming traffic—nor did he know who had reached out to pull her back. He'd seen enough to know her fall had been no accident. There had been something calculated in the push he'd witnessed.

And who had pulled her back? Why hadn't he stayed around to be thanked or at least be assured that she was safe? Had Nicole seen more of either man than he had? He had no intention of asking questions about the incident until they were alone, but he couldn't help wondering if the person who pushed her might make another attempt on her life. He thought of the man with the baseball cap. It seemed that man had been everywhere he and Nicole had gone today, and Braedon was almost certain he'd been the man running away after Nicole's injury. But he didn't quite fit the picture Braedon had formed in his mind of Nicole's assailant. He'd only seen a shoulder, but he couldn't help thinking the shoulder belonged to a larger man.

He studied the shadow in a doorway far down the street. It could be the same doorway the baseball-capped man had disappeared into. The distance was too far and the shadow too indistinct to draw any conclusions, but Braedon turned to the shopkeeper and asked, "Is there another door out of here? I noticed this store occupies a corner."

"Oh, yes. You can enter from either street." She pointed to where a couple was entering the shop from a side street.

"I think we'll leave that way," he said, once more gathering up Nicole's bags.

"Thank you for your kindness and for looking after our bags," Nicole told the woman. Braedon added his thanks. "And I'm sure my sister will love this nutcracker for her collection." She held up another small shopping bag. Braedon suspected the purchase was Nicole's subtle way of thanking the woman for her kindness.

"Would you like one large bag to hold all of your purchases?" the woman asked.

"Yes, thank you." Braedon surrendered the bags to the shop-keeper, who swiftly packed them inside a large, sturdy bag.

"I'd like these too." Braedon picked up a twelve-inch Mountie nutcracker and another one with a tall fur hat and set them both on the counter before reaching for his wallet. His mother would love getting a nutcracker, and he could give Nicole the red-coated policeman. She had seemed intrigued with it, and he too wanted to repay the kind woman for her help.

After thanking the woman again, they stepped through the door to the side street. They'd have to hurry to reach the ferry before it left, but Braedon figured it would be better to miss the ferry than to encourage Nicole to walk any faster than was comfortable for her. He also meant to be far more vigilant about watching their surroundings and the people they encountered than he'd been before. He thought of the shadow in a doorway that might have been a man.

He looped the handle of the shopping bag over one arm, then placing his other one around Nicole's waist, they began to walk.

He was careful to avoid walking or standing near curbs and approached street crossings with maximum care. Feeling exposed as they hurried across the Inner Harbour Causeway, he regretted that there was no time to pause in appreciation of the magnificent view of the setting sun across the sparkling harbor. He was vaguely aware of colorful sailboats, bright yellow pontoon rafts, and graceful catama-rans below the bridge, but he was also aware of jostling pedestrians, swiftly moving cars and buses, and the bicycle-drawn rickshaws where someone could hide behind an umbrella awning. Out of the corner of his eye, he kept seeing shadows that might be a small man wearing a blue baseball cap pulled low over his eyes.

Reaching the end of the bridge, he led the way toward the government buildings a short distance away. A sharp wind gusted off the water, warning that evening was approaching. Nicole pulled her light sweater close with one hand but didn't comment on the sudden temperature change. She hadn't spoken since they started their return to the ferry, and he wondered if he'd rushed her too much. He could hear her breathing and tried to analyze whether she was breathing harder than normal. When they ran together, she never seemed to show exertion, but she'd fallen hard. He should have called a cab, he chided himself, but he'd been so focused on getting her back to the ferry, he hadn't given enough thought to whether or not she was up to the hike.

"Are you okay?" he asked as they stepped inside the customs building, which seemed dark and dingy after hours in the bright light. He began at once searching the shadows for anything suspicious.

"I'm fine." She brushed a hand through her thick hair, and he saw a tiny tremor in the motion. "I'll be glad to get back to Fort Lewis though."

He felt a wave of concern. The crossing would take a couple of hours, then the drive back to base would involve at least two more, probably three. If Nicole were injured more severely than they had first supposed, they'd need to find a doctor in Port Angeles. And if she were only tired and frightened, should he take her home or find hotel rooms for the night? He presumed that whoever had pushed her into oncoming traffic was the same person who had fired at them the day before and was still out there somewhere watching them. It was even possible that more than one person wanted to hurt her.

"Let's see how soon we can board." He placed an arm around her and led her toward a security guard who told them that if they had nothing to declare, they could proceed to the waiting area.

The waiting area was the same concrete walls and plastic chairs of a million bus stations, and he selected a couple of seats where he had a good view of the doors and hallways. Nicole winced as he helped her to one of the uncomfortable seats but didn't complain. He took care to sit between her and the rest of the room. A middle-aged couple with half a dozen children wearing school uniforms sat by them, and Braedon decided to wait until they were aboard the ferry-boat to pursue any discussion.

Boarding the ferry was more formal on the Canadian side than it had been that morning in Port Angeles. The waiting seemed interminable, but the passengers were finally allowed to line up to file past a uniformed guard who glanced at their tickets before permitting them to proceed.

At last Nicole sank into a window seat and wearily laid her head against the glass. Though sitting wasn't exactly comfortable, she didn't think she could stand for one more minute. She was so tired. She'd been less exhausted after running a marathon than she was now. Her training both as a runner and as a medical administrator told her the overwhelming fatigue she was experiencing was more emotional than physical. She felt Braedon settle next to her and didn't object when his arm came around her, holding her as though he would hold at bay the chilly night air and all her fears.

They were well out on the water when she roused herself enough to look around. There were fewer passengers on this return trip than there had been on the outgoing trip that morning. She thought of that trip with a touch of nostalgia, as though it were a distant memory. It had seemed so glowingly perfect. Her eyes searched with nervous intensity for familiar faces, and she wondered if the person who had pushed her was now sitting in the same cozy cabin. She didn't see anyone remotely familiar. But there were several people toward the back who appeared to be sleeping with their faces partially covered by newspapers, and there were people up on deck in spite of the chill wind.

The water was becoming choppy, and lights were on in the cabin with the onset of evening. Her stomach felt a little queasy, and she wondered if she might be suffering a touch of motion sickness. More likely it was the culmination of the fall and their rapid retreat to the ferry. She'd been too busy, and perhaps too shocked, to think about what had happened until now, but as she pressed her face against Braedon's light sweater and heard the steady rhythm of his heart against her ear, her mind began exploring and asking questions.

Pulling back from Braedon's arms, she looked up into his face. "This is because of Dad, isn't it?"

"I think so."

"It has to be." She pulled herself straighter and looked around to be certain they couldn't be overheard. "This makes three attacks—the dump truck, that bullet hole in your truck, and being pushed in front of a bus. Nothing like this ever happened to me until I started looking for Dad."

"Did you see who pushed you?"

"No, but I know I was pushed. I felt something hard hit my back, and as I stumbled forward a hand shoved me toward the street. It couldn't have been an accident." She said the last as though she expected an argument.

"I saw just enough to be certain it wasn't an accident," he assured her with a sigh. "There was deliberate intent behind the shoulder I saw lunge into your back. It happened so fast, I can't even say what color shirt or coat your assailant was wearing, just something dark. Because of the angle, I think he was near your own height or possibly a little taller."

"Did you see who pulled me back? Was he the same person?"

"I don't know," he answered the second question first. "I didn't really see anyone. You were suddenly flying back toward me, and the crowd was shifting, beginning to move toward the intersection. I felt the air from the bus going by, and I must have dropped your shopping bag, though I don't remember doing it. When I knelt beside you, I thought I caught a glimpse of that man with the baseball cap we both noticed earlier."

"Do you think he pushed me?" She was surprised he was aware she'd been suspicious of the man.

"I just don't know. But he was everywhere we went today." He paused, then asked, "Why did you ask if the person who pushed you was the same person who pulled you back?"

"Last night you said the attacks lacked professionalism and may have been intended as warnings. I thought this might have been a warning too." She appeared thoughtful. "It just seems strange that whoever pulled me back didn't stay around to make certain I was all right."

"If it was a warning, it was a particularly nasty one." Braedon didn't appear convinced the incident was a warning, and her own fear was too close to the surface to allow her to believe someone hadn't intended her to die, or at the very least be seriously injured.

Nicole leaned back, staring out the window. She supposed it was called a porthole, but it was hard to think in nautical terms when she knew little about boats or bodies of water. It was true her mother was married to a man who lived on a small yacht, but she'd only visited them once, and then only briefly. During that visit to Florida, Teddy had kept his yacht anchored at the wharf.

She saw long, white lines form on the water, and as they rushed toward the ferryboat, they grew in size until they broke against it or dissolved in shifting hills and valleys around them. A large fish leaped high in the air, then shot straight back down into the black water.

"Did you see that?" She clutched Braedon's arm.

"See what?"

"It was a fish, a really long, thin one. It jumped just like a trout, only much higher."

"No, I didn't see it. I wasn't watching the water." His voice told her he was holding himself responsible for today's attack and that he was focusing on the other passengers, trying to make certain they weren't taken by surprise again.

"Do you expect there'll be trouble driving back to the base?" she asked.

"If someone followed us from Port Angeles, they'll know where we left my truck and that we'll be returning to get it. We need to stay alert."

As they neared Port Angeles, the wind almost disappeared and the waters grew calmer. Braedon suggested they go on deck where they could disembark first to give themselves a head start should Nicole's attacker be aboard the ferry. Clutching her shopping bag with one hand, he led the way.

Emerging from the cabin, Braedon noticed the air felt chilled even though the wind had died down. He moved to where they could watch both the dock they were approaching and the cabin door. He took care to position himself between Nicole and the few hardy passengers standing on the front deck, none of whom seemed to show them any particular attention.

Once the gangplank was in place, he gripped Nicole's elbow and moved forward. Other passengers streamed toward it too, carrying packages and sleeping children. Keeping an eye on the other passengers, he took cautious but hurried steps, breathing a sigh of relief when he felt the solid wharf beneath their feet.

"Okay, let's cut through the building where there's plenty of light and people," he said under his breath so only Nicole could hear, while moving toward the lighted doorway. Two steps inside the building, a low voice from somewhere to their right stopped them.

"Don't turn around. Just keep walking toward that far door. I'll be right behind you."

Chapter 12

Braedon recognized the gravelly voice of Chief Daniels. His first instinct was to turn around and confront the man. He'd known something wasn't right from the moment they'd met, but he hadn't considered that the chief was involved in the plot against Nicole. He was the one person who knew of his and Nicole's plan to visit Victoria, and he'd had plenty of time to arrange for someone to follow them. He never should have trusted the man, and he wouldn't blindly walk into a trap now.

"Chief . . ." He stopped, turning partway toward the man who had told them to keep walking.

"Not now. Our priority has to be to protect Nicole." The police chief was walking on the opposite side of her. Braedon moved closer, and as he did so he noticed Daniels never glanced toward him or Nicole, but his eyes were busy scanning each darkened doorway as he propelled Nicole across the barnlike hall. Hurrying to keep up, Braedon found himself watching shadowed doorways too and calculating the distance between the building and the lot where he'd left his truck. He wished he knew if the police chief was leading them into a trap or sincerely trying to protect them.

"I'll go first." Daniels stepped ahead to push open the door. He walked through, then held it open for them. Braedon looked around, searching for a group of fellow travelers, but the other ferry passengers seemed to have disappeared. Exiting the building as part of a group would be safer, and he continued to hesitate. Seeing a handful of people leaving from a door on the other side of the vast building, he considered dashing across the hall to join them, but a tug on his hand signaled that Nicole was already following Daniels through the door.

Cool air brushed his cheeks as he glanced up and down the street, seeing nothing that appeared out of place or threatening. Was he overreacting? Or was the calm hiding a sneak attack?

"Hurry," the chief's voice urged them toward the crosswalk. Still leery of the man rushing them toward the street, Braedon hung back, then noticing a group of seven or eight people approaching the crosswalk from the side of the ferry building, he took Nicole's arm and hurried to cross with the group. Halfway across the street, he caught sight of a dark car without lights idling farther down the street. It might be a coincidence, but he wasn't waiting around to see. He increased his stride, and by the time they reached the curb, all three were running.

A patrol car with two uniformed officers was parked in the space behind his truck, blocking other vehicles' departure from the lot. Braedon opened the passenger door of his truck, and Nicole slid inside. He closed the door before sprinting around to take his place behind the wheel. He was reaching for the door handle when Chief Daniels clapped a hand on his shoulder.

"Drive carefully and don't stop until you're back on base," he warned. "Follow that patrol car as far as Gardner." He pointed to the vehicle behind his. "I'll follow in my own truck until you reach the freeway. Once you're on base, you'll be all right, but call me at the beginning of the week. We need to talk." He spun away and with long-legged strides hurried to a dark green F-250 parked a few slots away.

Braedon wrenched open the door of his truck and settled inside. He glanced briefly at Nicole, who sat with her seat belt fastened and a worried expression on her face. A twist of the key and the engine roared to life.

"Keep your head down," he admonished as he threw the truck in reverse. Moments later, he was speeding down the street, barely managing to keep up with the patrol car ahead of him. In his side mirror, he found a pair of headlights staring back at him.

* * *

When he walked, he waddled like a penguin, except no self-respecting penguin would ever be found in all this heat and sand.

One hundred and twenty pounds of gear and Kevlar armor with carbide ceramic plates might make him look like the Michelin man, sweat like a pig, and walk like some kind of strange fowl, but he thanked God every day for the miracle gear that stood between him and a bullet or grenade each time he scouted for a convoy headed down one of the highways of this bleak country. Today was no exception. The terrorist attacks on convoys as well as civilian targets were escalating, increasing the risk to the soldiers who rode out ahead of the convoys with rifles and scopes to scour the road for bombs and the surrounding hills for hostile forces.

Only those soldiers who were crack shots and who were physically strong enough to run in full armor were given the dubious honor of riding on top of a modified Humvee watching for the enemy from a highly exposed position. J.D. didn't relish the assignment, but he was a soldier, and he took satisfaction in being able to do his part to defend the convoys and serve his country. Anyway, he'd far rather lead a convoy than take part in any of the unpleasant tasks associated with keeping a wartime military base clean. Most of the soldiers in his unit were stuck collecting and burning human waste today. Every soldier on base would be glad when the KBR contractors arrived to take over that chore.

There was no adjusting his helmet or easing the weight on his arms. His full attention was focused on the surrounding countryside. Ahead they would pass through a small village, the kind of village that always brought an element of the unknown to the job.

He tensed as a group of children ran from the few squat houses toward the convoy. Children were so misleading: sometimes they were the innocents they appeared to be, excited to see the Americans and eager to shake the soldiers' hands or accept a stick of gum. Other times, dark-haired little girls were wired with bombs, or they might be a diversion for hidden terrorists waiting with guns, and too often, small boys threw rocks that turned out to be grenades.

The driver continued his steady pace, only waving briefly at the children who lined the road waiting for the convoy that followed. A movement behind the children caught J.D.'s eye, and he turned his rifle toward the movement. Two little girls in long robes or dresses ran to join the other children. The older child appeared to be about six or seven and held the hand of the smaller child. They pushed past the other children to dash for the far side of the road where they would have a better view of the coming spectacle.

An explosion rocked the Humvee, but J.D. knew at once it hadn't been hit. They continued to move forward for several lengths with J.D. turning from side to side, seeking a target of aggression before they came to a halt, but no rifle fire or grenades followed the single explosion. A woman's high-pitched scream brought his sites around to where several women and an old man could be seen running toward the road where two small girls lay, their slight bodies mangled and torn. One woman knelt in the dust, screaming beside the lifeless young bodies.

Banking his anger and sorrow for the two needless deaths and the pictures of his own two small children that flashed through his mind, he noted the arrival of the convoy and the soldiers who quickly formed a protective perimeter around the fallen children and their grieving families. It was useless to ask how the Humvee had passed so near the roadside bomb without detonating its terrible violence, only for it to be tripped seconds later by innocent children. He didn't waste time blaming himself for his failure to spot the bomb. He was well aware of the cleverness of Saddam loyalists and al Qaeda insurgents in the way they hid their bombs and their complete absence of concern for the lives of those who got in the way of their drive for power.

As the soldiers responsible for Bradleys and automatic weapons assumed defensive positions, the first soldier to sprint from behind the heavy war machine to check on the children was his tentmate, Specialist Cassaday. J.D. spared just one brief moment to thank his Heavenly Father that his own children were safe at home in America. He promised Him too, that he would do all in his power to prevent the senseless hate and violence that took the two little girls' lives from spreading further.

*   *   *

It wasn't raining as Braedon and Nicole made their way back to Fort Lewis, making the trip smoother, though it seemed long because of their anticipation of some kind of attack. At first, Braedon drove in grim silence. Nicole was busy mulling over in her mind all that had happened that day.

"How did Chief Daniels know we needed protection?" Nicole finally voiced her thoughts aloud.

"I've been wondering about that too." There was anger in Braedon's voice. "I don't know why he would send someone to follow us unless he's somehow connected to your father's disappearance, but what other explanation is there for his knowing you had been attacked while we were in Victoria?"

"You don't think . . . ?" Her voice trailed off. "I'm certain he isn't either of the men who were with Dad that day, but if he was involved with them, that would explain why he's taken such an interest in our search." One part of her head told her that was the only explanation, but another continued to tell her she could trust the police chief.

"But if he was involved in what happened to Dad, why did he meet the ferry and help us get out of Port Angeles?" She asked aloud the question that troubled her.

"I don't know," Braedon answered. "He might be leading us into a trap. If anything happened to us in Port Angeles, it might be traced to him."

"I don't think that's it. I think he really is trying to help us. I just don't know why."

In Gardner, the police cruiser pulled to the side of the road, allowing them to pass, leaving Nicole with a sense of abandonment until she noticed the same strong headlight beams in the mirror that had followed them from the ferry parking lot. Perhaps that should frighten her more, but it didn't. There was something reassuring about the steady beam of light following them into the night.

* * *

J.D. followed a fast, cold shower with an even faster hike to his tent. When he stepped inside, Cassaday was already there. The other man didn't look up from the small Bible he held in his lap. His head was bowed, but J.D. sensed he was neither reading nor praying.

"Bad day?" he asked as he readied himself for bed.

"Why would God let something like that happen?" Cassaday turned reddened eyes toward him, and J.D. remembered his tentmate had been with the convoy earlier that day. Cassaday was a good soldier and never flinched from any security detail. He was a good man to have beside him in a firefight, but like many of even the toughest soldiers, he struggled with the suffering war heaped on children. "They were just little kids. They didn't do anything to deserve dying like that."

"There's something about the death of a child that offends our sensibilities. I think we're conditioned to expect an orderliness to life and death, believing we should depart in much the same order we arrive. Children shouldn't precede parents or grandparents. Not only does the loss of innocents who did nothing to deserve abuse stir us to anger, but the pain of those who loved them and looked forward to their future accomplishments strikes some chord of empathy within us. All that loss feels unbearable."

"God should have stopped it. The Bible tells us God loves little children, but what kind of love allows little children be blown apart by bombs?"

"Wait a minute," J.D. reached out to the angry young man seated across from him. "You're blaming God when you should be blaming the terrorist who set that bomb. God didn't hurt those children. In fact, I feel confident He welcomed them with open arms. They'll never be subjected again to the hate and bigotry that took their lives. But they will continue to grow and progress, blessed by the Savior's love for them."

"Why shouldn't I blame God? Everything happens according to His plan, doesn't it?"

"Not exactly." J.D. wished he were better versed in the scriptures. He read and studied them regularly, but he'd never had the ability to memorize passages or recall their exact words during a discussion. "I know your faith in God is strong and that you're a praying man. Ask God to help you understand. If you like, we could pray together tonight."

"Right now I'm too angry to pray. I'm not sure we're accomplishing any good by being here."

J.D. sat on the edge of his bunk with his clasped hands between his knees and his head bowed. "I get frustrated too, but I'm here because I believe freedom is worth any price."

"I believe that too." Cassaday spoke slowly. "Before I enlisted, I read somewhere that America's Founding Fathers pledged their lives, their fortunes, and their honor to the cause of freedom. President Roosevelt said something similar when he announced our country's entry into World War II. He acknowledged that the war would cost more than we could afford in lives and money, but he believed liberty was worth any price. That's part of what I find discouraging—too many people think the economy and politics are what really matter."

"My grandfather taught me that in the long run it's God's opinion that matters, and if I listen to that quiet prompting inside of me that tells me when something is right or wrong, I'll be okay."

"And does that prompting inside you tell you this war is okay?"

"I'm not sure war is ever okay." J.D. took pains to give his thoughts careful expression. "But I do know it's right to honor your commitments to God and country. It's right to stand up in defense of those who are weaker than you. And it's right to stand up for freedom."

Cassaday was quiet so long, J.D. thought he'd gone to sleep or didn't want to talk anymore. He got off his cot and knelt beside it to pray, then climbed into bed, pulling only a thin covering over himself. He lay on his back, wishing he could somehow offer his friend a greater measure of peace.

He was almost asleep when Cassaday spoke again. "Thanks, Duran. Talking helped. I haven't really doubted our cause was just, it was being unable to help those children or understand their senseless deaths that got to me."

J.D. raised up on one elbow and spoke into the darkness. "God understands how much you wanted to save those little girls just as He understands how many other children are safe and free because of the work you're doing here. You can't save them all, but remember, God holds us responsible not only for our successes but for the intents of our hearts."

Chapter 13

Nicole was surprised to see Braedon waiting for her when she left her sister's house Monday morning. It had been late when they returned Saturday night, and Marcie had insisted she stay in bed and nurse her injuries Sunday, so they hadn't met at church. Marcie had spoken with him briefly when he'd asked about her, but he hadn't called or said anything to Marcie about running with Nicole this morning. Seeing him gave her spirits a lift she attempted to ignore.

"Hi," he greeted her. "I wasn't sure you'd feel up to running this morning. I thought you might be a little stiff but decided to take a chance."

"I'm fine." She started her warm-up routine and discovered she did have a few tender spots, though she didn't admit to them out loud. She let Braedon set the pace when they started running, and she didn't complain when he chose a slow, steady jog.

"What brings you out this morning?" she asked. "I don't remember discussing running this morning. In fact, I had intended to sleep in again."

"Why didn't you?" He ignored her question by asking one of his own.

"Habit, I guess. I woke up at the same time I always wake up and decided I might as well run."

"I couldn't sleep. I missed you at church and thought about coming over to check on you, but your sister thought it best to let you rest. After lying there counting sheep, or more literally recounting all that has happened since we started looking for answers about your father, I got up and turned on my computer. I figured if I couldn't sleep, I might as well be productive. Besides, I have to work today, and I probably wouldn't be able to concentrate on anything else until I learned a little more about Chief Daniels."

He left the road for a path that angled toward American Lake, and she wondered if the sight of an approaching car was the reason he chose to leave the road for the more narrow path.

"What were you researching?" she asked while keeping her head slightly turned to watch the car pass the spot where the trail branched off from the road. Satisfied that it wasn't stopping or slowing down, she concentrated more fully on Braedon's answer.

"I did a little checking on our police chief friend."

"And?"

"He retired from the army eight years ago, moved to Virginia, and took some government job. Because there's so little information available, I suspect it was in a high-security area. Two months ago, he applied for the police chief position and was hired almost immediately by the city of Port Angeles. Other than a few basics, his military record is classified. A story that appeared in the local paper when he was hired as police chief said he's a widower with two adult children who live in the east and that he gained his law enforcement credentials in the army."

"Do you think he was an MP?" Nicole wondered aloud.

Braedon ducked beneath a low-hanging tree branch before answering. "Possibly, but if your father was working for the Criminal Investigation Division as I suspect he was, Daniels may have been CID as well."

"How can we find out?" Nicole slowed her steps. Her body ached, and her mind wasn't really on running. "Couldn't you get into trouble for snooping in records that have nothing to do with your current assignment?"

"I could, but there's nothing more I have access to that might be helpful, and without a higher security clearance, I can't go any further into military records anyway. Daniels said to call him this morning, and I think I should. If I can, I'll arrange for him to meet us in some public place."

"That sounds melodramatic." She felt a silly urge to giggle but managed to stop herself.

Braedon pulled up beside a large tree that leaned out over the water of the picturesque lake. "You're right. Making arrangements to meet someone I don't quite trust but who may have some of the answers we're looking for and specifying a public place does sound melodramatic. I keep asking myself if this whole case is something I conjured up in my mind because I was primed to go to war and instead found myself in Washington State without a lot to do and a beautiful woman I'd like to impress. Then I remember there's a bullet hole in the tailgate of my truck and someone shoved you in front of a bus two days ago."

"Don't forget the dump truck, and there was a car Saturday night near the wharf without lights that could have been waiting for us to cross the street."

"You noticed the car too? I thought I was being paranoid."

"We might both be a little paranoid," she admitted. She chose to ignore his "beautiful woman" comment, though it brought a pleasant warmth to her heart. "I'm sorry I made that crack about being melodramatic. I really do appreciate the help you've given me. It's just that a part of me would like to think what's been happening isn't real."

"I know what you mean. Things like this don't happen to ordinary people like me, so it feels more like some elaborate party game. But all I have to do to convince myself it's real is run my finger across that hole in my truck's tailgate." She shivered, and he wasn't certain whether it was from cold because they'd stopped running or if it was the reminder of the bullet hole, which proved all that had happened to them wasn't some fantastic game.

"I feel safe here on base, even though I know that could be an illusion." She walked toward the water.

He followed behind her, and when she stopped at the water's edge, he expressed the conclusion he'd reached. "I think we should meet with Daniels as soon as possible. This whole thing started here on base, and there's no guarantee we're safer here than we'd be anywhere else. But if you're uncomfortable, you don't have to go. I'll meet with him myself."

"No, it's my father's disappearance we're investigating, and wherever it takes us, I have to be there."

* * *

Marcie set a glass of orange juice in front of John David before switching on the computer. While it warmed up, she scrambled eggs and put bread in the toaster. She glanced longingly at the brightly lit screen, then placed her son's breakfast in front of him and helped him say a brief blessing before seating herself in front of the computer to pull up her e-mail. A smile lit her face when she saw she had a message from her husband.

> *I only have a minute, honey, but I just wanted to tell*
> *you I love you. Yesterday some children were killed by a*
> *roadside bomb near here, and it made me so grateful that*
> *you and our children are in a safe place. I miss all of you*
> *and look forward to when we'll be together again.*
> *Love,*
> *J.D.*

She reread the message several times before dishing up her own breakfast. Hearing from her husband gave her a lift, yet the message saddened her. She didn't like to think of children being the victims of terrorist bombing. She thought of her own children and echoed her husband's sentiments—she was glad they were far from the war zone.

Instead of sitting at the table, she carried her plate back to the desk where the computer sat. While she ate, she started a reply to her husband's e-mail, telling him about the children's activities and how nervous she felt teaching Relief Society, even though her first couple of lessons had gone well.

> *Friday I took Lexie for her checkup. She's doing great*
> *and has gained four pounds since you saw her last. John*
> *David wandered off while we were waiting for the*
> *doctor. He didn't want to sit still and kept running*
> *around the waiting room. Nicole wasn't with me because*
> *she and Braedon went to Port Angeles for the day.*
> *Anyway, I lost sight of him and had just gathered up the*
> *baby to go look for him when an older man walked into*
> *the room carrying him. John David was screaming and*
> *struggling to get down. I took him and tried to calm him,*

but he stayed upset and kept yelling "no" while the man was trying to explain that he'd found my son in the hall looking for a drinking fountain. He said the strangest thing; it was almost like a threat. He said a child who isn't watched closely enough can get into a lot of trouble, and children who tell tales might disappear. John David was making such a fuss that the man's words didn't sink in at first, and after I got him calmed down I looked around to thank him for bringing my son to me, but he'd left. He really creeped me out. I asked the pediatrician about him, but he didn't recognize him from my description. Next time I go there, if Nicole can't go with me, I'll find a sitter for John David.

Sandra Keyes has decided to go live with her parents in South Dakota while her husband is deployed. She moved out over the weekend. Sgt. Willdon's wife, Gretchen, is working day shift at the hospital now, so our triplex feels awfully quiet all day, and John David misses having the Willdons' twins to play with. I'm glad Nicole . . .

Hearing a key turn in the lock, she turned around to see Nicole entering the house. Through the window, she caught sight of Braedon's truck pulling away. The two were spending an awful lot of time together. She hid her smile of satisfaction before turning to greet her sister.

"Hi. This is starting to look serious," she teased. "You two are spending a lot of time together, but I'm glad you're feeling better. I've been anxious to hear all about your trip. I assume you had a good time in Victoria."

"Mmm, yes and no." Nicole glanced toward John David, then started toward the stairs. "I think I better shower, then I'll fill you in on all that happened."

Nicole's reply whetted Marcie's curiosity, and as soon as she finished her letter, she settled her son in front of the television with his favorite Bible video. It was time for a sister-to-sister chat, she told herself as she made her way up the stairs.

When Nicole emerged from the bathroom, Marcie was seated with the baby in her arms at the end of Nicole's bed.

"All right, tell me all about it." Marcie patted the spot beside her on the bed. Nicole didn't sit, but began to pace.

"Come on," Marcie coaxed. "I've been to Victoria. It's beautiful, and even though you fell and were injured there, I doubt a simple fall is the reason you appear to be upset. Since you saw Braedon this morning and seem to be on good terms, a serious disagreement with him apparently isn't the problem, so what happened to upset you? Did you find out something about Dad when you got back to Port Angeles?"

"I just don't know where to begin," Nicole said. "Victoria was fabulous, and I'd love to return there some day, but something happened that marred the day for us. You know we went to Port Angeles to meet with the police chief there and talk about a body that washed up near there about the time Dad disappeared. I soon realized the body couldn't be Dad's, but the chief seemed unusually anxious to help us continue our search with other possible leads. Braedon doesn't trust him, and I don't know what to think. We both think he's hiding something, yet I felt then, and still feel, we should trust him." She took a deep breath and continued pacing.

"We went to Victoria and were having a great time until someone pushed me in front of a bus. I didn't just fall. A quick-thinking stranger jerked me back onto the sidewalk and saved my life." Marcie gasped, but Nicole hurried on. "When we got back to Port Angeles, the police chief met us and seemed to know all about the incident, though we hadn't reported it."

"Nicole! You could have been killed!" Marcie reached for her sister, who sank down on the bed beside her.

"I'm fine, but that isn't all. The chief followed us back here. We aren't sure whether he was trying to protect us by following us, or if he was somehow involved in the incident. And . . . there's a bullet hole in the back of Braedon's truck. Someone fired a shot at us when we stopped for lunch on our way to Port Angeles."

"Someone shot at you?" Marcie's voice rose, and she felt something tight clench in the pit of her stomach. There had been two attempts on her sister's life in one weekend.

"We're both all right." Nicole offered quick reassurance. "We didn't even know someone had shot at us. We stopped to eat our lunch at a little pullout where we spotted a picnic table. It started to rain, so we grabbed everything and ran for the truck. Braedon stepped on a corner of the tablecloth I was carrying, and we both fell. There was a loud sound as we fell, but we just thought it was thunder until Braedon saw the bullet hole in his truck."

Nicole stood and took a few steps to the mirror where she picked up a hairbrush and began brushing out her hair with quick, hard sweeps. "We're pretty sure the attacks have something to do with our search for Dad, and that's why I'm telling you this. I think we're safe here on base, but we can't be sure. We also think whoever is doing these things is only after me because he thinks I can identify him, but just in case, you need to be careful. I couldn't bear for anything to happen to you or the children."

Marcie felt her head begin to spin. She must have made some sound because Nicole spun around to face her. "Marcie, what is it?"

"Friday," she gasped. "When I took Lexie to her pediatrician . . . A man . . . He said John David left the waiting room, but John David insists he didn't. He said the man took him, then brought him back. He said . . . Something bad could happen . . . I thought he meant John David . . . But he might have meant you."

"All right. Slow down. Tell me exactly what happened." Nicole returned to the bed to sit beside her. Her sister's arm came around her. Words spilled from her mouth as she tried to recount all that had happened at the pediatrician's office. Nicole asked questions, filling in the blanks in her narrative. Then it was Nicole's turn to catch Marcie up on missed details of her recent experience.

"So, Braedon is calling Chief Daniels tomorrow morning to set up a meeting. He knows something. I'm sure of it," Nicole finished.

"I want to go with you." Nicole wasn't sure she'd heard her sister right. Marcie looked as shocked by the words that came from her mouth as Nicole was at hearing them. She couldn't blame her. Nicole knew Marcie rarely took chances or volunteered for anything that involved risk.

"What about the children?" Nicole asked. Surely Marcie didn't plan to take them where they might be in danger.

"The children are why I have to be there." Marcie's voice was low, and Nicole could see her hands shaking. "I loved Daddy as much as you did, and it's as much my responsibility as yours to find out what happened to him. I've always known he wasn't the kind of man who would abandon us or the army, but I closed my eyes to the inconsistencies surrounding his disappearance. J.D. and Daddy are the bravest people I've ever known, and they don't deserve a coward for a wife or daughter. If my children are in danger, I have to know so I can protect them."

"You're not a coward." Nicole hugged her so tightly the baby who was caught between them began to protest. They both wiped their eyes and grinned at each other.

"I better go downstairs and see if John David's video is over and give you a chance to finish dressing." Marcie straightened, then holding her daughter in her arms, started for the stairs. Even as frightened as she was, there was a new buoyancy in her steps.

* * *

Braedon wasn't certain including Marcie in their meeting with Chief Daniels was a good idea, but he could understand her desire to be involved. Master Sergeant Greg Evangart had been her father too, and if Nicole was in danger, there was a good chance whoever was threatening her would go after her sister and her family as well, if for no other reason than as a means of silencing Nicole. It was just that he didn't know how Chief Daniels might react to their inclusion of another person in their luncheon meeting. He intended to take a tough stance with Daniels, and he couldn't help worrying that including Marcie in their meeting might increase the danger to her and her children.

At least Marcie hadn't brought the children today. Nicole told him her sister had made arrangements with her visiting teaching partner who lived a few houses away to keep them until she returned.

His shoulder brushed Nicole's, and he was glad for the bench seat in his truck. Maybe there was a bright side to Marcie joining them this morning. Flipping on his turn signal, he indicated his intention to exit I-5. He couldn't help thinking of the trip he and Nicole had taken just a few days ago as he turned toward the coast. Automatically he checked his mirrors to see which other vehicles were exiting the freeway. He didn't recognize any of the cars behind him, nor did any of them appear to be specifically following them.

Daniels had suggested they meet at a restaurant just outside of Bremerton, and Braedon had agreed. But the chief had later hesitated, giving the impression he was reluctant to include Nicole when Braedon informed him that she insisted on being present when they talked. He had a feeling the chief would be even more unhappy to see Marcie accompanying them. He just hoped her presence wouldn't hamper the discussion.

"I love this drive," Marcie said looking out the window at the lush growth and glimpses of open water. "Washington is so beautiful, and J.D. and I tried to explore as much of the western part of the state as we could before Lexie was born and he was deployed."

"It is beautiful, and I remember how excited I was to be here when I was a kid," Nicole added. "But everything that happened those last few weeks made me never want to see it again."

"Do you still feel that way?" Marcie asked. "I really wouldn't have twisted your arm to come if I'd known." Braedon listened for Nicole's answer. He hoped not all of her associations with the area were unpleasant. Even with all that had happened, he'd never felt more alive than he had the past months in her presence.

"I'm still a little uncomfortable with the really dense, forested areas. When I went with Braedon to the hill behind where we used to live, it helped some to relieve my feelings toward the blackberry thickets, but those thick tangles of thorny branches still make me uneasy. This coastal area with its combination of beaches, open water, islands, and pines only brings back pleasant memories of outings with Dad."

"And Victoria? Would you want to go back someday?" Braedon couldn't resist asking.

"I'd love to go back. There was so much we didn't have time to explore. Maybe it's because I'm an adult now, but one unpleasant experience didn't spoil the wonderful time I had up until I was pushed."

"I'm glad you feel that way," Braedon looked her way quickly, then turned his attention back to the road. "I think it's a fascinating city, and I'd like to return to see more of it and the rest of the island."

Recognizing the sign Daniels had told him to watch for, he moved to the outside lane and took the first exit. Following the directions he'd been given over the phone, he drove a few more blocks, then spotted the restaurant. He pulled in to the restaurant's parking lot and looked around for anything unusual before unlocking the doors. Marcie didn't jump out as soon as the vehicle stopped the way Nicole tended to do, but waited for him to come around and hold the door for the two women. As Nicole took his hand to step down, he noticed she was wearing the bracelet he'd given her. It brought a pleased smile to his face, distracting him momentarily from the serious confrontation ahead.

It took a moment for his eyes to adjust to the dim light inside the restaurant. Turning his head from side to side, he checked the other patrons for anyone familiar or anything out of place as he searched for Chief Daniels.

"Table for three?" a bright voice chirped, and he turned toward the hostess.

"They're with me," a deep voice interrupted, and Braedon saw Daniels step forward from behind a large piece of shrubbery. Braedon's eyes had adjusted well enough that he caught the quick flash of annoyance on the chief's face when Daniels's eyes rested on Marcie, though he didn't say anything, and the look was swiftly replaced by one of pleasure. Something about Daniels's behavior convinced Braedon that Daniels knew Marcie's identity without being introduced.

"This way." The other man ushered them toward an almost hidden table tucked in a secluded corner behind the treelike plant. Braedon noticed there were no other tables within eavesdropping distance. That was a point in Daniels's favor.

As Braedon approached the table, he became aware of another man seated at the table, a man with broad shoulders and a military bearing though he was dressed in a casual golf shirt. There was something familiar about the short-cropped gray hair, and as the man turned, Braedon struggled to appear unruffled.

"Sir!" He straightened his shoulders and stared in dismay as he saluted the tough new head of Fort Lewis's intelligence unit, the man his own commanding officer answered to.

"Lieutenant Morgan." Colonel Strichter acknowledged his greeting. "There's no need for formalities here." Feeling awkward and stiff, Braedon lowered his arm.

Chapter 14

Braedon followed the police chief's lead, quickly seating Nicole as the other man seated Marcie. He made certain his own chair at the table gave him eye contact with the chief. An uncomfortable silence followed once they were all seated, with each of them waiting for someone else to speak first. The tension was relieved by the arrival of their waiter, and they busied themselves ordering food Braedon wondered if he'd be able to eat.

Once the waiter left with their orders, the colonel asked in a voice unaccustomed to argument to be introduced to the two ladies. Daniels gestured for Braedon to go ahead, and he couldn't help feeling he had lost the control he'd meant to maintain in this meeting.

"Nicole Evangart and her sister, Marcie Duran," he motioned to each of the women. "Nicole, you met Chief Daniels a few days ago. This other gentleman is Colonel Strichter, head of Intelligence at Fort Lewis."

Marcie looked troubled as she was introduced to Chief Daniels. "I think we already met . . . before . . ." Chief Daniels sighed, then with a rueful smile reached for Marcie's hand.

"I remember a skinny little girl with red curls answering the door when I stopped by to pick up your dad when we were both stationed at Fort Hood a long time ago and a pretty teenager who met her dad's plane when we returned from Desert Storm." Daniels winked at her. She immediately turned to examining the tablecloth before her.

"I met Dad's plane too," Nicole stated quietly.

"And had eyes for no one but Dad," Daniels reminded her. Braedon felt one more piece had been added to the puzzle, but perhaps it was a beginning since apparently Daniels had known Greg Evangart personally.

Everyone lapsed into uncomfortable silence except Nicole, who politely acknowledged the introductions, then broke the ice with a blunt question. "Colonel, why are you here? My father disappeared from Fort Lewis twelve years ago, and I believe he was murdered. Braedon and I made this appointment with Chief Daniels because after meeting him, we suspect he knows more about Dad than he was letting on." Braedon was glad for her forthright introduction of the subject that concerned them all. He, too, was wondering about Colonel Strichter's sudden involvement, an involvement his mind was having trouble putting in its place among the facts he'd either unearthed or guessed.

"You're a lot like your father, young lady," the colonel addressed her.

"You knew my father too?" Nicole's head jerked back. And she glanced at Chief Daniels, then leaned forward, eager to hear whatever Strichter had to say. Braedon was curious too, not only about how both the colonel and Daniels knew Master Sergeant Evangart, but what the colonel's connection to Chief Daniels might be.

"You can rest easy about your father," the officer was saying. "He was a good man, and I never believed he deserted his post. But before we go any further, there are a few things I need to say to Lieutenant Morgan." He turned a stern eye toward him, and it was all Braedon could do not to squirm.

"You've been the subject of an internal investigation since the day you first pulled up Evangart's record. Sharing information from a military file with a civilian could place you in a great deal of trouble, Lieutenant."

"He didn't tell me anything I didn't already know," Nicole broke in, indignation in her voice as she came to his defense. He appreciated her support but worried she might antagonize someone who could make his life pretty uncomfortable. The colonel ignored Nicole's outburst and continued to berate Braedon.

"Only the dental chart, which Chief Daniels said he didn't receive, came from Sergeant Evangart's file, sir," Braedon defended himself. Hindsight told him he should have let his captain know what he was doing.

"I have a copy of that in storage back in Utah," Nicole broke in. "Using the military copy simply saved time. It isn't classified information."

"If you'd asked, I have a copy of Dad's dental records and a number of other papers Mom was going to shred but I decided to keep. They're in a safety deposit box in Tacoma." Marcie turned to Nicole, "I should have shared them with you before now. Other than the dental chart, I don't even know what's in the envelope. I never looked at the papers. I just didn't think Mom should destroy anything of Dad's."

"I did receive the dental chart," Daniels broke in. "I told you I didn't, since otherwise you would have known I'd arranged to meet you under false pretenses. The most cursory glance at that chart proved the Port Angeles John Doe couldn't have been Evangart."

This time the colonel turned toward Nicole and spoke directly to her. "No, your father's dental records aren't classified, and your friend is not in trouble, but he could be. Private investigations are highly discouraged in the military because the investigator may learn information that could cause harm to someone or muddy an official investigation. In this case, questions concerning your father have stirred up an old case that had appeared dormant for twelve years. Fortunately for Morgan, we found no connection between him and that case other than a personal interest in the daughter of a former CID agent. However, his curiosity seems to have attracted attention from more than his superior officers. That's why I decided to meet with you myself."

"I'd like to see that envelope you mentioned." Daniels leaned forward to speak to Marcie, and Braedon didn't miss the eager light in his eyes.

"I'll give it to Lieutenant Morgan," Marcie spoke with quiet determination. "If he thinks you should see it, all right. I'll leave that up to him."

Chief Daniels appeared frustrated when he turned to Strichter. "I don't think we can avoid laying our cards on the table." When the colonel nodded, Daniels began.

"You were right to think I know more than I was letting on, and I understand your reluctance to trust me. Colonel Strichter can verify that Greg Evangart and I were working together on a tip that someone from Fort Lewis was passing classified information to a terrorist training camp somewhere in the Middle East after Operation Desert Storm. We were both transferred here to follow up on that lead. You don't need to know the details, but Evangart infiltrated the group enough to learn they were involved in more than passing on information concerning the specialized training given Rangers and Special Ops at the base. He learned the group was a small cell supported by Osama bin Laden, who as you know is a wealthy Islamic fanatic who was taking an increasingly prominent role in terrorist activities. Evangart called me shortly before he left for a field exercise in Yakima to tell me he thought the group was making long-range plans to attack hydroelectric dams throughout the Northwest. He didn't want to give me names and details over the phone, and he disappeared before we could meet to discuss his findings in full."

"He was murdered," Nicole stated bluntly.

"Yes, we believe so, but there was never any evidence and no body." Daniels's agreement was guarded. "All we had to go on was a child's description of a shooting and Evangart's last message to me, sent just before he left Yakima, saying his contact had arranged for him to meet the cell leader. He was to fill me in on the details as soon as he arrived. I never saw him again."

"But I did," Nicole spoke the words almost too low for anyone at the table to hear. "And no one believed me."

"I did." The colonel's voice was almost as low as Nicole's, but everyone's eyes turned toward him.

"Your lunch." The waiter arrived carrying a large tray covered with plates. They sat quietly while he dispersed the plates around the table and refilled glasses. Braedon sat as though at attention while his mind retraced all that had been said. If Daniels had been working with Evangart, that would explain a great deal, but it didn't explain how someone knew of his and Nicole's plans to travel to Port Angeles. Or how, presumably the same person, found out about their impromptu trip to Victoria.

When the waiter left, instead of the group reaching for their forks, four pairs of eyes turned toward the colonel once more. Before he could speak, Marcie made a sputtering noise then pointed her finger at the colonel. "I remember now. You brought Nicole home after she ran away to the MPs."

Nicole stared blankly at the colonel. "That was you?"

"There's no reason you should remember me," he said to Nicole. "Though I remember you very well. You looked like your father then, and even more so now, and you still have the same direct approach to a problem he was known for. I'm the one who's changed. In addition to aging twelve years, losing thirty pounds and a lot of hair, the one time you saw me I was recovering from nasal septum surgery and my face and nose were still swollen."

"That's what confused me." There was a note of triumph in Marcie's voice. "I remember you as being larger with a puffy face."

"You have a remarkable eye for faces, Mrs. Duran." There was both approval and speculation in Strichter's voice.

"Why didn't you start an immediate search for Dad?" Nicole demanded an answer to the question that had haunted her for years.

"If you believed Nicole, why didn't you tell Mom?" Marcie suddenly had some questions of her own. "And why did you let Nicole be sent to an institution? Do you have any idea how hard that was for her? It was hard for Mom and me too. We lost not only Dad, but Nicole as well." She began to cry, and Nicole moved closer to her sister, using her napkin to wipe away Marcie's tears.

"Perhaps you'll understand that we did what we thought was necessary at the time if I explain a little more." The colonel looked uncomfortable but continued. "I was in charge of a CID investigation that began with rumors a soldier at Fort Lewis was involved in passing secrets to a militant Islamic group during and immediately after the Gulf War. I sent for two of the army's best investigators to help me with the case, but one disappeared a couple of months into the investigation. I thought it was a lucky break in the case that I happened to be visiting a friend who was in charge of the MPs that night when you came into the station. When I took you home, I could see your mother was almost out of her mind with fear for her husband. I assumed part of that fear was that something had happened to you too. She surprised me when she insisted you were obsessed with your father and that you frequently made up dramatic stories when you didn't want to face the truth."

"Why would Mom make up a story like that?" Nicole wondered aloud.

"She might have known Nicole's story was true and suspected that if whoever murdered her husband knew her daughter was a witness, they'd come after her," Braedon offered a theory.

"I always suspected Sheila Evangart knew enough about Greg's investigative work to think he had gone undercover. Her reaction following Greg's disappearance was aimed at providing a cover for his absence. She may have worried that Nicole's story could bring unwanted attention to him. It was the only explanation that made sense for why she was so anxious to move as far away from Washington as possible and why she agreed to commit her daughter at a high-security hospital for children," Chief Daniels added his view.

"If she thought Dad was alive but working undercover, that would explain why she never stopped hoping he would come back." Marcie latched on to Daniels's explanation.

"All I know is she was barely rational when I appeared on her doorstep with her daughter. When I reported back to the investigative task force, someone suggested that Major Detford, an Air Force doctor who was on the psychiatric staff at Fort Lewis's Madigan hospital, see the child. He had recently been promoted to major and assigned to a research project that involved a team of medical specialists representing all military branches. I had met him previously and understood he had some experience working with children.

"After Detford saw her, he suggested we use her mother's story as a screen to send her to a place where we could keep her in protective custody until it was safe to return her to her family." Braedon noticed the colonel had switched from speaking directly to Nicole to referring to her as though the child she had been was an entirely different person from the young woman seated across the table from him.

"But what happened to the investigation?" Nicole redirected the focus from herself.

"We ran up against a blank wall," Daniels picked up the story. "The investigation went nowhere, and we eventually had to turn our attention to other issues. Even the leads we knew Evangart was following and the leaks that led to the investigation in the first place dried up when our chief suspect abruptly left the country. But before we ended the active search, the task force set up some safeguards. We all suspected that neither Evangart's killers nor the terrorists he was investigating had gone away permanently. One of those safeguards was a silent alarm that went to Colonel Strichter's computer in Washington, D.C., whenever someone attempted to access Evangart's file."

"That explains what tipped you off that we were investigating Sergeant Evangart's disappearance and why you're back at Fort Lewis, but how did that awaken members of the terrorist cell?" Braedon wanted to know.

"We don't know," Daniels responded. "Evangart and I worked together on a number of cases before we were assigned to Fort Lewis. He was my best friend as well as my partner. With him gone, I chose not to reenlist after I became eligible for retirement. I accepted a position with a government agency and remained in this area for a while to keep an eye on the men Greg drove away with the day he left Yakima. I was hoping I could learn whatever Greg had discovered that last day. When my research failed to produce results, I took on other assignments dealing with terrorism, but I continued to keep tabs on Greg's daughters. When I learned Marcie had informed housing that Nicole was coming for an indefinite stay, I asked for and got permission to transfer undercover to this area."

"What did you learn about the men who were with Master Sergeant Evangart that day?" Braedon asked.

"Nothing important." Daniels shook his head. "Specialist Shad Fahim rose to the rank of sergeant, then died in Kosovo. Sergeant Malen rose in the NCO ranks, then applied for and was accepted into officers candidate school. He is presently a first lieutenant serving in Afghanistan. Specialist Poursaid left the army when his enlistment was up but continues to live in the Tacoma area. None of them have done one suspicious thing in all these years."

"Poursaid was the driver of the Jeep they left Yakima in, wasn't he?" Braedon asked.

"Yes, it was signed out to him, and we had a crew go over it in minute detail. There were no traces of blood or any indication it had been used to transport a body."

Strichter added, "Two of the suspects Evangart and Daniels had been watching were questioned, and their movements during the period of time in question were checked out. We had nothing to hold them on, and within a year, both left the country. There's never been anything to link any of the soldiers in that Jeep to those two suspects."

"But you've continued to watch them all these years?" Nicole asked.

"Yes, and you might as well know," Strichter confessed. "I've kept track of you over the years, as well. I always suspected that the determined little girl I met at the MP office would someday return. As soon as I learned from Housing that you were coming to Fort Lewis to stay with your sister, I notified Daniels and had someone begin keeping an eye on you. With the little bit we knew about Evangart's last investigation and the events of 9/11, I didn't want to take any chances someone might consider you a threat. And it seems I was right to take precautions."

"Braedon?" She turned to him with a horrified expression on her face and suspicion in her eyes.

"Not me. I didn't know anything about you or your father before we bumped into each other jogging." He lost no time defending himself.

"No, not Morgan." The colonel seconded Braedon's avowal of innocence. Nicole gave them both a dark look. Braedon wasn't certain whether or not she believed them. If she thought he had been spying on her, his chances of becoming more than friends with her were over.

"I have some pictures I'd like both of you ladies to look at." Coming from Colonel Strichter, this was more order than request.

"Do you have photographs of the men who left Yakima with Dad that day?" Nicole asked. "I think I might recognize the men I saw from a photo. Even after all these years, that day is ingrained in my memory."

"Colonel Strichter has a full set of photos." Daniels looked regretful. "When I learned you were insisting on attending this meeting with Morgan, I wanted to fill my pockets with mug shots, but that of course was impractical. Besides, if you do recognize anyone from the pictures, it would be better if you're in a more formal setting than a restaurant so your testimony can be used in court. Make arrangements with the colonel to go over them as soon as possible."

"Speaking of photos," Braedon set two enlarged snapshots on the table. "Do either of you recognize the man hiding in the shrubs?" Out of the corner of his eye, he saw the surprise his announcement initially brought to Nicole's eyes change to remembrance of the pictures he'd snapped at Butchart Gardens.

The two men leaned forward to examine the pictures better, then Strichter picked one up. "Where did you get this?" he asked. Braedon explained about being asked to take pictures of the newlyweds.

A grim expression crossed the colonel's face. "A certain staff sergeant will soon be facing court-martial if his interest in you turns out to be more than idle curiosity."

Daniels's glance at the colonel was filled with sympathy and confirmed Braedon's suspicion that the colonel had seen the man before. *If the man worked in Strichter's office,* Braedon put the two men's reactions together and drew some conclusions of his own, *then he may have had access to communication between Strichter and Daniels. That could be how he knew we were meeting with Daniels. It could also explain how the people who killed her father knew Nicole was back at Fort Lewis.*

Her curiosity aroused, Nicole reached for one of the photos Braedon had shot and enlarged. He knew the moment she recognized the man who, with his wife, had practically fought to claim the front seat on the double-decker bus in Victoria. He suspected her reaction would have been much stronger had the man been one of the two men she'd seen with her father.

"Did you have us followed when we left Port Angeles for Victoria?" Braedon watched now for Daniels's reaction. He merely nodded without a sign of guilt or apology. Before Braedon could demand an explanation, Daniels shrugged.

"But not by this man. You had already been shot at, and I was concerned that someone might be following you, so I sent one of my own men to watch your back. He suspected you'd spotted him, so he was hanging back as far as he dared. He only moved in closer when he saw you become separated when you were about to cross a street with a crowd of shoppers. Wanting to be certain, he crossed with the same light and moved closer. He saw a man who fits the general description of the man in your photograph shove Miss Evangart. He reacted instantly to pull her back to the sidewalk. From the corner of his eye, he saw someone running down the street and tried to go after him. Unfortunately, it took so long to disentangle himself from the crowd, the suspect got away."

"Short guy wearing a baseball cap?" Braedon asked.

"He was pretty certain you'd spotted him, so he put on a different disguise for the ferry ride back and pretended to sleep the whole way."

"He saved my life. I'd like to thank him . . ." Nicole stopped, seeing Daniels shaking his head.

"It'll be better if you don't. He messed up big time. Besides, he's feeling guilty because he let the perp get that close to you—and he didn't even get a good look at the guy."

"I know just how he feels," Braedon muttered. "All I saw was a shoulder give her a push."

"Are you ready to order dessert?"

Braedon looked around uneasily. He'd been so engrossed in conversation, he hadn't been aware of the waiter's approach. A glance at his plate told him he'd eaten, but he couldn't recall exactly what it was he had swallowed. He shook his head and noticed the others also declined dessert.

"Two things," the colonel spoke up again in a grim tone once the waiter was out of earshot. "No more investigating on your own. And I need you, Miss Evangart, in my office this afternoon to look at those pictures. You don't need to worry about the man in Lieutenant Morgan's pictures. He won't be anywhere around when you arrive."

"I'm sure Braedon can show me where your office is," Nicole said. "But I can't promise not to continue looking for Dad."

"It's too dangerous to search on your own," Strichter warned, and Daniels nodded. "I think we've pretty well established that whoever killed your father knows you were a witness, and they also know you've returned. They aren't willing to risk the possibility you might be able to identify one or both of them."

"I think it's safe to assume more than that." Braedon lifted his glass, but he didn't take a drink or meet Nicole's eyes. "The terrorist group Sergeant Evangart was investigating is still here and still planning some sort of attack or they wouldn't be concerned with what Nicole may have seen. I think we can also assume that at least one of the killers still has some connection to the base and is worried that he and Nicole might run into each other."

"For Nicole's safety, she needs to leave the base." Strichter turned to her and softened his voice. "You should return to Utah or go visit your mother."

"I'm not going anywhere," Nicole resisted. "With all the people you have following me, staying here is the best option. Just my being here might draw out someone from the terrorist group so you can catch him."

"You're not going to be a decoy." Marcie turned on her sister. "Go back to Utah. I am strong enough to take care of my children and wait for J.D. without falling apart."

"It's not falling apart I'm worrying about," Nicole grimaced. "If I'm in danger, so are you. I won't leave you after the threat you received a few days ago."

"What threat?" All three men asked in what was almost a chorus. Marcie explained about the man who claimed to have found John David wandering in the hall outside the pediatrician's office at Madigan hospital.

"Accompany your sister to my office this afternoon to look at mug shots." There was a sternness in Strichter's voice that didn't invite argument. It was almost an order, and Braedon half-expected Marcie to salute when she mumbled, "Yes, sir."

"Nicole's right," Daniels put in. "Both women and the children need to leave here. We'll have to find a place that can take all of them."

"You're not shipping me off to another mental institution." Nicole folded her arms and glared at the colonel.

"No, not that." Braedon was interested to see the colonel appear flustered by Nicole's reminder of where his efforts to protect her had taken her before.

"I'm not going anywhere." Marcie dug in her heels. "I'm staying where J.D. can call and e-mail me."

"We'll maintain a communication link with your husband," Colonel Strichter promised. "I'll contact federal resources as soon as I get back to my office to see if there's a safe house that can accommodate all four of you."

"If I may make a suggestion, sir." Braedon checked to make certain no one was passing by their table and leaned forward so only those seated around him could hear. Strichter indicated he should proceed.

"My family owns a ranch in Utah. It's twenty miles from our closest neighbor. My brother Steve is a sheriff's deputy, and both of my other brothers do search and rescue when the sheriff's department needs them. The ranch house is large enough to accommodate Nicole, Marcie, and the children."

"Marcie and the children can go." Nicole folded her arms and glared from one stern male visage to the next. "I'm staying here. This is bigger than finding Dad. Now that I know he was working to uncover a terrorist cell, I have to stay to do all I can to prevent another 9/11 by finding his killers."

"Nicole . . ." Braedon protested.

"She may be right. Identifying anyone connected to terrorists has to be our top priority. I'll begin arrangements at once to send Mrs. Duran and her children to the ranch and enlist the help of the CIA to locate a safe house nearby for Miss Evangart." Strichter stood. "I'll expect you ladies in my office this afternoon as soon as you return to base. If any of those pictures looks even remotely familiar, I want to know." He turned to leave, but Nicole stopped him.

"Colonel, if you remember, when the man I believe was my father was shot, one of the two men with him was wearing an army uniform. I saw someone a few weeks ago I think was that man."

"Where?" Strichter sat back down.

"At the commissary. I tried to get a better look, but he seemed to disappear. He wasn't in the checkout line or any of the aisles."

"Where exactly in the commissary did you see this person?" Daniels leaned forward.

"He was at the back of the store, near the meat area."

"Was he in uniform?" Braedon noticed a hint of steel behind Chief Daniels's question. When Nicole shook her head, a gleam of satisfaction could be seen in the police chief's eyes.

"Someone with access to the loading docks," he muttered almost under his breath.

"Poursaid." Strichter drew himself up straighter and seemed to share Daniels's air of having proved some previous point.

"Poursaid?" Braedon was clearly puzzled.

"Specialist A. E. Poursaid, currently a government contractor who makes regular deliveries to the commissary." Daniels and Strichter were both on their feet now. "Daniels, follow the lieutenant back to base. The ladies will accompany me. I want no delay in their seeing those mug shots."

Chapter 15

Cassaday walked into the tent carrying a small box and a stack of letters. J.D. looked up from his cot where he was re-reading a letter from Marcie for the fourth time. They exchanged greetings before J.D. resumed reading, and Cassaday began ripping open an envelope, leaving the package until last.

"Wahoo," Cassaday shouted and J.D. looked up once more.

"Letter from your girl?"

"Yeah." The young specialist looked sheepish for a moment before sharing the news. "I decided not to wait until I get back home to ask Carol Ann to marry me. She said yes."

"Congratulations!" J.D. jumped to his feet and slugged the other man's shoulder. "This calls for a celebration."

"There's nothing to celebrate with." Cassaday laughed. "Besides, neither of us drinks, so even if we had a bottle it wouldn't do us any good."

"We don't need champagne. I have something better." He walked over to his footlocker, which served as a makeshift table. Scattered across its surface was a mangled cardboard box, an array of cookies, candy, chips and dip, and a plastic bottle that had been on its way to being tossed out by the mess hall staff before J.D. had claimed it. It now contained a bright red liquid.

"Kool-Aid," J.D. announced with a grand gesture.

"I'll get my cup."

J.D. filled two cups, then lifted his high. "To love and marriage."

After they had both drained their cups, Cassaday shuffled through his other letters, read one from his mother, then set a couple of others aside and reached for his package. Along with more snacks, which he stacked on the footlocker beside J.D.'s, he unearthed a video cassette and a stack of photos.

"Mom said the video is of the family and Carol Ann at the annual revival and congregational picnic that is held every summer in my hometown. I guess I'll have to wait until tomorrow to look at it." He looked regretful for a moment, then began to smile again. "Sarge, you've been married a long time, and I can tell you and your wife are happy. You're over the moon every time you get a letter or an e-mail from her. She sends you great stuff like jalapeño bean dip and Kool-Aid. You must have done something right. Care to share your secret?"

J.D. wasn't certain Cassaday was seriously asking for advice, but he decided to give him some anyway. "Put Carol Ann first, and everything else will work out," he told his engaged friend. "Share all of the important things like your faith in God, caring for your children, love for your country, and money, but don't try to be carbon copies of each other. Respect and value differences too."

An explosion sounded in the distance, and both men cleared away their personal items while listening for further sounds of attack. They weren't really worried about their safety; theirs was the most thoroughly sandbagged tent in the entire complex. A few distant cracks of rifle fire subsided into silence. Only partially undressed, they lay on their backs on their cots in silence for a long time before Cassaday spoke again. "I thought about what you said that day when those two little girls were killed. I prayed about it too, and after a while, I understood I'd fallen into the trap of blaming God for what happened to those kids. Saddam Hussein and his followers are the ones who deserve the blame."

"The senseless deaths of children always upset me too," J.D. spoke into the darkness above his cot.

J.D. lay awake thinking for a long time, and as always his thoughts turned to his family. Cassaday's thoughts too must have turned to home, because long after J.D. thought the other man was asleep, he said, "Taking on the responsibility of a wife and hoping to be a father someday has got me thinking about the things that are important to me, like God and my country."

Quiet prevailed once more, and J.D. found himself drifting toward sleep. He hadn't taken time to pray before lying down. He thought of praying where he was, flat on his back on his bed. Sometimes he did that when he shared quarters with men who lacked religious faith or who ridiculed things he considered sacred. But Cassaday wasn't like that. Slowly J.D. forced himself to a sitting position, then to his knees beside his bed. A rustle of bedding and the clump of feet hitting the ground behind him told him Cassaday too was on his knees.

* * *

Nicole stared at the pictures spread across the colonel's desk. Her focus narrowed at once to a tall, broad-shouldered young man wearing the basic uniform of an enlisted man. His dark hair was cropped short, and his mouth was wide with full, unsmiling lips. She pictured him a little older wearing civilian clothes and knew she wasn't mistaken about the man she'd seen at the commissary.

"That one." She pointed.

"You're sure?" Strichter encouraged her to look again.

"I could never forget him. He's the man who accompanied the gunman the day my father was shot. He's also the man I saw while shopping with my sister."

"All right." He reached for the picture and held it in his hands for a moment before placing it back on the table. "Study the other pictures carefully. I want to know if you've seen any of these other men."

Picture by picture, she scanned each face as though attempting to memorize it. Most of the pictures were portrait shots, but a few were enlarged snapshots taken by a telephoto lens from a great distance. One shot of a man wearing western clothes and a Middle Eastern headpiece caused her to pause. Her hand lingered over it for several seconds. There was something vaguely familiar about the man's stance, but the picture was too grainy to be certain. It was impossible to make out his facial features. At last she touched one corner of the photograph. "I may have seen him before."

"That is Akbar Hattam. He was living in Seattle twelve years ago but abruptly returned to the Middle East two weeks after your father disappeared. To my knowledge, he was never on this base."

"He might be the man who shot my father, but I think I saw him standing just like that more recently. I wish his face were more distinct." She found it frustrating to be unable to remember when she might have seen the man in the photograph.

Colonel Strichter picked up the picture and looked at it for a minute before carefully placing it back on his desk. His face was grim. "If Hattam's back in this country, I want to know why I haven't been notified." He glared at Daniels who was sitting almost motionless in a chair at one end of the desk. Strichter drummed one fist on the edge of his desk for several seconds. "Wait in the other room while your sister looks at the pictures. Try to remember where you might have seen Hattam."

"I'm not certain it was him. I might have seen someone else who happens to stand the way he does in this picture." She took a few steps toward the door, then paused.

"Sir," she felt hesitant to say anything, but she knew Marcie would be uncomfortable mentioning anything so personal. "Marcie needs to go home. She's nursing her baby, who doesn't take a bottle well and is probably screaming for her mother by now."

"Oh, um, very well." He picked up the phone on his desk. "Send Lieutenant Morgan in here."

Minutes later, Braedon and Nicole were on their way to pick up the children while a highly nervous Marcie was ushered into the colonel's office. She sat when invited and stared at the array of photos on the desk without seeing them.

"Mrs. Duran, take your time." She knew the colonel was attempting to put her at ease, but she felt awkward and nervous. She'd never done anything like this before, and she didn't like being in an officer's office without J.D. What if she did something stupid? Would she damage J.D.'s career? It seemed like everything on a military base could impact a soldier's career, including his family's misbehavior. It would have been so much simpler if they'd just let her look at the photographs with Nicole. Taking a deep breath, she made herself look at the first picture.

There were only about a dozen pictures scattered across the top of a large metal desk, and at first it was hard to focus on them, but gradually she forced herself to calm down. The first picture showed a young man with dark hair and large, white teeth. She'd never seen him before. She turned her attention to the second picture, then the third. It wasn't until she started on the second row that a face became almost familiar. She studied it carefully, then went on to the next. This one reminded her of someone, but the picture wasn't quite right. Hastily she went to the next one, and this time there was no doubt. She'd seen this man with a prominent gold tooth before, but he'd been wearing a uniform, and he hadn't been smiling. Forcing herself to go on, she continued searching the photos for anything familiar.

Having completely forgotten that the colonel and Chief Daniels were watching her as she examined the photographs, she jumped when Daniels asked, "What do you see in those three pictures in the middle you keep returning to?"

"The middle one," she touched it lightly, "looks familiar, but I'm not certain . . . It may be that he just resembles someone I see quite often at the commissary, though that man is quite a bit older than this one."

"That picture was taken at least a dozen years ago, but your sister also recognized him." There was a note of satisfaction in the colonel's voice that encouraged her to mention the photos on either side of the one she'd chosen first.

"I know who this man is." This time she touched a picture of a dark-complected man dressed in a western-style suit, smiling broadly for the camera. He had a prominent gold tooth right in the front. "The day Nicole came, I was running late when I left for the airport in Seattle. This is the patrolman who gave me a speeding ticket."

"No mistake?" Daniels's hand snaked toward the photograph. His eyes glittered, and his mouth turned down in a grim gesture that almost frightened Marcie. She gulped before going on.

"I saw him again at the airport near the baggage carousel when Nicole and I picked up her luggage. I noticed his tooth again and looked more closely because I didn't think there could be two patrolmen with a tooth like that. He was talking to this man, but they left as soon as they saw me looking their direction." Her finger moved to the third picture. It was a blurred, long-range photo of a man wearing Western clothes and a checkered Middle Eastern head-piece. In spite of the poor quality of the picture, she was certain he was the same man she'd seen talking to the patrolman. "But I think he was wearing a wig instead of that scarf thing."

"A wig? What makes you think he was wearing a wig?" Strichter leaned forward, an eager expression on his face.

"Oh, I wish I could be certain, but at the airport I remember he was wearing sports clothes and his hair was neatly combed, but that wasn't the only time I saw him. I'm pretty sure I saw him again later with only a fringe of short gray hair around his ears."

"Where did you see him the second time?" The colonel asked with a calmness that belied the eager glitter in his eyes.

"I don't know."

"Could you have seen him with your father when you were a young girl?" Daniels inserted a question.

"It wasn't that long ago." It was frustrating to be unable to remember where she might have seen the man in the photograph a second time.

"Thank you, Mrs. Duran. You really do have a remarkable eye for faces. If you remember where you saw this man again, let me know at once. He's extremely dangerous." Colonel Strichter stood abruptly and held out his hand. Daniels remained seated, continuing to study the photos she had selected.

Marcie rose to her feet and reluctantly accepted Strichter's hand. "You've been extremely helpful," he said. "I have a few calls to make, so you can wait in the front office for your children to arrive, then we'll give you a few minutes of privacy before we call in some people to talk with you and your sister. I have an aide making arrangements for your transfer to Lieutenant Morgan's ranch."

"Sir," The soldier who had been sitting behind a desk in the outer office stepped into the room without knocking. "You're needed out front. It's an emergency."

* * *

Braedon drummed his fingers against the steering wheel as he waited for the ID check that would permit Nicole and him to enter North Fort. The line was long, and the delay irritated him in a way it usually never did. He couldn't explain the urgency or the impatience that filled him today.

At least Nicole was seated beside him on the front seat of the military car the colonel had arranged for him to drive. He doubted he could explain to anyone, least of all himself, the desolate feeling he'd experienced earlier when Nicole rode off in the colonel's vehicle instead of being beside him.

Finally it was his turn to show his ID, then they were on their way. Reaching the housing area where Marcie lived, he followed Nicole's instructions to a house a few doors down the street from where the Durans lived. He pulled into the driveway and parked behind the house next to the unattached garage.

Nicole jumped from the car, almost before it stopped, with Marcie's keys in her hand. She extended them toward him.

"You get the car seats while I collect the children. Lexie is probably screaming her head off by now." She, too, seemed to be in a rush, though in her case it was likely concern for her hungry niece that motivated her.

Braedon grasped the keys before sprinting toward the Duran garage a few houses away. He had no trouble getting the garage door unlocked or the car open, but releasing the car seats from the restraints that held them firmly in place took several minutes longer than he thought it should. When he finally got them free and the car and garage locked again, he carried the unwieldy seats back to the sedan he and Nicole had arrived in.

If he thought freeing the seats from Marcie's car was difficult, securing them in the military car with uncooperative seat belts was worse. He remembered the smaller seat faced the rear in Marcie's car and duplicated the position in the government car. Just as he finished assuring himself the seats were properly installed, Nicole arrived behind him with a sleeping child in each arm. He managed a smooth transition of the little boy to a car seat without waking him, then stared at the straps, wondering how to finish the task.

"I'll fasten him in, you take the baby," Nicole said, and before he could protest, a small bundle wrapped in a lightweight, pink blanket was in his arms. He stared down at the baby's face just as she shuddered and hiccupped. Her face was red and her hair damp.

"She cried herself to sleep, but she won't sleep long. When she wakes up, she'll be one unhappy baby and not at all shy about letting us know she wants her mother and dinner." Nicole took the infant back and circled the car to fasten her in the smaller infant seat. Braedon watched her insert first one side then the other of the locking mechanism into a slot at the bottom of the seat, then adjust the slide that fit over her small chest.

"Something tells me we need to hurry," he whispered. It wasn't entirely the sight of the sleeping baby stirring restlessly that spurred him to rush back to the colonel's office. A nagging sense of urgency had accompanied him from the moment Colonel Strichter sent him on this errand.

"I know," Nicole responded in an equally hushed voice. "But I just have this feeling I must make certain Lexie and John David are safe." She looked back at the children, checked their seat belts once more, then allowed Braedon to usher her into the front seat of the car.

As he rounded the hood of the car on his way back to the driver's seat, a high-pitched whistle sounded somewhere behind him. He whirled back in time to see flames shoot into the air a short distance away, followed by a deep rumble. Burning debris began arching back toward the peaceful neighborhood. Jerking open the car door, he slid inside with the key already in his hand. The engine started on the first attempt, and he shifted into gear. Instead of turning toward the street, he tore across two lawns to the next street.

"Braedon!" Nicole's voice bordered on a scream.

"Do up your seat belt," he shouted as he pulled onto the road leading to the main gate.

"Mine's done up! Yours isn't!" She reached across him to clip his belt into place. A thin wail rose in increasing intensity from the back-seat. She was helpless to do anything to comfort the two frightened children.

"What happened?" Nicole turned in her seat to look back the way they'd come. "It sounded like someone shot a rocket at us."

"They weren't shooting at us. Hopefully they didn't even see us. The explosion came from a house." Braedon slowed down. The gate was just ahead, and he didn't want to attract attention.

"A house? Then why are we running? We have to go back. Someone might need help." She clasped his arm as though she might physically force him to turn back.

"Nicole!" He had to raise his voice to be heard over the screaming infant behind him. "The house was firebombed. Going back would place the children in danger."

"But . . ." Nicole began, then she sank back against the seat, lowering her head to her hands. "It was Marcie's house, wasn't it?"

Braedon turned away to open his window and hand their IDs to the MP at the gate.

Chapter 16

Holding her niece in her arms, Nicole composed her features as she preceded Braedon, who was carrying John David, into the building that housed Colonel Strichter's office. How was she going to tell her sister that her home was on fire? Marcie would want to rush home to attempt to save anything she could, but she'd have to convince her it would be too dangerous for her to go there. Braedon opened the door to the colonel's outer office with one hand.

"John David! Lexie!" Marcie rushed toward her children with tears streaming down her face.

"They're fine." Nicole shifted the baby, who was now awake and beginning to whimper, to Marcie's arms. Marcie's emotional greeting caught her off guard. "Do you know . . . ?"

"The house? Yes. I know it burned, but my babies . . . I've been so worried." She cuddled Lexie, and John David stared at her with huge, round eyes while she continued talking. "Colonel Strichter got a report that no one was in our triplex, but the roof of the house next door caught fire. The fire department put it out before it could spread to the rest of the house, and everyone got out safely. A garage is burning with two SUVs inside, and a child is on the way to Madigan with an injury he got when a piece of hot debris fell on him several doors away." She held the baby with one arm and scrubbed at her eyes with the other before bending forward to kiss the top of her son's head. John David began to struggle to get down, and Braedon placed him on his feet. Immediately he wrapped his arms around his mother's leg.

"I'm sorry, Marcie. There was nothing we could do." She stepped forward to hug her sister, and as she did, Lexie's whimpers turned to screams.

"Sh-sh-sh," Marcie whispered as she rocked the baby. "I better feed her." She turned toward the colonel's inner office, then looked back hesitantly toward her son.

"Don't worry, I'll watch him." Nicole took John David's hand. He looked uncertain as he watched his mother close the door behind her, but Nicole led him to a chair where she sat and pulled him onto her lap.

"Aunt Nicole," the little boy turned a sad face toward her. "Mommy said our house got burned. Once I got burned when I touched the cookie pan. It hurt really bad. Does our house hurt?"

"Not the way people hurt," she told him. "What Mommy meant was your house burned down, and now it's all gone."

"Is my bed gone too?"

"Yes, but your mommy and I will find a bed for you to sleep in tonight, and the army will give your family a new house pretty soon. Then we'll go to a store and buy you a new bed." She wondered how to explain the disaster that had struck his family in a way a young child could understand without making him afraid.

"Did my toys get burned up too?"

Nicole groaned silently.

"Yes, sweetie, but I promise I'll take you shopping for new toys."

"I want my old toys." His voice was forlorn.

"I know where there are some toys that need a little boy to play with them." Braedon knelt in front of John David. "Perhaps you could play with them until Aunt Nicole and Mommy can take you shopping."

Nicole had been only peripherally aware of Braedon and Colonel Strichter conversing quietly on the other side of the room with two other officers. She hadn't seen him leave that group to join her and John David. She looked at him now, and he read the question in her eyes.

"Colonel Strichter is making arrangements to fly Marcie and the children to Hill Field north of Salt Lake City. From there, they'll be taken to my family's ranch. My brothers will watch them until it's safe for them to return here." He turned back to John David.

"Would you like to fly in a big airplane to visit my ranch? There are horses at the ranch and, if your mom says it's all right, my mother will let you ride a pony she keeps for children to ride. My dog, Cooper, is at the ranch too, and he gets lonesome for someone to play with. Do you think you could play with him?"

"Does he bite?" John David looked worried.

"No, he's pretty big, but he doesn't bite."

"I guess that would be okay." He looked up as the inner office door opened and a smile lit his face. "Mom!" He slid from Nicole's lap and ran toward his mother. "Braedon said I can ride his horse and play with his dog. And there are toys." Marcie hugged him with one arm while holding Lexie, who was now sleeping, with the other.

Nicole turned to Braedon. "We were going to hire a teenager who lives a few blocks away from Marcie to tend the children while we met with Chief Daniels, but her phone was busy and that's when Marcie thought about her visiting teaching partner. If the children had been in that house . . ." She couldn't help the shudder that shook her shoulders. "I don't think it has hit her yet how much she's lost."

"She has what matters most." Braedon moved to the seat beside Nicole and placed a hand over her trembling one. Nicole watched the scene across the room as her sister settled in a chair with her baby in her arms and John David on his knees in the adjacent chair, with his head bent close to his mother's. Yes, she was forgetting what mattered most. She closed her eyes and bowed her head to give silent thanks for her sister and the children. Still, practical matters had to be considered.

"You're right. But unless some of their belongings can be salvaged, none of us has a change of clothes. All of Marcie's pictures of J.D. and the children are gone, her computer, financial records, keepsakes, even her wedding dress that she wanted to save for Lexie are lost. I just hope she has J.D.'s address memorized." She could have added that her own clothing and even the souvenirs she'd purchased in Victoria were gone. She touched the bracelet on her wrist and felt some comfort. She was glad she'd worn it today.

"It's not quite as bad as you think," Braedon assured her. "The colonel put through a call to J.D. to inform him of the fire and let Marcie assure him that she and the children are safe. J.D. was pretty shook up, but he reminded Marcie that they took certain precautions before he left for Iraq. He placed his will, insurance policies, and other personal and financial records in a bank storage box, and Marcie contributed a few items to the box as well, including their babies' first pictures, a favorite wedding photo, and the envelope of papers belonging to your father."

"Do you think there's anything important in that envelope of Dad's that might help us find who did this?" Nicole's shoulders slumped. "After this much time, there probably isn't."

"We'll check as soon as we can. Right now, the important thing is to make certain you and your family are somewhere safe." Braedon ran his arm along the back of her chair and gave her shoulder a reassuring squeeze.

"I told you, I'm not going . . ."

"It happens that the colonel agrees with you. He wants you close enough to assist should he need you. And he believes your family will be safer away from you, so he's making arrangements for a safe house nearby for you." He withdrew his arm from her shoulder and extended a hand to urge her to her feet.

"Go say your good-byes. Arrangements have been made for them to leave almost immediately."

Marcie was on her feet too when Nicole reached her. Two MPs stood at the door, and the colonel's aide approached them as the sisters hugged each other. The aide spoke quietly to Colonel Strichter, who nodded his head and stepped out of the room. The aide crossed the room to stand by Marcie while she and Nicole bade each other a teary farewell. Nicole gave each of the children a quick kiss, then stepped back as the aide led them and Marcie from the room. In moments, Nicole stood alone, staring at an empty doorway. One of the MPs stepped back to close the door sharply behind her departing family.

Colonel Strichter returned to the room to announce to Braedon and Nicole that the man Braedon had snapped a picture of a few days earlier had been stopped at the north gate. His car had been searched, and the MPs had found empty explosives canisters and a canceled ticket for the Port Angeles/Victoria ferry dated two days earlier.

* * *

"Thank you, sir." J.D. returned the telephone to the captain who had summoned him to his quarters to take the call. Still reeling with shock, he made his way back to his tent.

"Are you all right?" Cassaday sat up in bed and turned on a dim light.

"Yeah, I'm fine." He sat on the edge of his cot with his elbows propped on his knees and his hands cupping his face.

"Your family?"

"They're fine, but they almost weren't." Braedon told his friend of the close call his family had experienced. "So now my family is going into hiding in another state. Even I don't know where. Marcie is going through all this alone, and I can't even be there to look after her."

"Didn't you say your sister-in-law is staying with her?"

"She's being sent to a different place. This will be really rough on Marcie. Nicole came to stay with her because she's nervous with me away. Her father left when she was just a kid, and her mother turned her into a timid mouse. The colonel let me talk to her for a few minutes, and she said she was fine, but . . ."

"Do you want me to get the chaplain? He doesn't belong to your church, but he's a good man, and sometimes just talking to him helps."

"Not right now, but I appreciate the offer. Just voicing my fears to you helps more than you know. I think I'll—"

"Sergeant Duran. Specialist Cassaday," the familiar voice of their commanding officer's corporal reached them through the closed flap of their tent. "Report to the sergeant major's quarters. Full gear."

"Roger." Cassaday acknowledged the summons. Then more quietly, he asked J.D., "Are you going to be okay?"

"Yes." J.D. drew on the faith that had sustained him through hard times more than once. Always partially dressed, he took mere seconds to don helmet and armor.

He'd been taught early in life to keep a prayer in his heart. Now he prayed as he ran. *Help Marcie,* he pleaded. *Help her to be strong.* As he came to a stop in front of the sergeant major's tent, a quiet peace filled his heart, and he knew Marcie truly was strong enough to handle this crisis. He made a conscious effort to block out all thoughts of home. For now, the mission was all that mattered.

* * *

Marcie felt the jolt as the plane touched down on the runway and the old, familiar panic rose like nausea in her throat. What was she doing leaving everything familiar to come to this strange place where she must trust strangers to protect her and her children? She wanted to stand up and scream. Her heart beat faster, and she thought she might faint.

Marcie, princess, you can do it. Startled she sat up straighter.

Take a deep breath and remember you're never alone. Someone who loves you is always nearby. Calmness settled over her as the advice her father had given her long ago when she'd been afraid to step into the baptismal font filled her head. She knew the someone he'd referred to was the Holy Ghost, but for just a moment, she felt her father's presence beside her. *God doesn't expect more of you than you can give. When your strength is gone, He'll give you some of His.*

"Look, Mommy. I see mountains!" Her son's excited voice brought her back to reality and did its part to restore to her a measure of confidence. She could do this! J.D. was counting on her to keep the children safe, and she would. She wasn't a young girl anymore charged with looking after a willful younger sister who was beyond her ability to handle. Nicole was right too, she was stronger now than the teenage girl she'd been all those years ago. She wouldn't let any of them down.

Thank you for restoring my confidence. She bowed her head for just a moment before beginning the task of gathering up her meager possessions.

The plane taxied to a stop, and she draped the diaper bag strap over her shoulder, picked up Lexie, and took John David's hand. The young man sent to accompany her on this leg of her journey carried the children's car seats. On trembling legs, she moved toward the exit where a young airman reached for her son and indicated she should precede him down the stairs. Once on the ground, she looked around and felt a warm breeze brush her heated cheeks. She barely had time to glance toward the mountains that held her son enthralled before she saw an SUV approaching the place where they stood. Her heart raced, and for just a moment she wondered if she'd made a mistake by coming here.

You can do it. You're stronger than you think. She heard her father's voice inside her head again. A sense of peace replaced her nervousness. She straightened her shoulders and looked toward the vehicle.

A tall man dressed in jeans and a long-sleeved cotton shirt stepped from the SUV. He bore a striking resemblance to Braedon.

Her remaining fears evaporated. She might not like being dependent on strangers for her children's safety, but Braedon had proved his dependability when he brought her children and her sister to her following the firebombing of their home. Now she would trust his brother.

The airman beside her was still holding John David, so she stretched out her one free hand. It was swallowed in the firm grip of calloused fingers.

"I'm Kendall Morgan, and you must be Mrs. Duran." Even his voice sounded similar to Braedon's. "Cameron is driving. Steve is close by in another outfit. He'll stay close all the way to the ranch."

"Call me Marcie," she said as Kendall guided her toward the SUV. "And these are my children, John David and Alexia." Another airman transferred the children's car seats, which, along with the diaper bag she'd left with the friend who watched the children while she went to lunch and the purse she'd taken with her, were her sole possessions other than the clothes she and the children wore.

Once the seats were secured and the children strapped in, there was barely enough room for Marcie, but she didn't complain. Kendall rolled down the window beside her, and the officer who had accompanied her from McChord Air Force Base, which adjoined Fort Lewis, leaned his head in to bid her farewell and assure her she would be safe with the Morgan brothers.

"What about Nicole?"

"Colonel Strichter will make certain she's safe," the man said before saluting sharply and returning to the plane that had brought them. Marcie watched him walk away, then she smiled for the first time since she'd entered that restaurant beside Nicole and Braedon. *Colonel Strichter may think he's looking after Nicole, but I know my sister. She'll look after herself, though I suspect Lieutenant Morgan will also have a hand in keeping her safe.*

* * *

Chief Daniels accompanied Nicole to Tacoma to retrieve Marcie's envelope from her bank's safety deposit box. As she entered the impressive stone-fronted building, she expected someone to challenge her or at least accuse her of fraud when she asked to see her box, but the young man who led the way to the vault seemed almost bored with the activity. The key Marcie had removed from her key ring and handed to Nicole before leaving the colonel's office slid easily into the lock.

There were few people in the vault, and Daniels encouraged her to open the envelope at once. Right on top were the dental charts Marcie had said were there. The next paper proved to be Nicole's parents' wedding certificate. Under it was a copy of her father's will and several documents from insurance companies. Nicole wondered if her mother had ever filed claims on the policies. Several sheets of paper chronicled her father's service record. There were letters addressed to her and her sister, which she scanned quickly. Her father's words of love for his daughters brought tears to her eyes and erased any lingering doubts she might have ever harbored concerning his disappearance.

"Nothing too exciting in it," she found herself almost apologizing. The papers might mean little to their search, but they meant the world to her.

"What's this?" Daniels asked, picking up a newspaper clipping that fell from between the papers she held in her hand. She glanced at it and was puzzled to see an environmental article describing the salmon stairs built into the dams along the Columbia River.

"Mind if I keep this?" Daniels asked.

"You can have it," she told him. "I don't think it's important. Dad talked about taking me fishing for salmon, but he was killed before we had a chance to go." Daniels tucked the clipping inside his billfold while Nicole returned the other items to the box. When this was over, she and Marcie would decide what to do with them.

"I'm sorry there was nothing helpful in Dad's things," Nicole said as they walked toward the exit.

"Don't let it concern you," Daniels said as he held the door open for her. "I really didn't expect anything. Your father was far too professional to mix his work with his personal life. But we had to be certain."

"I understand."

He turned to her and handed her the key he'd been holding. "Those items have no value to the case, but they may be of great value to your family. They're proof he cared about the three of you enough to ensure your financial future."

"He cared about more than our financial future."

"Yes, he did." Daniels took her arm, and together they walked out of the bank. "He loved you with complete devotion. He used to tell me how proud he was of you and that you would be his girls forever. He used to say, 'There's nothing my Nicole can't do if she sets her mind to it.'"

Nicole thought about Daniels's words as they drove back to Fort Lewis, basking in her father's confidence in her abilities. She admitted to herself that at first she'd been disappointed to find no clue to who had shot him, but she didn't consider the trip a waste. It had been reassuring to be reminded that her father hadn't abandoned her. A warmth she hadn't felt since that long-ago time when they'd hiked and explored together filled her heart.

* * *

Daniels drove her to a building on base that looked like the barracks single, enlisted soldiers lived in. The room she was given was smaller than her freshman-year dorm room and boasted fewer amenities. In fact, it bore a chilling resemblance to the room she'd occupied for almost a year at the institution in California. At least there had been a ceiling-mounted television in that room. Restlessly, she paced from the narrow bed to the small, heavily screened window and back again.

She glanced at her watch and fumed. The last thing Daniels had told her before he left was that Braedon had promised he'd be here by six to take her shopping. He'd mentioned dinner too, but she wasn't hungry. She wanted to purchase a laptop even more than she desired a change of clothes, and she wanted to check into a motel. She wanted to be able to move around freely, but she supposed her wants were impossible at the moment. It annoyed her that she couldn't purchase a toothbrush or a change of underwear without Braedon's help as long as she remained on base. Without her own military ID, she couldn't shop at the commissary or PX, and if she left the base for any reason, she couldn't return without military sponsorship. Even if Colonel Strichter hadn't warned her not to cash a check or use a credit card because they could be traced, they wouldn't be accepted on base anyway.

She reached for the handbag she'd left lying on the bed. She was glad she'd had it with her when Marcie's house was destroyed. Retrieving her wallet from the purse, she counted the bills inside and groaned. She had very little cash, not nearly enough to purchase an airline ticket or rent a hotel room. She could manage a toothbrush, if there was someplace she could shop, and that was about all.

Sitting on the bed, she stared gloomily at the thin stack of small-denomination bills in her hand. She didn't want to be dependent on Braedon or Colonel Strichter or any other man. The only man she'd ever counted on had disappeared from her life when she'd needed him the most. She remembered the letter her father had written to her much younger self and felt a little better. It hadn't been Daddy's fault he'd left her.

She considered walking off the base and never returning. She could do that. She wasn't a prisoner—at least she didn't think she was. Thrusting her wallet back inside her purse, she rose to her feet and tiptoed to the door. Easing back the security bolt, she twisted the doorknob and peered through the crack in the door at an empty corridor. She closed and locked the door again. At least there wasn't anyone standing guard at her door. But if there was no one guarding her door, how safe was she?

She felt like she was losing her mind. If Braedon didn't arrive pretty soon, she'd be nothing but a puddle on the floor. Then again, she wasn't certain she wanted to see him again. He said their meeting was accidental and he hadn't been using her to draw her father's attackers into the open, but there had been something unreal about their relationship from the moment they met. He'd been too persistent—and he'd believed her story. No one else had ever believed her, and that alone should have aroused her suspicions. Once more she rose to her feet to pace. She needed a long, hard run. But she didn't have running shoes. Just thinking about her hundred-dollar running shoes being gone, likely burned to a crisp, made her want to cry.

Tears splashed on her slacks, and she stared at the water splotches with a sense of déjà vu. She couldn't remember the last time she'd cried. No, that wasn't true. She and Marcie had cried and hugged each other when they'd finally talked about their father and acknowledged their mutual sense of guilt over the past. She'd cried, too, after telling Braedon about her father. But she hadn't cried because she was uncertain and afraid—not since that night her mother and Marcie had left her at the sanatorium. She'd been shown to a small, second-story room with bars on the only window and been told that was to be her new home. She'd sat on the edge of a strange bed and watched silent teardrops splatter onto the knees of her pajamas.

Angry with herself for reacting as that long-ago child had done, she scrubbed at her eyes then jumped to her feet. As she did so, another memory from the past came to her mind, and she slowly sank to her knees. He had comforted her then and made her strong; He would do so again.

Chapter 17

If she'd wanted to be a blonde, she wouldn't have chosen this dirty-dishwater shade. Nicole glared at herself in the mirror. Braedon had finally shown up, bringing with him a change of clothes for her that were too large and a female soldier he'd introduced as Sergeant Russell.

Sergeant Russell arrived carrying a briefcase full of torture implements she used to cut, bleach, then dye Nicole's hair, along with an assortment of makeup to change her skin tone. The sergeant had also reshaped and dyed Nicole's eyebrows, added contacts to turn her eyes brown, and handed her padded underwear that added twenty pounds to her appearance. Nicole gave Braedon a dirty look as she figured out why the slacks and shirt he'd brought her were too large. Oh well, she'd only agreed to the transformation because it appeared to be the only way she'd manage to get out of this room she'd come to think of as a prison.

Her one consolation was catching sight of Braedon going through some of the same ordeal. Colonel Strichter had given orders that both their appearances be changed to lessen the chance of their being recognized. Since they were both taller than average, she wondered if their height, especially when they were seen together, would give them away in spite of any cosmetic changes made to their appearances.

When Sergeant Russell finished, she packed everything back in her case and scrubbed away all traces of her handiwork from the sink and floor of the tiny bathroom where she had worked. Before leaving, she pulled one last item from her case, a small imitation leather handbag, which certainly didn't make a fashion statement.

"Empty the contents of your handbag onto the bed," she told Nicole. With a shrug, Nicole did as instructed, then watched as the woman sorted through the contents before stuffing all but a bottle of nonprescription eye drops and her pitiful amount of cash back inside. She held the little bottle and paper bills out to Nicole, along with the purse that looked far from new. Her almost new and very expensive bag disappeared into Sergeant Russell's briefcase along with the bracelet Braedon had given her and her watch, leaving her with a sense of loss almost as great as the one she'd experienced when she'd realized all of her clothing and personal possessions she'd brought to Washington were lost in the fire that destroyed her sister's home.

"This bag contains military dependent ID and a new California driver's license in your new name, along with other items you'll find useful," the sergeant told her as she thrust the bag into Nicole's hands. "Familiarize yourself with it as soon as possible." She picked up her briefcase and headed for the door. It closed softly behind her.

"What did she mean by a new name?" Nicole turned to face Braedon with her hands on her hips.

"The colonel thinks you'll be safer with a new identity. I thought you understood that."

"I hadn't thought about changing my name." She reached inside the bag and pulled out a slim brown wallet. Opening it, she stared for a moment at a grainy military ID that strongly resembled the face she'd seen a short time ago in the mirror. The name that went with it was Jean Haskell. "I not only have to answer to a new name," her voice came out in an almost childlike wail, "but I'm fat too."

"The extra pounds look fine," Braedon grinned at her. "But I miss your red hair."

"My hair isn't red!"

"Not now, but I sure hope it will be when it grows back." His frank appraisal made her want to squirm, but she'd been an army brat long enough to learn how to control that impulse. Daddy had insisted military children should stand straight and deny anyone who gave them a bad time the satisfaction of seeing them squirm in discomfort.

"Do you think we might go eat now?" She wasn't all that hungry, but it was the only thing she could think of to end Braedon's scrutiny.

"Not yet." He seated himself in the only chair in the room, leaving her to perch on the edge of the bed. She found herself examining him as critically as he had looked her over a few minutes earlier. His hair, though a much lighter shade of brown, didn't change his appearance significantly. It was so short that once he put his beret back on, it wouldn't make any real difference. He was still the same handsome man who'd gotten under her defenses, causing her to trust and depend on him far too much. Just sitting on the edge of the bed watching him was making her uncomfortable. She rose to her feet and sauntered as casually as she could manage toward the window.

"Stay away from the window," Braedon warned.

"A person would have to have x-ray vision to see through this window," Nicole objected.

"Even though it's tinted and heavily screened, it's better to not take chances. It won't be long now until we can leave."

"You don't really look different," she said, leaning her head to one side and eyeing him critically. "Won't anyone who sees us together guess my identity?"

"Yes, that's why we're not leaving together. Your date will be here to pick you up in about ten minutes. And for your information, I have contacts that will change my eye color before you see me again."

"My date?" Until Braedon implied she would be eating dinner with someone else, she'd thought she'd like nothing better than to put some distance between them. Now she felt a twinge of fear. She didn't want to be with someone else. Even when she'd been attacked in Victoria she'd felt safe knowing Braedon was with her. She might be ambivalent about his personal interest in her, but she trusted his instincts when it came to her safety.

"Colonel Strichter made arrangements for us to meet later tonight." He attempted to reassure her as a knock sounded on the door. He turned on his heel to open it. There stood an enlisted soldier, looking uncomfortable. He saluted, and Braedon gave him a sharp once-over before putting him at ease.

"Jean," Braedon began introductions, and she felt confusion for just a moment until she remembered the name Sergeant Russell had pointed out on her new military ID, "this is Corporal Ronald Haskins. He will be taking you to dinner."

She offered Haskins a tentative smile. He wasn't bad looking, and though several years younger than Braedon, they shared a number of common features. They were almost a match in height, though Braedon might be a tiny bit taller. Ronald's eyes were hazel, and he was heavier and definitely less poised than Braedon. In one ear, he sported a small gold earring, something she couldn't imagine Braedon wearing.

"All right, off with you." Braedon placed a hand at her waist and urged her toward the corporal standing just inside the door. "I'll see you about nine," he whispered loudly enough for her ears only.

The ride to the restaurant where Ronald had reservations passed almost in silence. She would have been happy to settle for a hamburger at the closest fast food place, but her date was determined to take her to a nice restaurant. Fortunately, it was only a few miles from the base. Checking in and being seated by the hostess took a few minutes and seemed to help Ronald get past his shyness.

Nicole fiddled with her silverware and wracked her brain for something to say. The corporal seemed like a nice enough young man, but he was obviously as ill at ease as she. She had to give him credit for trying though. His awkward but persistent attempts at conversation had served to remind her that she had no interest in football, saxophones, wrestling, four-wheeling, motorcycles, or Arnold Schwarzenegger movies. Even with a lack of common interests, he was scrupulously polite and insisted she order anything she liked from the menu.

Reading the menu and ordering helped to fill the time, and once she began eating, she discovered she was hungrier than she'd thought. Even a good meal and the sense of freedom that came from leaving both the room she'd been assigned and the military base behind couldn't dispel the little stab of fear she experienced each time someone new walked into the restaurant or an unexpected sound reached her ears.

At least the man sitting across the table from her seemed to be enjoying his meal. He ordered the biggest steak she'd ever seen one person consume and slowly savored each bite. She was through with her entrée before he was halfway through his steak. A discreet glance at the watch Sergeant Russell had handed her in place of her own told her they'd have to start back soon if she were to meet Braedon at nine. To her dismay, Ronald signaled their waiter and insisted they both order dessert.

She pushed her pie one way then the other with her fork, slowly tearing it to shreds. She was too full and much too nervous to eat it. Finally Corporal Haskins stood and excused himself. Nicole watched in exasperation as he headed for the men's room. She'd given up all pretense of trying to eat by the time he returned.

The corporal slid onto his chair and she leaned forward, ready to urge him to hurry when something stopped her. There was something different about her date. The hazel eyes were the same, his shoulders stooped a bit as though he were in the habit of disguising his height, and he had the same small earring in his left earlobe. Maybe it was his teeth. They appeared straighter and whiter, and there was just something in his bearing. A metallic chink as he picked up his glass alerted her to a gold band on his left ring finger she'd swear hadn't been there before.

He drew his chair closer to hers and whispered, "Put your left hand under the table. There's a matching one for you." She knew that voice, and it didn't belong to Corporal Haskins.

"Braedon, what—?" she started.

"Shh, give me your hand." She glared at him for several seconds, then slowly let her hand drift to her lap beneath the tablecloth. Almost at once she felt a ring slide past the knuckle of her ring finger.

"Mr. and Mrs. Ron Haskell," he murmured. She remembered the name on her ID.

Braedon signaled for the bill, handed the waiter a credit card, then signed the slip of paper as though Ron Haskell were the name he'd been signing all his life.

Nicole didn't speak until they were inside the car she'd assumed belonged to Ronald Haskins. "All right. What's going on?" she demanded.

"Pretty clever, don't you think? Even the names are similar. Someone pointed Ronald Haskins out to me right after I arrived at Fort Lewis, and even I was struck by the resemblance. Now anyone who might have seen you leave the base saw you leave with Ronald. If you were followed, you're still in his company, but this is where we lose them." He pulled into a car wash. "Jump out quick. Head for the car in front of us," he ordered as he flung open his own door.

Seconds before a deluge of water poured down, they passed a couple sprinting in the opposite direction. She assumed they were on their way to claim Ronald's car. She dived into the open door of the other car, feeling the first splash of water as she slammed it shut behind her.

Braedon, without a speck of moisture on him, was laughing when she looked his way. She couldn't resist chuckling too, until they pulled back out onto the street and turned toward the freeway. "I want to hear it all," she said.

Braedon glanced from the road long enough to flash her a triumphant grin. "First things first," he began. "I talked to my mother an hour ago. Your sister and the children arrived at the ranch safely. John David is already asleep in my old room, and Marcie and Lexie are across the hall in Cameron's old room. Mom is delighted to have them there and is looking forward to spoiling the kids and becoming friends with Marcie."

"Thank you. I've been worried, but I didn't know how to find out anything about them."

"Colonel Strichter has given me orders to contact my brother Steve every day and to continue calling my mom a couple of times a week using a secure phone. Steve's phone is also a secure line, and he has direct contact with the closest military base. He's made some adjustments to Mom's phone as well so Marcie can talk to you and J.D."

"That relieves a lot of my worries, but what about this ring? And where are we going?" She peered at the highway signs. "We're headed the wrong direction to be returning to Fort Lewis."

"We're not going back to Fort Lewis." She heard a nervous note in his voice and knew at once it was her reaction to what he had to say that concerned him. "Base intelligence is working with Homeland Security, and the consensus is that a major terrorist attack is imminent on the West Coast. The CIA has intercepted an elevated amount of chatter referencing the West Coast and particularly the Pacific Northwest. There's a strong possibility of a link between those terrorist plans and someone wanting you out of the way."

"So I'm going into hiding?" She would have said more if she hadn't vowed to let him finish before objecting to anything.

"In a way," he conceded. "But Colonel Strichter believes the attacks on you demonstrate excessive paranoia on someone's part. He says it's unreasonable for anyone to be so certain a child who saw two people twelve years ago would accidently see and recognize them today."

"I did see and recognize Poursaid," she reminded him.

"Yes, and he immediately disappeared. His apartment in Tacoma is empty, and he hasn't shown up for work since you spotted him at the commissary. That means he also recognized you."

"I think I know what you're getting at." Nicole paused and pursed her lips as she concentrated on the thought that had come to her mind. "If Poursaid simply disappeared after he suspected I had recognized him, why couldn't the other man do the same? Why continue the attacks against me when it would be so simple for both of them to disappear until I leave Washington again?"

"Exactly. The conclusions Strichter's people have reached are that whatever the terrorists are planning is going to occur too soon for their plan to succeed if key people suddenly leave the area and that Poursaid's partner is a prominent figure you're not likely to miss seeing."

"Wouldn't someone know if any of the people in those pictures Colonel Strichter showed me were prominent people? Besides I'm new to this area. I wouldn't recognize the governor if he walked by." The theory that she might come in contact with any prominent people while in Washington didn't seem too plausible to her.

"He wouldn't have to be prominent in the typical sense," Braedon said. "Just because you saw him in civilian clothes doesn't preclude the possibility he's in the military or he could be a civilian who works on the base as Poursaid did. By the way, you and Marcie both identified Poursaid. Your sister also picked out two men who were at the airport when you arrived, one of which you also found vaguely familiar. He is a well-known terrorist suspect, Akbar Hattam, who left this area abruptly about the time your father was killed."

"And now he's back."

"Yes, we think he's back. The second man was the one who met him at the airport. He's now in custody, thanks to the ticket he gave

Marcie earlier. He's a WHP officer, and he claims he received orders from his superior to meet the man in question and escort him to a Seattle hotel that morning. Chief Daniels identified the patrolman as one of the suspects he was investigating twelve years ago under a different name. There's no record of Hattam or a man with the name the patrolman gave us registered at any hotel in Seattle."

"What about the man who worked in Colonel Strichter's office?"

"He claims it was a coincidence that he went to Victoria the same day we did, and he insists neither he nor his wife know anything about the attacks on you. He also claims he has no idea how those explosive cases got in his car. He'll be held while his story is investigated, but I think he might as well start looking for an attorney."

The car came to a stop, and Nicole turned her attention to her surroundings. They were in a parking lot surrounded by townhouse-style apartments. The apartments looked fairly new, though she could see the silhouettes of large trees behind the buildings, and she had the sense that they were in the country. Braedon picked up a remote control and pressed a button. The door of a single-car garage in front of them opened.

After pulling inside, Braedon shut off the engine and opened the car door. For once, Nicole was still seated when he reached her door. He touched her waist as she stood, guiding her toward a door that opened into a kitchen. Braedon watched Nicole as she stood just inside the kitchen and slowly looked around. The apartment was exactly what he had expected, but it was all new to Nicole. The kitchen was small but well equipped. It was also well stocked with groceries. A table and two chairs occupied the small nook area.

Nicole took a few steps to the living room. It was furnished with a comfortable-looking sofa and chair, a large television complete with DVD and stereo equipment, a framed print of a gray wolf with two pups on one wall, and a bookcase filled mostly with DVDs beside the chair. Magazines were scattered across a low coffee table. A staircase rose to the second floor along the west wall. She turned to face him and raised her eyebrows in silent query. He put off answering her unspoken question.

"Well, this is going right now." He unfastened the small ring in his earlobe and pulled it out. "If it weren't common knowledge that

Haskins wears an earring when he's off duty, I wouldn't have let Sergeant Russell stick the thing in my ear." He pocketed the tiny piece of jewelry.

"I didn't think it was your style," Nicole teased, forgetting for a moment the more serious questions troubling her. "I would have sworn a good Mormon boy like you wouldn't have an ear pierced."

"Like I said, it wasn't my idea. Besides, it hurt." He grimaced.

"Poor baby." She almost laughed before her situation settled heavily on her mind once more. "This is the safe house?" she asked once more, looking around. "Will I be alone here?"

"Uh, Colonel Strichter thought it best for both of us to live off base. His people arrived here a few hours ago in a moving van. They put in a secure phone line and furnished and stocked the house. There are clothes, toiletries, and all that stuff upstairs for us."

"Both of us? And the two of us will be staying here all by ourselves as a married couple?" She tapped the ring on her finger, and something in her voice warned Braedon to be careful. "Colonel Strichter said I'd be going to a safe house, like it or not, but he didn't mention you would be coming too."

"This was purely Strichter's idea. He wants me out of sight, and I've been assigned as a kind of bodyguard to protect you. He said it would look more natural to our new neighbors for us to pose as a married couple . . . Uh, there are two bedrooms upstairs. You can have the bathroom up there, and I'll use the one down here." He pointed to one of two closed doors along the short wall between the kitchen and living room. "And . . . uh . . . We're not exactly alone. There are two CIA agents next door."

She sat down on one of the steps and looked at him through wrought-iron rails. "Is there anything else you haven't told me? Like are there cameras in all the rooms? Microphones? Is the telephone bugged?" Her voice dripped with sarcasm.

"It won't be that bad." He looked apologetic. "There are alarms on the upstairs windows, but surveillance equipment is limited to the first floor."

Without another word she fled up the stairs.

Chapter 18

Marcie watched the tall cowboy patiently lead a small pony bearing two excited three-year-olds around the enclosed area. John David gripped Cameron's son's waist, and his smile lifted her own heart until thoughts of her sister intruded. Coming here to the Morgan ranch had turned into a delightful experience for her son, and she felt welcome and at ease with Margaret Morgan herself. A large Australian shepherd lay at her feet, never taking his eyes from the two little boys. At first, the big dog had frightened her, but she soon saw his devotion to her son and the loud clamor he set off every time anyone other than family arrived at the ranch as an added level of security. Her concern for her children's safety was greatly eased, but thoughts of J.D. and the war he fought were never far from her mind, and now she worried about Nicole's safety as well.

She lifted her eyes to the soaring mountain peaks and felt a strange peace. She wasn't terribly familiar with mountains, but they seemed to speak to her soul as she remembered her father's love for wilderness of any kind. Instead of staring at them, she supposed she should be worrying about how to replace her furniture and the family's few possessions with the meager amount of money they'd have coming from their renter's insurance. With J.D. in a combat zone, his pay was a little higher than usual, and Margaret had let her know she wouldn't accept any reimbursement from her for the time she and the children spent at the ranch, so she should be able to budget the necessary money to buy furnishings for their new home when they returned to Fort Lewis. She just hoped they wouldn't be at the bottom of the waiting list for on-base housing.

"Look, Mommy!" John David's voice broke into her thoughts, and she looked his way. He was riding the pony alone now with Cameron Morgan walking beside him. Cameron's wife, Lynette, was in the corral on a much larger horse with her son seated in front of her. Marcie envied the other woman the courage to ride such a large animal. It had taken all of her courage to allow Cameron to seat her son on the shaggy little pony.

His father would be so proud of him if he could see him on that pony. A second impression followed. *His grandfather would be proud of him too.* Her father had never expressed disappointment or behaved as if he regretted that both of his children were daughters, but an outdoorsman like her dad must have longed for a son. It struck her as another reason to mourn her father, that he hadn't lived to know his grandson. She thought of the one quick conversation she'd had with Nicole since arriving at the ranch. Her sister had told her about the letter from her father waiting in her safety deposit box. It had gone far to ease the ache his seeming abandonment had caused her for so many years.

"Marcie! Come quickly," Margaret's voice floated from the wide porch of the old ranch house. "There's a telephone call for you."

Marcie glanced toward her son, then back toward the house.

"Go ahead," Cameron told her. "I'll watch your boy."

"Thanks," she called back over her shoulder as she ran toward the house. For just a moment, she wondered at the easy trust she had developed in Braedon's brother. She had no doubt that her son would be safe in the man's care. In less than a minute, she clutched the phone in her hand.

"Hello," she gasped.

"Marcie, are you all right?" J.D.'s concerned voice reached her ear.

"Yes. I'm just out of breath. I was down by the corral watching John David ride a pony. I wish you could see him. He loves all the attention he's getting, the animals, and playing with Cameron's son, Trace."

"I wish I could see him too," J.D. said. "I'm glad that staying at that ranch is working out so well for you and the kids, but I can't help worrying. Has there been any more trouble at all?"

"No. Steve keeps close watch for any strangers to the area, and he and his brothers really do look after us."

"What about Nicole? Have you heard from her?"

"She called yesterday. She said she's fine and that she's spending a lot of time on the computer. She's still searching for Dad and seeing Braedon every day." She almost giggled. "I suspect Miss I'm-not-interested is a whole lot interested in Braedon Morgan. Oh, and she said the pictures I identified have given them some strong leads to follow. I never thought I'd ever have anything to do with tracking down terrorists."

"You're really all right? You're not lying awake at night afraid to close your eyes are you?" J.D.'s voice was serious.

"Really, honey, I'm okay. You told me once that I was stronger than I gave myself credit for. Nicole said the same thing. I was terribly frightened when I thought our children were in danger, but on that flight out here, something changed inside me. I remembered Daddy saying 'God never expects more of us than we can give, and if we aren't strong enough He makes us stronger.' I felt closer to him then than I have at any other time since he disappeared. It was almost as though he were sitting beside me, assuring me I could do it, just like when he taught me to ride a bike and when I was baptized. That's when I knew you and Nicole were right. I can do what I need to do, and I can keep our children safe."

"You've changed, honey."

"Not so much you won't still love me when you get back?" she asked in a half-teasing voice.

"I'll never stop loving you, and I can hardly wait to meet this new side of you. What I'm trying to say is you amaze me, and I'm proud of you."

"Wow, if I'd known all I had to do to impress you was to fight a few terrorists, I would have started a long time ago." For some reason she felt almost euphoric hearing the admiring note in her husband's voice.

"Hey, leave the terrorists to me. That's why I'm over here, remember?"

"Seriously, J.D. One thing I've learned from this is that evil people can hide anywhere. They fool good people and people who are just too busy to pay attention into thinking they're ordinary people. This war can't be won by soldiers alone. We all have to keep our eyes open."

Long after their farewells were said, J.D. lingered over his wife's words. In reality, he wasn't sure how he felt about Marcie's newfound strength. He hadn't lied when he told her he was proud of her, but the possibility that she might not need him anymore raised troubling thoughts in his mind. Then the remainder of her words sank in. "This war can't be won by soldiers alone. We all must know the difference between good and evil." He and Marcie and Cassaday and Nicole and Braedon and many, many others were engaged in a war not just in Iraq and not just against terrorists. They were all embroiled in a war between good and evil.

* * *

"If I don't get out of here soon, I'll go crazy!" Nicole paced the narrow space between the living room and kitchen. She was dressed in nylon sweats and a pair of cheap athletic shoes. He knew the short hair beneath the scarf she wore for a sweat band was showing the faintest signs of darker roots and would need to be touched up soon. He hoped this whole mess would be cleared up before that became necessary. In the meantime, he sympathized with her plight. Nicole was much too physical by nature to be confined to the limited space of this small town-house apartment.

"I'm going for a run," she announced with a hint of defiance. She reached for the door handle. "If you want to come along, fine, but I'm not waiting." She was out the door before he could stop her, but he wasn't sure he wanted to stop her. He needed exercise as badly as she did, and if the CIA agents didn't like it, they could try to keep up. He let the door slam shut behind him, knowing it would automatically lock and that he had the key in his pocket. Two weeks had produced no sign of the terrorists, and he was fed up with the wary distance Nicole maintained between them.

She was already across the parking lot, heading toward a path that led into a thick grove of trees, and he'd have to stretch to catch up. He lengthened his stride, concentrating on catching her. Out of the corner of his eye, he noticed a car pulling into the parking lot and moved to the side, allowing it plenty of room. Seconds later he was in the trees, where he caught just a glimpse of Nicole before she disappeared around a bend in the trail.

Two weeks of not running, as well as failure to warm up before starting this run, slowed him some. It slowed Nicole too, or she was deliberately allowing him to draw closer. He had no illusions about being the better runner—Nicole could beat him any day. But little by little, he was closing the distance between them. Finally, puffing from the exertion, he pulled level with her.

"Slowpoke." She grinned, and it was like getting the old Nicole back, the one he'd been rapidly falling in love with before Colonel Strichter and Chief Daniels got involved in their search. He hoped it was a signal their polite but distant relationship of the past two weeks was at an end.

He didn't attempt to speak. It was all he could do to run by her side and watch for tree limbs and shrubs that required ducking his head or dropping back to single file. He did manage a smile acknowledging her taunt.

After about ten minutes, he noticed she was slowing and welcomed the slower pace. At last her stride became a walk, and he became aware of the stillness around them. He wondered where Nicole's mad dash had taken them. Lacey wasn't like the towns he was familiar with back home. There were no neat streets running north and south with clear city limits. Instead, it sprawled through the dense forest with bands of trees and winding roads separating homes and schools from one another. A network of informal footpaths wove through the forested areas, and if his sense of direction hadn't failed him, he guessed they weren't too far from where they had begun. Nicole confirmed his guess.

"The elementary school that is about a block down the street from the apartment is just ahead," she informed him. He looked but couldn't see it through the trees.

"How do you know that?" he queried.

"I have a pretty good sense of direction."

"You've never seen that school, so how do you know it's there?" He only knew of the school's existence because he'd been shown a map of the area before he'd gone to meet Nicole at the restaurant before they'd moved in.

"The Internet." She laughed at his incredulous expression. "There are dozens of ways to map a neighborhood, starting with just a few facts."

"I know that, but did you go to all that trouble just to be able to escape the apartment for an hour?"

"Don't you think that's a pretty good reason?" Her grin was sassy, then her expression turned serious. "There was more to it than that. If we should be discovered, I want to be familiar enough with the area to have a chance of escaping."

"Why didn't you just ask the colonel for a map of the area?"

"Because I was angry. He left me out of the planning for staying here, and when he calls, he tells you what is going on but never me. He should have briefed me on the area in case we're discovered and have to leave."

"You know we're going to get yelled at when we return, don't you?" He didn't comment on her reasons for plotting a map of Lacey or for taking an impromptu run. In a way it wounded his pride that she didn't trust him enough to count on his protection, but he admired her ingenuity and even understood her frustration. She'd been looking out for herself for a long time and had learned early on not to count on other people. It really was unfair to leave her out of the information loop when it was her life on the line. Besides, he didn't like feeling trapped or dependent either.

Ahead, he caught a glimpse of the school through the trees and began to skirt it. Without discussing the matter, they took care not to expose themselves to view any more than could be helped. The brush was too thick to allow them to resume running, and they had to pick their way through thick growth until they came within a few feet of the road that separated them from their apartment.

They stayed hidden until they were certain there was no traffic on the quiet street, then, clasping hands, they dashed across the road to a group of mailboxes.

"I don't recognize that car." Nicole pointed to a vehicle parked in front of their apartment. He remembered the car he'd passed earlier while concentrating on following Nicole and realized this was the same one.

Still holding her hand, Braedon backed up a few steps and motioned toward the thick stand of trees across from the mailboxes.

"Stay in the trees until I signal for you to come," he whispered. For a moment, he thought she was going to refuse to hide while he checked out their visitors, but after a slight hesitation, she darted across the lane to where the trees swallowed her up.

Not wanting any of the neighbors to find his actions suspicious, he boldly approached the apartment and inserted his key in the lock. He opened the door and stepped aside, allowing the door to partially shield him from whoever was inside the apartment. The corner of his mouth twitched on seeing Colonel Strichter dressed in golfer's attire filling the armchair, a newspaper in his hands.

"It's about time you got back." There was an ominous quietness in the colonel's voice. He lowered the paper and looked beyond Braedon to the empty stoop behind him. "Where's Nicole? If you lost . . ."

"It's all right, sir," Braedon hastened to assure him. "She's waiting for my signal that it's safe to return." He stepped back out onto the stoop and raised one arm. Moments later Nicole joined him in the front room to face the colonel.

After dressing them both down for leaving the apartment without permission, he turned to the reason for his visit. "Marcie recognized a suspect with al Qaeda ties that Evangart and Daniels were investigating twelve years ago. He's the same man you, Nicole, thought looked a little bit familiar. He returned to the Middle East about the time Evangart disappeared. Akbar Hattam's name has popped up in the Middle East with increasing importance in terrorist circles through the years since. He's been known to drop out of sight for long periods of time, be active briefly, then disappear again. An inquiry into his whereabouts produced nothing during the past six months until last night when we got a break. His description and an artist's sketch closely resemble one of two men suspected of starting a string of fires over a week-long period in California's drought-dry forests. The fires were blamed on careless campers until it was learned a chemical igniter and an accelerant were involved, making the fires arson. There are physical indications each fire began with a small explosion, presumably set off by a remote device. Yesterday, multiple descriptions of the same campers near various affected areas came to the attention of a forest service fire investigator who once attended the same American university as our camera-shy Hattam."

"Has he been arrested? Where did Marcie see him?" Nicole asked rapid-fire questions.

"No, he hasn't been picked up yet, but every law enforcement agency in the country is on the lookout for him. The fires burned thousands of acres and destroyed more than eighty homes." Strichter sighed. "Unfortunately, your sister only remembers one of the places she saw him."

"What I really came here for," Strichter looked uncomfortable, then tightened his jaw and went on, "is to tell you that our investigation has led us to believe someone currently at Fort Lewis, possibly an officer, is involved with a suspected terrorist group outside of my jurisdiction. We think Poursaid, the young man from my office who was arrested, and at least one other individual were links between this individual and the terrorists. Homeland Security has requested a joint investigation to include several federal agencies, state and civil law enforcement, and the military in an effort to prevent another possible 9/11."

Braedon understood how much it pained the colonel to admit a military officer was involved. "Sir? Can you share with us the suspected individual's identity?"

Colonel Strichter reached across the small space separating him from Nicole and took her hand. "Even as a child your instincts were right. We sent you to the one man who could harm you the most. The Air Force, unlike the army, has for years made base assignments somewhat permanent, and Major Detford continued to work at McChord Air Base adjoining Fort Lewis until his retirement a few years ago. Since retiring, he has continued to be affiliated with Madigan hospital as a civilian doctor. The CIA reports he deposited large sums of money in his account on a regular basis for nearly three years in the early nineties. Those deposits have resumed during the past year, and in recent months have included several very large lump sums. Among the handful of patients Detford continued to see after his retirement were Poursaid, my first sergeant, and a handful of navy and air force enlisted and lower-ranking officers. Unlike the other suspects, we suspect money rather than ideology was his motive."

Nicole gasped, and Braedon reached for her even though he too was reeling from the news. "But how . . . ?" he managed to begin a question.

"Detford was found dead in his office this morning. He'd been shot at close range. His files and cupboards had been ransacked to make it appear he'd been shot in the course of a robbery, but a small safe he had concealed in the floor was discovered during the investigation. It was opened, and the investigator recognized materials he determined should be brought to my attention."

"Do you know who was paying him?" Nicole asked, seeming to regain her balance.

"No, but all of his papers have not been analyzed yet. In addition to a meticulous record of all of his private and professional appointments and his bankbook, we found your file with frequent updates made over the past twelve years. From it, we learned someone was angry with him for sending you to an institution instead of killing you and canceled their arrangement with him. It appears that Detford saved your life, then made it his business to follow your movements until you returned here. We think he's also the man who attempted to pass on a warning to you through Marcie and her small son."

"But who killed him?" Nicole asked in a dazed voice.

"We're not sure, but we suspect it was a former navy man who met with him several times over the past couple of weeks. The CIA has suspected him for several years of having ties to Islamic extremists."

* * *

Marcie stood at her bedroom window looking at the trees on the hill. She loved the view from this window. When she first arrived, she could hardly distinguish the green of deciduous trees from the deeper green of conifers. Nicole was the nature lover in their family, but Marcie had recently discovered both comfort and peace in the view from this window. For some reason she couldn't explain, she felt closer to her husband here. Perhaps it was because he had grown up in a place like this. His parents and older brother had died in a boating accident when he was only three, and he'd lived with his grandparents on an Idaho farm until they both passed away when he was seventeen. The army had been his family after that, until he married her.

If only J.D. were here. Some instinct told her he would like the Morgan ranch almost as much as their son did. Her husband had been gone since early spring, and she missed him terribly. She wished she could call him to tell him about the kittens John David had discovered in the barn yesterday afternoon and that he had ridden the pony alone this morning without Cameron walking beside him. Lexie was sitting up by herself and her first tooth now had a companion. Most of all she wished he were safe, snuggled up in the big four-poster beside her.

Lexie stirred, making small whimpering sounds, and Marcie went to her, lifting her from the cradle the Morgan brothers had brought down from the attic and placed beside the bed where Marcie slept alone. She changed the baby and dressed her before heading across the hall to check on John David. As was often the case, she found her son's bed empty.

The empty bed brought a smile rather than concern to her heart. At first, Braedon's big bed had seemed far too large for such a little boy, but John David seemed determined to match the Morgan men in stature. Except for his father, she couldn't think of any finer role models for her son to emulate. He would soon be four and was becoming quite independent. Lately he'd become adamant about dressing himself, and though some of his selections were bizarre combinations, she didn't want to discourage him, so she let him choose his own outfits from the generous selection of clothing donated by Steve's twin sons.

Carrying Lexie, she continued on downstairs expecting to find her son at the breakfast table, but his customary spot was empty.

"Has John David already eaten?" she asked Margaret.

"That boy." The older woman turned to face Marcie with laughter sparkling in her eyes. "He was waiting here in the kitchen when I got up this morning. He didn't want to waste any time eating breakfast. He just wanted to go check on the kittens."

"Oh dear," Marcie sighed. "I'll have to talk to him. I don't want him to go to the barn by himself."

"Don't you worry about him. Steve and Kendall installed dead-bolts on the doors and windows just hours before you arrived as a safety precaution. That boy may be growing like a weed, but he can't reach the bolts yet. Anyway, he's not out there alone. My grandson is out there too, and Cameron and Lynette are in the barn getting ready to work the colts Lynette is training. They showed up before John David was half through eating the breakfast I convinced him would help his muscles grow. Of course, the moment he saw Trace, he was too full to eat another bite."

Both women laughed, then Marcie busied herself preparing cereal for the baby and eating her own breakfast. When she finished and Lexie was clean once more, she set her daughter in the playpen Lynette had loaned her.

"I'll vacuum this morning," she promised. "As soon as I've checked on John David."

"You don't need to be cleaning all of the time," Margaret assured her. "This house has never been so polished as it has been since you arrived. You go spend a little time with your boy, and I'll keep an eye on this little lady." Lexie was rubbing her eyes, indicating she was ready for her morning nap.

When Marcie reached the barn, she followed the sound of children's voices until she found John David and Trace romping on a low stack of hay bales with Cooper. The dog's excited bark echoed through the barn.

"Good morning," she greeted her son. She picked him up to give him a hug, then sat down on a bale of hay with him in her lap. "What are you guys up to?" She included Trace with a smile and invited him to sit beside her too. Not to be left out, Cooper laid his head on her knee. She reached forward to stroke his thick tricolored coat. Her hand smoothed the silky hair back over his neck several times before she noticed the dog wasn't wearing a collar.

"Why doesn't Cooper have a collar?" she asked Cameron, who was forking fresh straw into a nearby stall.

"We've given up buying them," Cameron said with a laugh. "We haven't found one yet that canny old mutt can't—"

A strangled scream escaped Marcie's throat.

"Marcie, what is it?" Cameron dropped the fork and came running toward her.

"I have to call Colonel Strichter. I have to tell him I stopped to buy flea collars. I ran right into him!"

"Who did you run into?" Lynette joined them.

"The man who was delivering bags of fertilizer to the nursery. He was the man in the picture." She rose to her feet. "I have to let Colonel Strichter know I remember where I saw Akbar Hattam."

Chapter 19

Returning from the mess hall, J.D. heard Cassaday long before he reached their tent. For a religious man, Cassaday knew more than his fair share of cuss words, and though he didn't swear often, J.D. knew just what the swear words signified. There was a spider in their tent, and not just any spider, but a hand-sized camel spider.

Cassaday hated the things, not that J.D. was too fond of them himself, but at least he recognized them as overgrown wolf spiders like he'd run across while vacationing in Arizona once. The little beasts had a well-deserved nasty reputation, though they didn't quite measure up to the stories soldiers passed from unit to unit extolling the spiders' exploits. They could move quickly, about ten miles per hour, but they really didn't attach themselves to camels' bellies and eat them alive, and they didn't aggressively chase down GIs or attack them in their sleep. However if cornered or threatened, they would bite, and the bite, though not venomous, was excruciatingly painful. A few soldiers had been sent home because of encounters with camel spiders.

"All right, where is it?" J.D. asked as he entered the tent. He stopped to look around and found the answer to his question. The ferocious-looking spider was cornered inside an empty ammunition crate Cassaday had been planning to use for storage. Cassaday was standing several feet away with his M-16 trained on the creature.

"Careful, you'll have the animal rights people down on us if you shoot him," J.D. warned with a straight face.

"Spiders ain't animals. They're one of God's curses. Anyway, I know I can't shoot him, but it isn't those animal rights folks I'm worried about. It's Sergeant Dennison. She threatened to shoot the next person who discharged a gun in this camp that isn't aimed at a terrorist."

"I suppose you might make a case for having spiders declared terrorists, especially that one. He's the biggest camel spider I've seen yet." J.D. could barely suppress a shudder.

"Quit fooling around and help me find a way to get rid of the thing. He's going to charge any minute." There was a definite plea in the younger soldier's voice.

J.D. picked up a thick, wooden chessboard some well-meaning service group had sent and began moving cautiously toward the spider.

"Sergeant Duran, Captain Davenport sent me to find you." A voice came from behind J.D. "He said he needs to see you as soon as possible and that if you need any help clearing up whatever you're doing, I should assist you."

"Here, get rid of this for me." J.D. slapped the game board on top of the ammunition box and thrust it toward the hapless private. The private's eyes widened as he took the box.

"You might need this." Cassaday came forward with a roll of duct tape. J.D. took it from him and gave it a couple of quick twists around the box.

"Wha . . . what should I do with it, Sergeant?" the young soldier stammered.

"I understand the 528th is burning garbage today," Cassaday suggested.

J.D. resisted the impulse to whistle as he made his way to Captain Davenport's quarters. It was almost strange how much better he'd felt since his last telephone call to Marcie. It was almost as though her newfound strength strengthened him. It was more than that though. She'd made it possible for him to see a concept he hadn't fully grasped before. This war had no borders. They weren't fighting the Iraqi people—most of them were victims, not enemies. Hate and oppression, the desire to dominate and control, could occur anywhere terrorists chose to strike.

* * *

There were advantages to having her hair short, Nicole thought as she fluffed her hair after blowing it dry. She'd felt cold and sticky sitting in the front room discussing Major Detford following her run. She felt vindicated for her distrust of the man, but she had no desire to dwell on whether he might have saved her life. As soon as Colonel Strichter left, she'd headed for the shower.

She hadn't spent time luxuriating in the steamy water because she knew Braedon was anxious to shower as well, and the apartment didn't have an abundance of hot water. Dressed in jeans and a long-sleeved sweater, she went downstairs to prepare lunch. She could hear the shower running and knew Braedon wouldn't be ready for lunch anytime soon. Picking up the remote from the sofa arm, she turned the television on as she wandered toward the kitchen.

Opening the refrigerator door, she stared at the contents while she considered what to prepare. She wasn't in the mood to cook, and meal preparation was something that hadn't worked out quite the way they'd planned. They were going to take turns cooking, but it hadn't taken long to discover Braedon's culinary skills were limited to grilling steaks and scrambling eggs. She didn't really mind doing most of the cooking because Braedon was so pleased to have her do it that he voluntarily did most of the cleanup.

Pulling from the refrigerator the remnants of the roast she'd prepared the day before, she cut a pile of thin slices, which she heaped onto pieces of whole wheat bread. She added tomatoes, pickles, lettuce, cheese, peppers, mayo, and another slice of bread to complete the sandwiches. She placed one on a plate with a handful of potato chips and set a can of root beer beside it. She poured herself a glass of milk and scooped up a handful of cut veggies from a plastic box in the fridge.

Setting her plate on the table, she felt a moment's hesitation before bowing her head to mutter an almost silent prayer. She would never, ever get used to the idea of being watched by unseen strangers while she ate or said a blessing. For the first three days, she'd carried her plate up to her room every meal. She grinned, remembering Braedon's persuasive speech when he convinced her to join him at the kitchen table. "Do you think *they're* eating like this?" He'd jerked his thumb toward the wall that separated their apartment from the one the CIA guards occupied, then held up his plate, loaded with lasagna, green bean casserole, and the hot rolls she'd prepared that afternoon. "Watching me eat like this is killing them. Think what it would do to them if a beautiful lady were sitting across the table from me as well."

He'd made her laugh, and she'd carried her plate to the table. It was the beginning of a truce of sorts, and today had felt like a resumption of the friendship they'd formed earlier. As she had wondered more than once, she considered whether or not her relationship with Braedon was more than friendship. Was she falling in love while he was merely doing his job?

She didn't want to think about that possibility. She looked around for a distraction and remembered she'd turned on the television. A soap was playing, so she clicked through the channels looking for something more appealing without luck. Then she spotted a newspaper on the floor beside the armchair where Colonel Strichter had sat. She decided to read it while she ate. The television was frequently on, and she heard the news every day, but she hadn't seen a newspaper since they'd arrived at the town house.

Once she settled in her chair with the newspaper in front of her, she discovered something interesting. The open paper blocked her view of the tiny ceiling camera in one corner of the room. If it blocked her view of the camera, it probably blocked the camera's view of her. She settled down to enjoy her sandwich and the newspaper.

"Looks good," Braedon complimented, entering the kitchen. Just as he started to sit down, the phone rang. Giving his sandwich a longing look, he scooped up the phone.

"Haskell residence, Ron speaking." He winked at her, leaving her annoyingly flustered. The grin faded from his face, and his expression showed concern as he listened quietly. Once he grimaced. She forgot about her sandwich and openly watched him.

"Sure I'll put her on," he said after a long pause. He thrust the phone into her hand and sat down, straddling the chair opposite her. Instead of reaching for his sandwich, he watched her as avidly as she had watched him moments earlier.

"Your sister contacted me right after I reached my office," Colonel Strichter spoke abruptly, wasting no time on pleasantries. "She remembered where she saw Hattam. The day she picked you up at the airport, she stopped at a pet store not far from Sea-Tac to buy a couple of flea collars."

"I remember," Nicole picked up the story. "She almost walked into a nursery by mistake. She collided with a truck driver in the doorway and realized she was entering the wrong business."

"Did you recognize the man who bumped into her?"

"No, but I really didn't get a look at his face. He was wearing a cap, and his back was to me."

"We believe the truck driver she collided with was Akbar Hattam. Did you see what kind of truck he was driving?"

"Yes, Marcie's son noticed the truck first and was excited about it. It was white and there was a logo on the door, but I don't remember what it was. I do remember it was a large flatbed loaded with pallets of bags like those gardeners buy at nurseries to improve their soil."

"Fertilizer," Strichter shouted into her ear and abruptly broke the connection.

"Fertilizer?" She stared in confusion at the phone in her hand until an ugly picture surfaced in her mind. She remembered news photos of a building with a huge chunk ripped out of one side. "Oklahoma," she murmured in a shaky voice as she sank back onto her chair.

"The Alfred P. Murrah Federal Building," Braedon's soft exclamation was followed by a low whistle. "I think I know now why Poursaid was making regular trips to Fort Lewis."

"Do you think he was planning to bomb the base?" It was just too unbelievable.

"No, he gained a lot of detonation experience during the years he was in the army, and both Daniels and Strichter suspect he was stealing explosives. But they haven't been able to discover what or how much is missing."

"I don't understand the connection. If no explosives are missing . . ."

Braedon picked up the newspaper Nicole had dropped on the table and set it to one side. He reached for Nicole's hand, holding it gently as he went on. "Poursaid wasn't stealing explosives. He was making his own."

"How do you know that?" Nicole freed her hand, feeling confused. "I only know Specialist Poursaid was one of the two men with my father when he was killed."

Braedon's eyes narrowed. "I think he was stealing small amounts of aviation fuel each time he visited the commissary."

Nicole remained skeptical. "The commissary doesn't carry jet fuel. Besides Fort Lewis isn't an air base."

"No, but McChord is. The air base is adjacent to Fort Lewis, and the commissary, hospital, and PX are shared. I suspect someone from McChord has been meeting Poursaid each week at the commissary or some other designated place on base to slip him a gallon or two of jet fuel each time he arrived with a delivery. Detford may have even been the go-between. The small amounts haven't been missed by the air base but have added up significantly wherever Poursaid and Hattam have been stockpiling it."

"Does the colonel have any idea what they mean to blow up?" Nicole rose to her feet once more, gathering up her plate and glass as she stood. She walked to the sink with them, rinsed them, and placed them in the dishwasher.

"Well?" She turned back to Braedon, who was still seated at the table and hadn't attempted to answer her question.

"There are a lot of possible targets in this area. The Northwest is full of hydroelectric dams and major seaports. Seattle is a worldwide trade center. The army, navy, and air force all have bases here and . . . The list could go on and on, but your father and Daniels were following leads that led to a dam on the Columbia. Daniels believes either the Dalles or Bonneville dam is their target."

"That's why he was interested in the news clipping Dad kept. He wasn't thinking of the salmon. It was the dams themselves he thought might be a clue. But all we really know is that terrorists are planning to attack. We don't know for sure what they plan to blow up. Or when." She snatched the rest of the dishes off the table and carried them to the sink.

"Hey, I'm not through with that." Braedon protested as she dumped the last of his sandwich and chips down the garbage disposal.

"Sorry." She said the word absently. Her mind wasn't on lunch or straightening the kitchen. Clearing the table was merely something to absorb her nervous energy. Her mind was elsewhere, trying to put pieces of the puzzle together.

"I can't help feeling everyone is losing sight of something important in all this mess." She met Braedon's eyes from across the room.

"We got involved because we set out to find my father's body, then someone started trying to kill me. I don't understand what any of this has to do with me. Poursaid is the only person connected with my father I recognized, and he's disappeared. There is no way I can guess what he and his friends plan to blow up, so there's no way I can try to stop them."

"Either you have a piece of information you don't know you possess or the terrorists believe you do." Braedon's observation didn't make her feel any better.

"Do you think they're still looking for me?" she asked while attempting to ignore the knot forming in her stomach.

"Yes," Braedon said. "At first we hoped the people who blew up Marcie's house would believe you had been inside, but since no death notices or news accounts mentioned anyone killed in the tragedy, they must know you're alive."

"How long do you think it will take them to find me?" He watched her pace to the next room where she picked up the television remote and began mindlessly switching channels. After a few minutes, she sat on the edge of the sofa but continued her restless channel surfing. She could figure out as well as he could that their safe house wouldn't stay safe indefinitely. As long as they continued contact with their families or the army, there was always the possibility someone would find a way to trace them.

Braedon gathered up the newspaper Nicole had left on the table and followed her to the front room. He settled in the armchair and turned to the sports page. He found himself unable to concentrate on any of the stories he started reading. His mind kept reviewing the events of the past couple months and particularly the weeks he and Nicole had spent in the town house. The closest they'd come to a romantic moment was when he'd reached for her hand a few moments ago. Still he had to admit he'd selfishly enjoyed pretending to be Nicole's husband during the past seventeen days. He had it bad, he admitted to himself, if he'd enjoyed simply sitting across the table from her, being driven nuts by the smell of her shampoo, arguing over who was going to do the dishes, and taking out the trash.

He looked across the room at her and realized he didn't want to pretend anymore. He wanted a real life with her. He wanted to take her on dates, run every day with her, and in time raise a family with her. He couldn't do any of that as long as a threat hung over her head. He wanted this ended for her sake as well as his. Whether she chose to spend her future with him or not, she deserved a chance to get on with her life. She gave him an odd look and ducked her head to the side as though examining him from another angle.

He buried his head behind the paper. He wasn't ready for her to see what must be plain on his face. He certainly wasn't going to declare his undying love for her in front of a CIA camera.

"Braedon, let me see that." Braedon tensed when he realized she'd forgotten to call him Ron. The paper was suddenly ripped from his hands.

"This isn't a good idea," he started, then realized she wasn't paying any attention to him. Her whole attention was focused on something in the newspaper.

"That's him. He's gained weight, but I would recognize him anywhere."

"Who? What are you talking about?" He stood up and stepped around Nicole to look over her shoulder. He couldn't tell what had captured her attention. There was the usual political statement by some candidate for something, a spokesman for some environmental group was blaming the president for an oil spill halfway around the world, four new forest fires were threatening homes in western states, and a group of longshoremen in Tacoma were planning a union meeting.

"There! That's the man who shot Daddy." Tears ran down her cheeks as she stabbed her finger at a black-and-white newspaper photo.

Chapter 20

To Braedon's eyes, the picture was just that of another well-dressed businessman. Dropping his gaze to the picture caption he learned that the man was Anthony Fournier, the newly elected union representative for the Port of Tacoma and the featured speaker at tonight's union meeting.

"Are you sure?" He didn't want to doubt her, but as he scanned the article, her assertion appeared unlikely. Fournier's background read like the American dream. He immigrated from France in 1982, settled in Tacoma, and went to work loading and unloading cargo at the sixth largest container port in North America. He joined the union the day he began working, and by the late nineties, he had become a foreman and a leader in the Tacoma longshoremen's union. He married a local woman from a prominent family. Their daughters were students at a public high school in a middle-class Tacoma neighborhood.

"Yes, I'm sure. His face is fuller, not so weaselly, but the eyes are the same. I know it's him. We need to call Colonel Strichter." Her hands shook, making a closer examination of the man's picture difficult.

"Okay, but this guy doesn't sound like someone who would be mixed up with terrorists like Poursaid and Hattam." He stepped away from her and reached for the phone.

Before he touched it, a shrill ring startled him. Nicole reached past him, then withdrew her hand and looked at him. She'd been instructed to never answer the phone, but he knew she still struggled with following Colonel Strichter's order. Answering a ringing telephone was such a reflex thing to do. He snagged the receiver with one hand.

"Haskell here," he said skipping a greeting. He hoped the caller was the colonel with more information.

"Brae—" a female voice began, then cut off the name she was about to speak. "I need to talk to my sister."

"Okay, here she is." He handed the phone to Nicole while mouthing Marcie's name.

"I tried to reach Colonel Strichter, but he's out, and his office said they couldn't put me through to him," Marcie began. Her voice carried to his ears and something in the tone of her voice had him moving closer to the phone Nicole held.

"What's wrong?" Nicole asked, and he knew she had picked up on her sister's fear. He blatantly leaned his head next to Nicole's to eavesdrop.

"On the news there was an artist's sketch of the man wanted for starting fires in California. I'm sure he's that Akbar Hattam the colonel is looking for. Will you tell him?"

"The colonel already knows Hattam is the chief arson suspect," she assured her sister. "Someone called him last night to tell him. But why didn't you tell Steve to contact the colonel?"

"He's not answering his pager."

"What?" Braedon took the phone from Nicole. "Where are Cameron and Kendall?"

"They're rounding up cattle. There was some kind of difficulty with a fence down between your property and the government land next to your ranch, so Lynette left Trace here and went with them."

"You're there alone with Mother and the children?" Braedon asked the question as though he were merely curious.

"Yes, the baby is asleep, and the boys are watching *Sesame Street*. Margaret and I are working on a surprise for dinner since everyone will be hungry and tired by the time they return. We're going to call Steve and Kendall's wives and invite them over too." Marcie seemed to be over the fear that had prompted her to call, but his was just starting.

"Could you put my mother on the phone for just a minute?" he asked. In minutes his mother's cheery greeting came over the line.

"Mom, you and Marcie shouldn't be alone. And what's this about not being able to reach Steve?"

"I don't think it's anything to worry about. The sheriff's office is probably just having a busy day."

"It might be more than that." He didn't want to alarm his mother, but his training had taught him to be wary of coincidences, and he could feel the short hairs on the back of his neck standing up.

"Plan B?" There was resignation in his mother's voice.

"I think so, and hurry." He hung up, knowing he may have set off a load of trauma for his mother and Marcie, but he'd never forgive himself for failure to act if his brothers' absence from the ranch turned out to have been orchestrated.

"What is plan B?" Nicole asked the moment he set the phone back in its cradle. He started to answer, then stopped. Even though the agents next door were on their side and were supposed to listen to every call coming in or out of their apartment, he felt reluctant to share with them the details of his and his brothers' childhood secret hideout. "I'll explain later," was all he said.

"But they'll be safe?"

"Yes." He made his answer sound confident, but he couldn't help worrying that someone had tracked Marcie to the ranch and was already there observing her movements.

"Okay, I think I'll go upstairs for a while." She was too nonchalant. He'd have to keep an eye on her. He didn't know Nicole as well as he'd like to, but he knew her enough to know she never dropped a subject that worried her that easily. He made a quick call to a contact in his old reserve unit in Cedar City, requesting an immediate check on his family and the ranch, then followed Nicole upstairs.

He'd made it a point to never enter her bedroom, but he noticed she hadn't closed the door behind her as she usually did, and he could hear the click of computer keys, so he followed the sound. Standing in the doorway, he watched her for several minutes, then let his gaze wander around the room. It was as scrupulously neat as he'd expected, but unlike his room, there was a complete absence of wall decorations. Then he noticed small pieces of white tape covering each spot where a picture hanger had once been. Obviously she didn't trust the agents next door to confine their snooping to the first floor.

"Look at this." Though she hadn't acknowledged his presence, she clearly had been aware of him. He stepped closer, and she waved toward the screen. Leaning closer, he saw she had brought up the online edition of the newspaper Strichter had left behind that morning. With the tap of a few keys, the Port of Tacoma union boss's picture filled the screen. A few more taps and the screen divided to show side-by-side shots with the sketch Marcie had called to tell her about.

He looked from one to the other. Fournier was clean-shaven with only a pencil-thin mustache, while the arson suspect sported a couple of days' stubble and a thick mustache. The shape of their heads appeared the same, and he could see a strong similarity in their eyes.

"I don't know . . ." he began hesitantly.

"Watch this." Nicole wiped the stubble from the fire suspect's face with a few clicks of the mouse and trimmed the man's mustache to match Fournier's. The resemblance became unmistakable.

"If this isn't some amazing look-alike, your gunman is Akbar Hattam." Braedon gave a soft whistle before going on. "Strichter showed me the photo your sister identified. He also said the CIA was following up on the possibility the arsonist is Hattam."

"He's also Anthony Fournier. But why didn't I recognize him from the picture Colonel Strichter showed me? I saw the same photos Marcie did."

"The picture was grainy and shot from a long way off, but less than three years ago. You remembered the gunman as skinny with a narrow face. You had no way of knowing he'd gained weight. Marcie had seen him more recently and recognized him from that encounter," Braedon pointed out.

"I don't get it." She stared at the screen. "If he was worried about me recognizing him, why did he go on a fire-setting spree? He must have known there was a possibility his picture could appear on television and he might be recognized, not only by me but by anyone who knows him."

"I read Daniels's profile on him. He's suspected of personal involvement in planning and carrying out several strikes against Western interests in the Middle East. He must have thought the risk was worth taking for some reason. Maybe he was testing some kind of device or he expected greater damage from the fires. Whatever his reasons, it's likely there's a similarity between those fires and whatever he's planning. At the rate terrorists have been blowing themselves up along with their targets, maybe he doesn't expect to survive whatever he has planned, and he figures that by the time someone identifies him, it won't matter anymore."

Nicole hit print, then leaned back in her chair with her arms folded. "It could be plain old arrogance." She continued speculating with more than a little sarcasm as she picked up the page as it came from the printer. "He may have decided that since I'm a lowly female, I'm too stupid to see through his disguise."

"What are we doing speculating about his reasons when we should be calling the colonel?" He bolted toward the stairs with Nicole on his heels, the printout still in her hands. Grabbing the phone, he tapped in the code for Strichter's private phone. There was no answer. He immediately tried the office number and learned the colonel was in a high-level meeting and unavailable to everyone. He asked the aide to interrupt the meeting, but the corporal refused to disobey Strichter's order not to be disturbed.

"What're the odds of Colonel Strichter and Steve being unavailable at the same time?" he grumbled aloud, slamming the phone back on its hook.

"Try Daniels," Nicole encouraged.

A gruff voice answered on the second ring, and Braedon asked to speak to Chief Daniels.

"He's out of town," the voice volunteered. "Could I help you? I'm his second-in-command. I don't usually answer phones around here, but I'm filling in for dispatch while she takes a break."

"No, this is personal. Is there any way to reach Daniels at another number?" Braedon didn't expect an affirmative answer, but he was desperate enough to ask.

"Nope. I've been trying to reach him for a couple of hours on that itty-bitty phone he takes everywhere. I just get an out-of-service message."

"Could you tell me where he went?"

"That's against policy, but if you'll leave your name, I'll let him know you called when he checks in."

"Ron Haskell, and tell him it's urgent. He has my number." Braedon hung up and turned to Nicole. "Now what?"

"One more person unavailable." She stared thoughtfully at the paper she'd dropped on the kitchen table, then dashed for the stairs.

"We need some telephone numbers." He heard the soft whisper of her printer once more, and she returned a few moments later with a couple of pieces of paper in her hand.

"Here try this number," she thrust a page under Braedon's nose.

"But . . . who do I ask for?" He dialed the number. When he got the temporarily out-of-service message he hung up.

"That does it," Nicole grasped the phone and began punching numbers.

"Hey, you're not supposed to . . ." She twisted away from the hand he put out to restrain her.

"Hello," her voice took on a nasal twang. "I've been trying to reach my daughter in southern Utah all afternoon, but there seems to be something wrong with her cell phone. I know she never turns it off. Could you please check on it for me?" She listened for several seconds, thanked the person on the other end, and hung up.

"It seems some major microwave relay station in southern Utah is down, leaving almost no cell phone service between Cedar City and Phoenix," Nicole reported.

"That might explain Steve's phone."

"It could explain where Daniels has gone too," Nicole speculated. "You were concerned enough about a possible terrorist attack on your ranch to insist your mother use some backup safety measure, but Daniels is concerned about dams, and both the Hoover and Glen Canyon Dams are in the affected area."

"What if . . . ? No, that's too wild." Braedon backed away from what he'd planned to say.

"No, we have to consider every possibility," Nicole prodded.

"Poursaid and Hattam aren't acting alone. We know there was a highway patrolman working with them, and there's still someone at either Fort Lewis or McChord who was assisting Poursaid and reporting to Detford. Then there was the guy who blew up Marcie's house and the former navy guy they suspect shot Detford. There's also someone who was in California with Hattam who hasn't been identified. We don't know how many others are involved or what information they have access to." He paused to catch his breath.

"Whatever is happening is big. Chief Daniels is involved with protecting dams, so I think we can safely assume he's got people watching the roads near every dam in the west for any truck large enough to carry enough explosives to blow up a dam. Hattam probably knows that. Whoever he is, he isn't stupid, and he knows a great deal about you and the people closest to you. He probably guessed that your disappearance means you're working with the military and Homeland Security. What if the communications problems are meant to distract us?"

"I see what you mean," Nicole said, her mind working quickly to put together the pieces of the puzzle she possessed. "While we're busy worrying about our families, and Daniels is rushing off to protect hydroelectric dams, Hattam could be planning something much closer."

"The Port of Tacoma," Braedon barely breathed the words. "If you're right about Fournier being Hattam, his target could be to destroy one of our country's largest ports. Both the economic impact and the loss of life would rival 9/11."

"All right you guys!" Nicole stood with her hands on her hips yelling at the camera in the corner of the ceiling. "Get over here! We have to do something. If you're not here in two minutes, I'm out that door—and I know you can't catch me." Braedon didn't know whether to laugh or applaud, but he knew his admiration for Nicole had just climbed another notch.

Suddenly the main-level bathroom door opened and a familiar figure wearing jeans and a baseball cap slouched into the room. Nicole's mouth dropped open as the man she'd first thought was a threat, then learned had saved her life, stood before her. Braedon was nearly as shocked as she. Even he hadn't known there was a direct access from the apartment next door through the bathroom he routinely used.

"You're . . . you're . . . All the time you've been able to . . ." She was incapable of finishing a sentence. Discovering the CIA agents had access to their apartment at any time shouldn't have surprised her, but it offended her innate sense of privacy. Also, if this man was a CIA agent, and he took orders from Chief Daniels, then Daniels was CIA as well. She should have guessed as much, and the fact that she hadn't made her feel foolish. The supposed second-in-command in Port Angeles was probably the real police chief there.

"My partner is filling a few people in on your theories, and he's got someone checking on this Fournier character," he said without preamble. "We didn't figure we should both desert our posts."

Before she could respond, a second man stepped into the room. "We've got a problem, Cap," he announced. "I just received a coded message warning me that someone has traced a call to this sector. We need to get the Haskells out of here before the hunt is narrowed to this complex."

"Okay, take nothing but what you have on and follow me," Cap barked, and Nicole and Braedon moved quickly toward him. Passing the kitchen table, Nicole snatched up the printouts that were still lying there. Folding them in fourths, she thrust the papers into her back pocket just as Cap turned out the lights. She'd been so preoccupied, she hadn't even noticed daylight fading or that Braedon had turned on the apartment lights.

"I don't think they've found us yet, but they could have cars in the neighborhood." Cap paused before stopping to speak directly to her and Braedon. "Follow the route you took this morning. Bob and I will meet you about twenty yards into the trees. Walk normally and appear to be conversing with each other. Hold hands." He stepped back to allow them to pass through the front door. "We'll go out the back door."

They stepped into the shadow of the big fir tree that shaded the front yard, hesitated only a moment to check for any sign of being watched, then strolled hand in hand toward the end of the apartment complex. The walk seemed much longer than it had that morning.

Maintaining a casual walk was one of the harder things Nicole had ever attempted. It seemed to take an eternity to reach the trees on the opposite side of the parking lot. For a fleeting moment, she wondered why they didn't just hop into the car she and Braedon had arrived in. She almost asked, then remembered to only appear to be talking. It was probably because anyone searching the neighborhood for them might have the license plate number, she reasoned.

She welcomed the deep shadows of the trees like old friends, but the sudden pressure of Braedon's fingers brought her to a stop sooner than she expected.

"Down," he whispered and practically shoved her to the pine-needle-strewn path. He crouched beside her, and together they watched a late-model SUV turn into the lane they'd just left. Lights swept the drive, then went out. Without lights, the SUV pulled into the parking lot and cruised slowly toward their apartment. It stopped two doors away. They waited for what seemed an eternity, but no one emerged from the SUV.

Feeling a light tap on her shoulder, she started, then turned to see Cap. Bob stood behind Braedon. Cap motioned for them to follow, and she and Braedon both rose to their feet. He led them deeper into the trees at a careful trot. She followed with Braedon on her heels. It was too dark to see if Bob was behind them, but when Cap picked up the pace, she thought she detected more than one set of running feet behind her. For a small man, Cap moved swiftly, and she wondered if he'd explored this path earlier as she and Braedon had done. She was glad for their early morning adventure and the insight it had given her into the twists and turns of the path they followed.

It was hard to judge time, but they must have been running for twenty minutes before Cap brought their group to a halt. They were in a thick tangle of growth with several fallen trees beside the trail. She could barely make out their shape, but she found the sight of them reassuring since she remembered them from her morning run. The trail forked just ahead with one arm circling back toward the school and the other coming out at a small lake she remembered from the map she'd constructed of the area on her computer.

The map! Could someone access it on her computer and guess where they had gone? No, her files were double password protected, and it would take some time to hack them. By then, they should be a long way from here.

"There's a boat concealed just ahead." Cap's voice was pitched low. "Wait for my signal." He disappeared into the darkness. Moments later, a soft whistle reached her ears, and Bob urged them forward.

"Stay low," Cap cautioned as they stepped over the side of a metal rowboat, and he and Bob picked up the oars.

She didn't need the warning. It was far too easy to picture them as sitting ducks silhouetted on the open body of water. No one spoke as the boat moved across the water, and she found herself glancing nervously at the sky, hoping the moon wouldn't rise before they reached the other side. The sound of a car on the road between the woods and the lake reached her ears. The men stopped paddling and bent low until the sound receded. Her heart pounded, but after a few moments, she decided worry was a waste of time and her time could be used much more profitably praying.

The sound of water lapping against the shore was her first clue they were about to reach land. It was a good thing because her legs were numb, and she had a strong feeling she was never meant to be a human pretzel. The darkness grew more intense, and the boat nudged against something solid. Cap placed his mouth near her ear, "Stay here. You can sit up, but don't speak." The boat rocked, and she sensed he'd gone.

Sitting up was easier said than done, and it took all of her power of concentration not to let a groan escape. As her eyes adjusted and her limbs stopped screaming in pain, she noted she was facing another person and the intense darkness was due to being inside a boathouse. Without a word being spoken, she knew it was Braedon facing her, and when he reached across the narrow space between them to touch her hand, she gripped his tightly and was amazed at how much she longed to throw herself in his arms and hear him reassure her that all would work out and they would be safe.

They sat for what seemed a long time. From across the lake, she could see headlights at frequent intervals passing a spot where the trees were thin, and she wondered if any of the cars held terrorists searching for her. When a vehicle stopped and a searchlight swept across the water, she knew for certain someone was looking for them. The light seemed to be slowly moving along the shore near where she estimated they had entered the water. The beam didn't reach to the boathouse, but if the searchers continued following the shore, it would eventually reach them. She felt Braedon's fingers tighten in a way that brought a slight measure of reassurance and told her he was aware of the danger too.

"All right, come with me," a low voice came from the deeper blackness inside the shelter that hid the boat. She felt a hand reach for her, and she clambered onto a wooden dock to be led inside a house. No lights were on in the house, and the drapes had been closed, but she could still make out the shadowy shapes of furniture scattered across the room. "Through here. The garage is to the left," Cap whispered. She didn't know why it hadn't occurred to her before that the agents were following an escape plan, prearranged for the eventuality they were discovered. She wasn't the only one who had thought an escape plan necessary, and of course the agents had a lot more resources to draw on.

"Is there a telephone here?" She recognized Braedon's voice and moved closer to him. She felt his hand close around hers. With her hand in his again, she felt safer, and her thoughts returned to her earlier discovery. She had to find a way to convince the two CIA agents she was right. Something terrible was going to happen if Fournier wasn't stopped.

"There is a phone, but it's too risky to use it. We need to get completely out of this area before we attempt to contact headquarters," Cap answered.

"Where are we going?" she asked.

There was a slight hesitation before Cap responded to her question. "To check out a certain union meeting."

Chapter 21

"You heard Nicole's theory?"

"You think I might be right then?"

Nicole and Braedon spoke almost together.

"Yes." It was Bob who answered this time. "We asked headquarters to run a check on Fournier as soon as we saw the pictures you left on the table. It seems a very different Anthony Fournier returned from France eight years ago from the one who quit his job and went back home six months earlier. An investigation has already been launched to discover what happened to the real Fournier."

"If the CIA already knows Fournier is Hattam, why are we going to the union meeting?" Braedon asked. "Couldn't you have him picked up before he arrives there?"

"Agents were sent to his home and office. He wasn't at either place, and the Highway Patrol has orders to watch for his vehicle."

"Why are we headed for the union meeting?" Braedon asked. "If he plans to blow up the docks while thousands of workers are waiting for him at that meeting tonight, won't we simply be jeopardizing Nicole unnecessarily?"

Nicole glared at Braedon, though of course he couldn't see her in the darkened room.

"The port area is vast, and his plans may not include the meeting area at all. It's far more likely the terrorists will attempt to take out piers and bridges or block the harbor. If the California fires were practice, then we can probably expect a series of blasts from multiple outdoor targets. Law enforcement, even with military backup, will be spread thin, and that's why we've got to get moving again." Cap paused, then added, "You two won't actually be at the meeting. Bob and I will be leaving you at a safe location almost a mile away from the dockworkers' meeting. Reporters from the major television affiliates will be at the meeting, and I understand a local education station is planning to highlight a beautification project along the waterfront and to broadcast Fournier's entire speech, so you'll be able to watch the whole thing."

Nicole knew she shouldn't feel disappointment, but she did. She wanted to be in on the capture of Hattam, and she didn't have to see Braedon's face to know Cap's announcement left him with mixed feelings. She suspected he didn't want to be left out of the action but was pleased that she wouldn't be in danger.

Cap led the way to the garage and a late-model Jeep Cherokee with the rear seats tucked out of sight. Again he insisted she and Braedon stay low.

"Lie down," he instructed, and when they did, he covered them with a blanket, then piled fake packages and bags, which were lying conveniently beside the vehicle, over them. Braedon was close enough that she could hear him breathing, and she found it reassuring when he placed one hand on her waist.

She tried to keep track of the turns the vehicle made, and she stiffened each time it stopped. The car was equipped with a police scanner, but she couldn't make sense of most of the calls. Cap and Bob remained quiet, and she followed their example as she futilely strained to hear anything on the radio that might tell her what was going on.

She felt the vehicle climb, then as it smoothed out, she felt the increase in speed telling her they were on the freeway. She was aware, too, when they left the freeway and guessed they had reached Tacoma. Restless energy consumed her, and she found it difficult to stay hidden. Her limbs ached for movement. Braedon's hand tightened on her waist as though he sensed her longing to be free.

Nicole breathed a sigh of relief when the SUV came to a halt and the engine stopped. She inhaled sea air and guessed they were close to the sound. The deep bellow of an oceangoing vessel's horn confirmed her guess. Once out of the Jeep, she stood, stretching her arms and legs to regain their normal circulation. They were in a ramshackle garage filled with an array of items from used mattresses to an assortment of cans, bottles, tools, bicycles, and even an old push lawnmower.

Cap hurried her and Braedon to their feet and from the attached garage into what appeared to be an older house. Looking around, she noticed they had entered a cramped kitchen that probably hadn't changed much in the last forty years. An overflowing trash can stood beside chipped cabinets in one corner of the room. The bar was short and separated the kitchen area from a living area. It was piled high with papers, empty pizza boxes, and dirty paper cups. Slatted blinds were closed tightly, and they looked new. She noted the furniture in the living room was old and shabby except for some state-of-the-art electronic equipment. A slender, balding man looked up from the monitor he was watching. His cotton shirt was rolled to his elbows, and he sported black suspenders. On closer inspection, she could see what she first took for suspenders was a shoulder holster.

"Come in," the man beckoned with one hand without taking his eyes from the screen. "The military is guarding the bridges, and HP is checking vehicles entering the area. There's no way he's going to smuggle in enough explosives to blow anything up. We've got guys everywhere, including at Fournier's meeting. There's been a big push for nearly a year to get greater unity between the Longshoremen and the smaller unions along the Puget Sound, so the hall is packed with several thousand workers, and more are trying to get in. Representatives of every local, the Teamsters, and even an environmental group are seated near the front. Fournier hasn't arrived yet, though his wife and daughters are on the stand. No suspicious trucks have entered the area, and the FAA has shut down Sea-Tac and made Tacoma a no-fly zone. Homeland Security is in the process of issuing a red alert." He gave his rapid-fire update and rose to his feet.

In one casual move, he pulled on a heavy vest, followed by the kind of coat she supposed fishermen wore. It completely hid the gun he carried. Nicole turned to the two agents who had brought her and Braedon to this house. They both wore jackets like ball players wear, zipped in front. Before she could speculate whether they concealed Kevlar vests and gun holsters, the man who had been seated at the computer console turned to Braedon with a careless wave, indicating he should sit in the chair he had just vacated.

"This baby records everything that comes in," he said. "But the boss wants you to monitor incoming traffic as backup. He said you've had some experience with this type of equipment. The traffic center will alert him to incoming intelligence and keep him in touch with his point people. Don't transmit unless he asks for input from this station."

"I don't expect anything to go wrong, but your cover is already blown, and just in case . . . You might need this." Cap handed a wallet to Braedon. Braedon looked surprised, then slipped it into his back pocket.

"And you," he whirled about to face Nicole, startling her into taking a step back. "He said for you to park your fanny in front of the TV and stay put until this is over."

* * *

Marcie set down the infant carrier and looked around at her surroundings. She couldn't believe this was really happening. She was inside a mine. It didn't look anything like the mines she'd seen on TV with their rock walls, support beams, and railroad tracks running down the center. Other than having no windows, the mine where Margaret had brought them was just a crude room with a plank floor, four bunks, a table, and an odd assortment of chairs. In the corner, two old, wooden orange crates served as a cupboard of sorts.

"Are we going to sleep in Daddy's hideout?" Trace asked.

"We might." Margaret smiled at her grandson.

"Here, let me help you," Marcie offered. She set down the diaper bag and baby quilts she'd carried along with Lexie and John David when they made their hurried exit from the house through a cellar door. She took the bag of supplies Margaret had hastily gathered before leaving the ranch house and set it on the table. Handing each of the boys a cookie, she praised them for how quiet they had been.

Earlier, after a firm admonition from Margaret, the boys had cooperated as they'd picked their silent way through a grove of fruit trees to the gardening shed. Once inside the shed, Margaret had tugged on one corner of a workbench, and Marcie had gasped to see a whole section of the tongue-and-groove wall behind it move forward.

"Quick, inside." Margaret had motioned Marcie toward the dark hole behind the wall. With her heart slamming against her ribs, Marcie had led the reluctant children into the darkness. Margaret followed them, but before closing the door, she'd picked up a tin can she found on the floor. She took a handful of fine silt her sons had collected and blew it into the shed, where it settled like dust on the floor. She repeated the action several times before pulling the door closed behind her.

The darkness had disappeared almost immediately as the older woman turned on a flashlight she'd carried in her pocket. By the light from its beam, she turned a deadbolt, which she explained could not be seen from the other side and that ensured that the door couldn't be opened again from the shed side.

Margaret had pointed the way with her light down a tunnel. "It's safe," she'd said, then went on to explain to Marcie that the tunnel had been reinforced by her husband when he discovered their boys playing in the old mine and that Cameron had inspected it again recently.

"It's not much of a mine." The older woman laughed. "My husband's grandfather found traces of coal in the area. He thought if he burrowed into the mountainside, he'd find a vein that he could mine for use in the family cookstove and fireplace to keep the house warm. Instead of coal, he found a cave that had been buried by a mudslide at some time. He cleaned it out and used it as an icehouse to store meat. When electricity and refrigeration came to the ranch years later, the icehouse was no longer needed and nearly forgotten until my Ralph discovered the tunnel again while building a gardening shed for me. When he found we couldn't keep the boys out of it, he replaced the tunnel supports, reinforced the cave walls and ceiling, and installed a fresh-air pipe. The boys added a wood floor as they got older. It was Ralph's idea as well to give the boys' hideaway a secret entrance."

"Didn't you worry about your boys locking themselves in?"

"The lock is new. Kendall installed it just before he and his brothers left to get you and your little ones. Braedon convinced him it would be good to have a secure place to hide should your presence here be discovered." Margaret had set the flashlight down and pushed a button on a battery-operated lantern in the center of the table. Light filled the room, bringing a cheer from the little boys.

They'd brought the cherry pies they'd planned for dinner along with a thermos of hot water and one of milk to supplement the supplies neatly stacked on the orange-crate shelves. Margaret handed Marcie a sweater from a pile of warm clothing on one end of the nearest bunk. John David didn't object when she pulled it over his head. The underground room was noticeably chilly, but they had a good supply of blankets and sweaters.

No outside sounds reached inside the mine, and Marcie found herself wishing they had a way of knowing what was happening on the outside. As the hands on their watches moved toward the children's bedtime, she and Margaret fed them and settled them in the lower bunks. They fell asleep surprisingly fast. Margaret's assurance no one could find them went a long way toward alleviating her fears for the children. Still, she found herself listening intently for the prearranged signal on the hidden air pipe Margaret had told her about that would alert them to the return of the other Morgan family members. Calmness about her own situation filled her mind, but she couldn't help wondering if Nicole was safe.

* * *

Nicole wasn't certain being ordered to watch television was some kind of insult or whether Chief Daniels thought there was something she might learn from watching Fournier's speech. The TV was already running, so there was nothing to do but settle in one corner of the sagging sofa and watch.

An eager young reporter was filling in the listening audience on the history of the port. She then moved on to describe some of the history and recent activities of the union. Behind the reporter, Nicole could see a crowd of mostly men entering a large hall. News photographers from the major wire services were occasionally caught showing signs of impatience by a roving camera that frequently panned the crowd.

She thought of the publicity surrounding the meeting and understood why Hattam had been so sure she would see and possibly recognize him. She might have seen his picture sooner in ads and news stories leading up to tonight if she were in the habit of really watching television, but she usually let the television run as background noise and seldom actually looked at the screen. Of course, avoiding the room where the television was located for much of the past few weeks and being cut off from newspapers while in hiding hadn't helped.

The reporter yielded to a roving camera that showed shots of the docks and the massive cranes which hoisted container cargo into the holds of waiting ships. A return to the reporter showed the meeting still hadn't started, and Fournier's seat remained empty.

A close-up shot showed Mrs. Fournier, an attractive, well-groomed woman in her late thirties or early forties who remained calm and serene. The older daughter stared stoically ahead while the younger one fidgeted and glanced with increasing impatience toward the wings of the stage.

"Janet Fournier, a former Miss Washington, married Anthony Fournier just seven years ago in a romantic elopement between a society matron and a longshoreman," the reporter confided in a gossipy voice to her audience. "The young widow with two small daughters was making plans to expand her deceased husband's chain of nurseries when she entered the office of the shipping company that transports her bulbs and seedlings from Europe. While she waited for her appointment, she sat next to Fournier, who was carrying out one of his first assignments for the union he will be sworn in to lead tonight. They were married in a romantic seaside setting after a whirlwind courtship of just six weeks."

"Did you hear that?" Nicole turned eagerly toward Braedon. "Fournier's wife owns a chain of nurseries. That explains why he was at a nursery the day Marcie bumped into him."

"It also explains his access to chemical fertilizer," Braedon added.

When she turned back to the television, the reporter was showing shots taken earlier in the day of a landscaping project the city had undertaken with the backing of the longshoremen who had contributed numerous community service hours to beautifying a nearby park, warehouses, streets, and both administrative and union buildings near the waterfront. The reporter paused in front of a group of men who were unloading shrubs from a van to cover the sloping sides of a road leading to an area where massive elevators stored grain. She could see mechanical arms extending from the elevators to ships stationed below. A short distance beyond were oil tankers unloading their cargo.

The camera returned to a close-up of the reporter, then widened the shot to include the people digging holes for the shrubs. The reporter wrinkled her nose and made some remark about compost rich in natural nutrients and complaints from nearby residents that their neighborhoods smelled like a barnyard.

"Manure." Nicole smiled lightly at the reporter's dainty reluctance to name the overpowering odor coming from the recently prepared soil and the explanation she'd obviously memorized concerning the advantages of organic fertilizer for promoting rapid growth.

Nicole's gaze went beyond the cans of shrubs to another truck, slowly inching its way along the newly completed landscaping. There was something about it . . . From the large tank on the back of the truck a steady spray spewed toward the recently planted shrubs and trees, covering even the wood-chip-mulched areas. She couldn't think of any reason why the truck should set off alarms in her mind. She'd seen such trucks before, spraying a liquid fertilizer mixture that smelled just like mulched grass or fresh manure on large landscaping projects.

She turned her attention back to the reporter, who was beginning to look ill, just as a hand closed the side door of the van she stood beside, revealing a logo emblazoned on the door. She'd seen that same logo on a white truck months ago, a row of green, stunted trees like a bonsai project gone wrong, sitting in orange pots. Something clicked in her mind, telling her what it was about the truck that bothered her. There was no need to apply a liquid fertilizer to soil already so saturated with manure it was making the television commentator sick.

"Braedon," she practically screamed. "Mrs. Fournier's company did the landscaping. Her husband personally supervised the installation of the design. The explosives are already in place! They're hidden in the landscaping!"

"What?" Braedon looked up from the monitor he was watching.

"The explosives are already in place. They're hidden in the landscaping Mrs. Fournier's company completed this week along the waterfront and around important buildings. You've got to call Daniels."

"The odor of jet fuel would be pretty noticeable if it were out in the open." Braedon expressed skepticism.

"Not if it was camouflaged by frequent, generous applications of something that smells worse."

As her words sank in, Braedon knew what Fournier planned. With his explosives hidden beneath the mounds and small hills land-scapers love, Fournier could detonate his bombs with some kind of remote device just as he'd practiced in California.

"What if you're wrong?" Braedon hesitated a second. "But I don't think you are." He began tapping furiously on the keyboard.

"This better be good," Daniels's voice came from the speakers on either side of the monitor. Quickly Braedon explained Nicole's theory. A splutter of static was the only response he received in return before his monitor went black and the lights in the house flickered and went out.

Nicole rose to her feet. "Braedon," she whispered.

"I'm here." She felt him touch her shoulder. "I peeked through the blinds. It looks like the power is out over a pretty wide area. It isn't just us."

"I thought . . . Did Daniels get your warning?"

"I don't know for certain, but I think so. The power went off before he could acknowledge."

"Shouldn't there be a generator around here if this place is used on a regular basis by the CIA?" Nicole's eyes were growing accustomed to the dark, and she began looking around.

"Even if there is one, I don't think we should attempt to start it up. It could switch on lights, which would draw attention to a house in an otherwise dark neighborhood. Besides, generators used for crit-ical functions usually switch on automatically when the usual power source is lost, and we could be wasting time looking for something that isn't here or doesn't work."

"You're right," Nicole agreed. "We've got to find a policeman or someone who can find that union hall."

"I'll go out through the garage. You lock up after—" Braedon began.

"No way. We both go." She started toward the garage. "I saw some bicycles . . ."

"I saw them too." Braedon jerked the door open. "They might be useless, but let's give them a try."

It was difficult moving through the cluttered garage, and she winced each time she bumped into something. When they reached the bikes, Braedon skimmed his hands over them, trying to determine by feel whether they were in working order, then he pushed one toward her. Single file, they walked the bikes through a side door Braedon had noticed. Once outside, they were able to see much better.

"Which way?" Braedon asked.

"Where are you going?"

Nicole gasped and heard the clatter of Braedon's bike hitting the ground. She turned her head slowly to see a pair of children perched on a split rail fence. Though neither boy looked more than twelve, Nicole was glad she hadn't stumbled on them alone. There was a street-smart toughness about them that had her edging closer to Braedon, who had moved up behind her and placed a hand on her shoulder.

"We're supposed to meet a guy at the dockworkers meeting tonight, but the guy who was supposed to drive us there took off while we were asleep." Nicole didn't know whether she was impressed or dismayed by how easily Braedon invented a story.

"It ain't far."

"How far? And which direction?" Nicole's questions came rapid-fire. Braedon's fingers pressed into her shoulder, and she regretted communicating her sense of urgency.

"How bad do you want to know?" the other boy spoke up, proving what Nicole feared. There would be no information without paying for it. Braedon reached for his wallet, carefully turning it so the pair of con artists could see the single bill he extracted from it was all it contained.

"A twenty is all I've got."

"What about the lady?"

"I left my purse in our friend's car." Now she was lying. Her purse was back in their apartment—at least she hoped it was still there.

"Okay. It ain't much." The boys jumped down from the fence. "When you get to the corner over there," he pointed, "go two blocks left, then another six right. You'll smell it before you get to it, and there's about a million cars parked around it." He snatched the bill from Braedon's hand, and both boys disappeared into the darkness.

Hoping the boys hadn't lied to them, Nicole leaped on the bike she still held and followed Braedon down a steep driveway to the street. Seeing no traffic, they began pedaling down the street, avoiding darkened areas where punks like the two they'd already met, or worse, might be lingering. Nicole discovered in a hurry that the bike she rode was in serious need of being oiled. She suspected she could run faster than she could make the rusty derelict go. Breathing hard from exertion as she forced the rusty bicycle on, she began to notice an unpleasant odor. The pungent air made her want to gag, and she knew the boys hadn't lied. The hall was close.

Braedon's bike began to wobble, and he barely managed to jump clear as it fell to the pavement. Nicole managed to stop before running into him. He stood, dusted his knees, and looked toward his bike. "Stupid tire."

Seeing the twisted wheel, Nicole climbed off her bike. "I can't peddle this rusty heap another yard." She let it drop beside Braedon's bike. "Come on, let's start running. I know the well-lit building in the next block from the television special I was watching, and we've got to hurry. This whole place could go up any minute."

"Let's get out of here." Braedon grabbed her hand, and they began to run.

"Stop right there!" A spotlight blinded them and a voice came from behind a row of parked cars just half a block short of their goal. "Identify yourselves."

Braedon hesitated, and a figure carrying an assault rifle stepped toward them. Recognizing a familiar uniform, he gave his name and rank.

"I'll need to see ID." He kept the rifle trained on them while Braedon pulled out his wallet. He was glad Cap had returned it. They'd left the apartment so quickly, he hadn't given a thought to identification or money.

"We need to find Colonel Strichter or Walt Daniels. It's urgent," he told the soldier with the rifle.

"Stay right there," the soldier ordered, then backed toward the parked vehicle, keeping his weapon at the ready. Braedon stood at attention and stared straight ahead while he waited, but his mind frantically retraced the facts and theories he and Nicole had put together. Nicole didn't appear to move a muscle, but he sensed she was eyeing the mound of dirt and shrubs across from them with growing alarm.

"Come with me." A man wearing a Port Authority uniform emerged from behind the car. He motioned toward them and began a sprint toward the union hall. When they reached it, he led them to a side door. "Just inside, you'll find four stairs leading to a hallway that passes behind the stage. Go to the first door."

Before he could leave, Nicole caught his arm. "Warn everyone not to smoke. There could be jet fuel fumes escaping into the air."

"Everyone's already been warned," he assured her.

Following instructions, they made their way to the designated door. Braedon opened it, expecting to find a dressing room. Instead he found himself in a room filled with projectors and sound equipment. Standing near a tinted window he recognized as one-way glass stood Colonel Strichter. He motioned them forward.

"Sir, we weren't sure the transmission got through. The power went out before Daniels could respond."

"The booster station that handles that grid was sabotaged. We figure it was a distraction to draw law enforcement away from this area and slow their response time."

"Where's Daniels?" Braedon looked around at the various men fiddling with equipment or watching the scene below in the crowded hall.

"Down there." Strichter pointed toward the stage. Braedon strained for a glimpse but couldn't see him. The stage was similar to a theater stage with chairs set up in a single row on the apron in front of a heavy curtain. Three women and a half dozen men occupied the chairs. He didn't recognize any of them. A podium stood slightly forward, and a heavyset man was standing behind it speaking to the crowd, who approved of whatever he was saying by stomping their feet and whistling. Braedon paid no attention to the speech coming through speakers into the room that had become a command center.

"Fournier just stepped on stage," Nicole's voice came out in a harsh whisper. Dressed in a dark business suit, the man she identified as Fournier raised his hands and with dramatic gestures began to speak. The crowd roared their approval. She leaned closer to the glass, and her hands formed fists. Braedon wanted to go to her, but somehow he knew seeing her father's murderer again was something she needed to first deal with alone.

Nicole's whole consciousness focused on the man standing before the microphone, though she didn't hear a word he said. This was the man who had shot her father; all doubt was gone. A sick reflex, worse than that she experienced earlier from the pungent landscaping, twisted her stomach.

She was so focused on the man who epitomized evil in her mind that when, from somewhere to his left, a hand suddenly grasped Fournier's left wrist and almost simultaneously his right wrist, she was as taken by surprise as the crowd. A moment's shocked silence held the crowd as each of Fournier's wrists was shackled to the wrist of one of the men she assumed were CIA agents beside him. A roar like a herd of maddened bulls broke from the longshoremen and pandemonium erupted as the crowd surged toward the stage. She saw Daniels step from behind the curtain and approach the trio at the podium. She pressed her hands against the glass and leaned as close as she could get. A ring of uniformed police officers formed a circle around the union boss, who was struggling with his captors. Some part of her brain registered the identity of one of the men holding Fournier as the man she knew as Cap.

She became aware of angry workers storming the stage, ready to defend their new leader. Military police and Port Authority security officers stepped between the crowd and the men on the stage. The crowd continued to roar and shake their fists. Fournier jerked one manacled hand toward his breast pocket. He succeeded in extracting a small, black object. The agent linked to that hand flung Fournier backward, taking Cap to the floor with them. Cap lunged toward the object, applying pressure with his free hand to Fournier's wrist to incapacitate the hand holding the object. Daniels stepped in, emerging from the melee with what looked like a television remote control held beyond Fournier's reach.

Daniels stepped to the microphone with the remote held in a raised hand. After a few moments, the audience quieted enough to hear his shouted explanation. Voices raised again as he explained that explosives had been found around the building and in various spots along the waterfront. Shock visibly rippled through the crowd which suddenly hushed. She could see the men looking about uneasily and eyeing the exits.

"Fournier is being arrested for questioning since he is affiliated with the landscaping company suspected of placing the bombs. And this device in my hand is believed to be the detonator." Nicole noticed several camera crews jockeying for a better position to catch Mrs. Fournier's reaction. Nicole glanced toward the woman in time to see Mrs. Fournier's expression change from shock to fury. There was no way Nicole could miss the loathing expression the woman directed toward her husband, who was being led off the stage by Cap and another undercover agent.

While Daniels went on to tell the crowd they were free to leave and caution the union members to stay on the sidewalks as they exited the building and to refrain from smoking, Nicole sagged against a nearby chair. It was over.

She began to weep. Even with the capture of the man who shot her father, there was no way to prove the crime without a body. Silent tears streamed down her cheeks. She knew she was crying for the father she'd never been allowed to mourn, but more than that, it hurt to know the case would be closed now. Hattam would be tried for crimes that in most people's eyes far exceeded the taking of one man's life.

"Nicole," Braedon placed a hand on her shoulder. "You're safe now, and you've cleared your father's name." She looked up to see they were alone in the room.

"But we still don't know what they did with my father. When I saw that horrible man standing there, I was filled with so much hate and anger, I wanted to kill him."

"Don't . . ."

"It's all right, I came to my senses. There's enough hate and anger in this world. That's what drives people like Hattam. I just want to talk to Marcie, then find a room somewhere and sleep."

"I'll see if I can find Colonel Strichter and arrange for transportation back to Fort Lewis." He reached past her to switch off the speakers to allow her a few minutes' peace and quiet.

He left the room, and she leaned forward, resting her forehead against the glass with her eyes closed. Her mind felt numb, and she craved sleep. Gradually the numbness receded to be replaced by bits and pieces of a day that had been both too long and too stressful. She was grateful a major disaster had been averted, but as the events of the day played out in her mind, an awareness that Hattam hadn't acted alone crept into her thoughts, and she wondered how many terrorists had escaped. And Marcie. Had the terrorists gone after her?

A soft click alerted her that the door behind her had opened. "Braedon . . ." She turned to see not Braedon, but Poursaid standing in the doorway with a gun pointed at her. She edged toward the sound console. If she could get behind it, it would provide some protection. Her fingers felt the edge, but before she could squeeze behind it, he was across the room and grasping her by the arm.

She released a scream, and he clapped a hand across her mouth with a threat to kill her if she made another sound. He vented his rage for several minutes at first her father, then at her. He blamed her father for destroying carefully made plans to blow up dams on the Columbia, then her for interfering with Hattam's plan for ending exploitation by sea by American infidels. He shook her viciously until she thought her head would explode before dragging her toward the door. She suspected she would already be dead if he didn't need a hostage more than he needed revenge at the moment.

"We must go," Poursaid hissed in her ear. "If we're seen leaving here, the fools will not risk killing you. It's your fault the plan must be changed, so it's fitting you help me escape. Not all of the explosives are beneath the dirt. Hattam filled one cargo container with his mixture, and it's aboard a ship anchored near an oil tanker. His detonator would've caused the needed explosion. Instead I must die a martyr's death, and you're going to die with me."

With one arm wrapped around her shoulders and the other holding the gun against her temple, he ordered her to open the door. She turned the doorknob, pushed the door open, then paused. Someone was standing just beyond the door. Poursaid forced her forward. She deliberately stumbled, hoping to alert the person she'd glimpsed and create a diversion. Even if she died, it would be better than allowing him to carry out his plan. Enraged, Poursaid struck her with the gun, sending her senses reeling.

"Drop!" She recognized Braedon's voice and went limp, sliding downward. A gunshot sounded. Feeling no pain, she rolled away, dodging a forest of legs and shoes. She came to a stop next to a wall. While she struggled to catch her breath, her eyes roamed upward, and she saw where a bullet had struck the ceiling. The sound of pounding feet turned her attention toward nearly a dozen men in various uniforms running toward her.

"Braedon!" She snapped out of her daze and struggled upright to find the fight was over. Poursaid lay face down on the carpeted hall floor with several men standing over him. Braedon turned toward her, and she stumbled into his arms, burying her face against his chest.

"Someone will be by to return us to Fort Lewis soon," he whispered in her ear as he turned her away from Poursaid and began walking her down the hall. As they left the building, she saw several men in handcuffs being herded into a police van. In minutes, they were inside Colonel Strichter's car with his driver at the wheel. Nicole collapsed against the cushions and sobbed as the car pulled out of the union hall parking lot.

After a few minutes, she sat up, remembering her sister and feeling guilty for wallowing in grief before learning about her sister's welfare. "Marcie? Is she all right?"

"She's fine and asking about you. When I found Colonel Strichter, he told me law enforcement officers in southern Utah have been kept busy all day responding to nuisance calls and the destruction of a major microwave transmission tower. Steve finally got through to Colonel Strichter's office less than an hour ago. He reported that when Cameron and Kendall returned to the ranch, they found a broken window on the main floor of the house and a few sticks of dynamite on the ground, but with no fuses or blasting caps attached to them. There was quite a bit of blood on the ground around the broken window. Old Cooper came crawling out from under the porch with a bullet in his shoulder. Steve thinks whoever broke into the house was scared away by Cooper before he could do any real damage.

"Cameron called the sheriff while Kendall went looking for Mom and Marcie in the old mine my brothers and I used as a hideout when we were kids. That was our plan B. They were inside and doing fine. Steve and another deputy stopped a Jeep near the entrance to the ranch road. It contained two men and two high-powered rifles along with an almost empty dynamite case. Both men are being held for further investigation of the attempted break-in and the dynamited towers."

"What about the explosives Hattam planted?" She reverted to Fournier's real name.

"A careful search has begun," Braedon assured her. "From what I've learned from transmissions between Daniels and his men, the area's been cleared, and so far demolition experts have located what they believe is an ammonium nitrate bomb under a major bridge near the harbor. They've also discovered caches of dynamite they suspect are triggers for explosives hidden under the landscape mounds. One of the dynamite triggers was just outside the hall where Hattam was speaking tonight. A preliminary examination suggests the charges were set to go off in a domino fashion once the first one was triggered by remote."

"Would he really have blown up himself and his family?" Nicole wondered aloud.

"I don't think he would have hesitated to blow up his family, but I think he might've had an escape plan prepared for himself. He had a single airline ticket and a passport under another name in his pocket."

* * *

Nicole spent the night in the barred room she'd been taken to before going to the safe house in Lacey. She was too tired to care about the room. She spoke with Marcie just long enough to assure herself that her sister and the children were safe, then slept until the ringing phone awoke her the next morning. It was Braedon offering to take her to breakfast. Later, he accompanied her to Colonel Strichter's office. On the way, he told her the ship carrying explosives had been towed from port and the crew detained.

Colonel Strichter thanked her for her part in capturing Hattam and Poursaid. "Once we got digging into Fournier's past, we discovered he's made frequent trips to Paris during the past eight years. Those trips coincided with trips Hattam made between Paris and various Middle Eastern countries. We also think the accident that took Janet Fournier's first husband's life needs a little closer scrutiny."

"What about my father?" Nicole asked. "Is there any chance his body will ever be found?" Braedon moved closer and placed an arm around her. Gratefully she leaned back against him.

"I can't promise anything, but I have a theory about that. I'll let you know if it pans out. He turned to Braedon, "Lieutenant, your unit is being demobilized in two weeks. I had a little talk with your commander and suggested you leave tomorrow with Miss Evangart to join her sister. He agreed that would be acceptable."

Epilogue

A sound awakened Marcie, and her first instinct was to look at the clock beside her bed. Four o'clock. The sound came again, and she scrambled to reach the telephone.

"We got him!" The jubilant voice was her husband's, but it took a moment to grasp the meaning of his words. Before she could even respond, J.D. launched into the details of Saddam Hussein's capture. "After demanding that his people fight to the death, he didn't even offer minimal resistance. He cowered underground in a spider hole like a miserable rat."

"I remember my dad saying, 'Evil is a coward.'" Her father's words often came to mind now, and she could think of no better way to respond to her husband's news.

"I wish I could have known your father. The more I hear of him, the more I think we would have been friends." There was wistfulness in his voice.

"I know he would have loved you almost as much I do. He and your grandfather are probably great friends by now." She listened to his soft chuckle, then asked, "Does this mean you'll soon be coming home?" Her heart filled with hope they would soon be together again.

"No. His capture will erase a lot of fear for many people, but it will likely be used as a rallying cry by those who oppose the forming of a democratic government in Iraq. We'll have to be particularly watchful for the next few months. This may bring out every warring faction bent on taking over the country, and especially the fanatics who have the most to lose when Iraq forms a representative govern-ment. But on the bright side, we expect that many individuals who have been afraid to support the new government will come forward now with both information and support."

"I hope so. I want this war over and you home beside me."

"I want that too. I was going to call you a little later to tell you I've been given dates for my two weeks' R&R, but I couldn't wait until morning to tell you about Saddam. I'll be home four days after Christmas."

"We'll save Christmas until you get here." Tears of joy ran down her cheeks, but she ignored them, not wanting to waste a precious second of her husband's call.

Long after the call ended, Marcie lay in her new bed in the house she'd been assigned after returning to Fort Lewis. At first she made a mental list of all she'd need to do to prepare for a special Christmas celebration. Once she would have worried over whether her husband would approve of the new furniture she'd purchased or the car that sat in the garage. Now those things seemed insignificant. All that mattered was J.D. was coming home. She tried not to dwell on the short duration of his furlough or that after two brief weeks he'd have to go back. The war wasn't over just because one tyrant had been stopped.

She drifted asleep but awoke again shivering. She'd been back in the mine, only it wasn't the cheerful hideaway left behind by boys who had left childhood for the responsibilities of men, but a shivery dark hole where something evil lurked. She lay still, remembering back to the fears that had trapped her in holes of her own making all her life. Her fears and insecurities had imprisoned her much like being locked underground in the mine had, but that experience hadn't been so bad as long as she'd kept focused on helping the children and Margaret. She couldn't swear she'd never be frightened again, but she had learned she was capable of facing her fears. And maybe that was all courage was anyway.

* * *

Nicole turned her face up toward the falling snow and felt the flutter of winter's first snowflakes. Her hand was snug inside Braedon's, and they walked side by side along the path leading from the corrals to a small cemetery that held the earthly remains of some of Braedon's ancestors and a couple of cowboys who had died while working on the ranch without leaving any way to contact their next of kin. The storm wasn't the kind that lasted, nor would it do much to alleviate years of drought, but it brought beauty and wonder to the night.

She'd driven from Cedar City to spend the weekend with Braedon and his mother as she did more often than he came to the city to see her. She liked her small apartment near the hospital where she'd accepted an assistant administrator position, but she found herself drawn more and more to Braedon and the land that had been in his family for four generations. Now she turned to face him.

"Colonel Strichter called me this morning," she said, trying to keep her voice even. "He said he played a hunch and came up a winner."

"The colonel didn't strike me as a man who gambled." Braedon kissed a snowflake from the tip of her nose, almost distracting her from what she had to say.

"Oh, he's a gambler. He took more than one chance on me."

"In that case, maybe I'm a gambler too." Braedon's arms came around her, and she tipped her face up until their lips met. After a moment, she pulled away.

"He got a warrant to search a rundown shack on the edge of Auburn where Akbar Hattam lived before Dad died. The shack's vacant, but the taxes have been paid over the years, preventing it from being sold to anyone else. Using a metal detector, the people he sent found Dad's dog tags. He sent another crew to excavate the next morning. They found bones and remnants of an army uniform. The colonel said the results came back from the lab yesterday verifying the bones belonged to Dad."

"Have you told Marcie?" Braedon asked, brushing away a speck of moisture from the corner of her eye that might have been a snowflake.

"Yes, I called her right away. She wants a service held for him."

"What about your mother? Does she know?"

"I didn't know what to say to her, so Marcie offered to call. Teddy called back just before I left to drive here. He said Mom was sleeping peacefully, but she'd been very upset at first. He said she cried for hours and kept saying she'd always known Greg loved her and that he wouldn't just leave her. He said she admitted to jealousy of the time Dad and I spent together. Teddy said that the jealousy got all mixed up with her conviction he'd gone undercover and her fear I would jeopardize his safety with my story. He also said he'd bring her out here if we hold a service, which brings me to why I needed to speak to you. Would you mind if we brought his remains here?"

"I think he should be buried here." The playfulness was gone from Braedon's voice.

"Florida doesn't seem right, and Fort Lewis was his home for such a little while. Marcie doesn't know how long she'll even be there. When J.D. returns, they could be sent to another army base."

"And you want him near you," Braedon added. "After all this time, he should be laid to rest near the daughter who sacrificed so much to find him."

"I thought about buying a plot in Cedar City, but it just didn't feel right." She stood looking out over the valley, catching an occasional glint of light from the ranch house through the lightly falling snow.

"It didn't feel right because it isn't home." Braedon's arms tightened around her.

"This isn't my home either," she said with a touch of sadness.

"It will be when you marry me." The words were spoken against her ear.

"So it will." Her words were almost a sigh, taking away years of loneliness as she turned in Braedon's arms to savor the feel of his mouth settling over hers.

"You know I'll be in the reserves a long time, and I could be called up again," he said when they paused to catch their breath.

"Yes," she whispered back, then added in a stronger voice, "and if you go away, I'll wear a yellow ribbon in my hair until you return."

About the Author

Jennie Hansen graduated from Ricks College in Idaho and then Westminster College in Utah. She has been a newspaper reporter, editor, and librarian. In addition to writing novels, she reviews LDS fiction in a monthly column for *Meridian* magazine.

Her Church service has gone full circle from Primary teacher, to teaching in other auxiliaries and serving in stake and ward Primary presidencies, and back to her current position as a Primary teacher.

Jennie and her husband, Boyd, live in Salt Lake County. Their five children are all married and have so far provided them with eight grandchildren.

Code Red is Jennie's fourteenth book for the LDS market.

Jennie enjoys hearing from her readers, who can write to her in care of Covenant Communications, P.O. Box 416, American Fork, UT 84003-0416, or via e-mail at info@covenant-lds.com.